BUS...

by
LIA ANDERSSEN

SILVER MOON BOOKS LTD
PO Box CR 25 Leeds LS7 3TN

SILVER MOON BOOKS INCORPORATED
PO Box 1614 New York NY 10156

New authors welcome

Printed and bound in Great Britain

If you like one of our books you will probably like them all!
To order other titles see details and extracts on back pages

For free 20 page booklet of extracts from previous books (and, if you wish to be on our confidential mailing list, from forthcoming monthly titles as they are published) please write to:-

Silver Moon Reader Services
PO Box CR 25 LEEDS LS7 3TN
or
PO Box 1614 NEW YORK NY 10156

BUSH SLAVE first published 1996
Copyright Lia Anderssen

The right of Lia Anderssen to be identified as author of this book has been asserted in accordance with section 77 and 78 of the Copyrights and Patents Act 1988

BUSH SLAVE

Lia Anderssen

This is fiction - in real life, practice safe sex

Chapter 1

If it hadn't been for the air conditioner breaking down that day, Lisa might never have fallen under Conrad Lang's spell, and her life would have been completely different. Possibly even normal. Certainly she could never have dreamed of the fate that awaited her that hot June evening as she worked late over her computer terminal at the Bellco headquarters in London.

Lisa had worked for Bellco for nearly two years now as a computer programmer, and she enjoyed her job. Bellco was one of the largest arms manufacturers in the western world, exporting its products to every corner of the globe, and Lisa had been heavily involved in the design of their database, which held information about all their customers and products. Now, however, as she worked her way through some particularly complex program code, she was beginning to feel a little weary, and a glance at the clock on the wall confirmed to her that it had been a long day.

Seven thirty. It really was getting too late. She was due at her evening class in less than an hour, and she had already missed the last two sessions due to pressure of work. But how could she possibly get home and shower in time? She sighed, pushing the thick computer listing away from her and sitting back. It was stiflingly hot in the office, and she felt extremely sticky. There was no way she could go to the class without freshening up. She rose to her feet and began packing her things into her briefcase, but already she knew that by the time she had taken the tube home and had a shower, the lesson would already be half over.

Then she paused, a sudden idea striking her. There was always the executuve washroom. That had a shower in it. Of course members of staff were not supposed to use it, since it was reserved for the exclusive use of company directors. But there was nobody about. Surely it couldn't do any harm?

She hesitated. She hated breaking the rules. Throughout her life she had always done as she was told. In fact she took a genuine pleasure in obeying the orders of others. A pleasure that sometimes went beyond what she knew to be normal behaviour. But in this case it seemed such a simple thing. After all, who would ever know that she had used the executive facilities? And she really did want a shower.

All at once it seemed simple, and with a decisive nod of the head she put down her briefcase and headed for the door.

Somehow, using the elevator seemed a bad idea. She had visions of the doorman in the foyer watching as the numbers that showed on the panel above the lift doors betrayed her movements. So she chose the stairs. As she pushed open the landing doors she found the passage in darkness apart from the emergency lighting. She crept up the staircase, feeling like an interloper in somewhere that she did not belong, a feeling that increased when she set off down the corridor to where the suite of executive offices was situated.

The floor here was thickly carpeted, the walls lined with wood panelling that stood in stark contrast to the plain decor of the offices below. Lisa looked to right and left as she made her way along, locating the door to the washroom with a sigh of relief and and pushing it open. She ran her hand up the wall and found a switch which she pressed, flooding the room with light.

The room was large, with full-length mirrors all about the walls and expensive looking fittings on the row of sinks. Strictly speaking it was a men's bathroom, though the urinals were situated in a separate section, divided from the part she was in by a swinging door so that all she was confronted with was the washing facilities. On the other side of the room, though, was the shower, behind another of the swing doors, and it was toward this that she headed.

She found herself in a small changing room. This was devoid of furniture except for yet another huge mirror and a low bench set against one wall. Once again she hesitated, still slightly intimidated by where she was. She thought of the executives, who she seldom ever saw, yet to whom this place was dedicated. Yet what harm could it do to simply use their shower? She took a deep breath, then gave a little shrug and began to strip.

She was dressed for summer, in a short skirt that zipped up the back. She pulled the zip down in a single movement and let the dress fall from her shoulders, stepping out of it and placing it on the bench. Underneath she wore a plain white bra and panties. Reaching behind, she undid the catch of the bra and let it slide down her arms. Then she hooked her thumbs into the waistband of her panties and pulled them off.

Naked, she paused to examine herself in the mirror. Lisa was a stunningly beautiful young woman, and had been told as much on a number of occasions, though the compliment always embarrassed her. She was small in stature, no more than five foot four inches tall, with a slim figure that was perfectly proportioned. Her breasts were the shape of ripe oranges, firm and round with no hint of sagging. Her nipples were like circular buttons that protruded enticingly when they were hard. Below, her body tapered to a slim waist before curving out again to her hips. Her belly was flat, her pubic hairs forming a small dark triangle beneath which thick sex lips were visible. Her long legs were beautifully shaped, with narrow ankles and small, neat feet.

She raised her head to stare into her own eyes. They were green and radiated a childlike innocence from beneath long lashes. He hair was dark and wavy, hanging down to her shoulders and framing a face with a fine bone structure and small, kissable lips. Lisa was quite simply gorgeous and was capable of turning heads wherever she went.

She turned away from the mirror and pulled open the door of the shower cubicle. Stepping inside she switched on the tap and a warm spray sprang from the nozzle. She moved beneath it gratefully, closing her eyes and revelling in the freshness of the water as it splashed onto her body.

There was a piece of soap in the rack and she began to wash herself with it, rubbing it into a lather between her hands then massaging it into her body. The warmth of the water felt wonderful and she raised her face to the spray, feeling her weariness wash from her along with the suds. For a while she completely forgot who she was or where, happy just to enjoy the refreshing sensation of the shower.

When at last she had had enough she turned off the tap and stepped out from the steamy atmosphere of the cubicle into the changing room, feeling renewed and invigorated. It was only then that she realised she had a problem.

There was no towel.

Anxiously she checked every inch of the room, but in vain. There was nothing with which to dry herself. She cursed her stupidity at not having checked beforehand. Her body, she knew, would soon dry. But her hair was soaking, and it would be ages before she would be able to dress with it in such a state. In desperation she tried wringing it out, but without success.

Then she remembered the storeroom. It was situated at the end of the corridor on the executive floor and only the week before she had been asked to get something from it. At the time she had noticed that they stored the roller towels there that were used throughout the lower floors. She would simply have to use one of those.

She let herself out of the changing room and into the area where the sinks were. As she crossed the room she was confronted by her reflection on all sides. The sight of her wet and naked body made her hesitate. Despite the fact that she was certain the building was empty, it still seemed an outrageous act to walk about the corridors with nothing on.

She opened the bathroom door a crack and peered through. Outside it was as silent and empty as when she had arrived. With a guilty glance about her she slipped out and padded off up the corridor.

The store room was further away than she had remembered, and she had to walk down two more passageways before she finally found it. When she did she reached for the handle gratefully and turned it.

The door did not move. It was locked. Once more Lisa cursed her ill fortune as she realised she was foiled again. She pushed the door, but it was no good. There was no way in. With a sigh she turned and began to retrace her steps.

Then a light went on ahead of her.

Lisa froze, her heart almost stopping with the shock of the realisation that there was someone there, possibly just around the next corner. At first she couldn't believe it, but the sight of a second light coming on confirmed her worst fears. Someone had arrived on the floor since she had left the bathroom, and they were heading in her direction!

Lisa suddenly felt very vulnerable indeed. She was not even supposed to be on this floor of the building. To be discovered here naked was more than she could bear. She could hear footsteps now, and they were coming closer every second.

There was a door to her right and she grabbed the handle and turned it. The door opened and she slipped through, closing it behind her as quietly as she was able. Looking about her she found herself in one of the large executive offices. It was quite dark inside, the only light coming through the outside window. On the far side of the room was a wide desk on which stood a computer terminal. Beside it was a large cabinet close to the corner. There was a small gap between it and the wall, and Lisa scurried across to this niche, squeezing herself into it. No sooner had she done so than the door opened and the room was flooded with light. She shrank back against the wall as she heard somebody enter the office.

The footsteps crossed the room, then there was the creak of a chair, followed by a click and the rattle of the computer disk as the machine started up. Lisa stayed where she was, cursing her ill-luck at choosing precisely the wrong office in which to conceal herself.

Minutes passed, during which the familiar beeps of a personal computer booting up were the only sounds. Then came the noise of fingers tapping on the keyboard. This went on for some time. Every now and again a man's voice would swear, then the tapping would begin again. Lisa remained with her back pressed against the wall, wondering how long she would be forced to remain where she was.

At last, though, after she had listened for what seemed ages to the obvious lack of success of the man at the keyboard, curiosity got the better of her. She leaned forward and peered out from her hiding place. There, sitting with his back to her and staring at the computer screen, was a dark figure, strumming his fingers on the desk.

Afterwards, when Lisa analysed the situation in her mind, she realised that even then she might have got away with it. It was obvious that the man was losing patience with the computer and would surely have left soon. She could easily had remained where she was until he had gone.

But then, all of a sudden, she needed to sneeze.

She held her breath, praying that it would pass, but the tickle in her nose increased until she could hold it back no longer.

When it erupted she slammed her hand over her mouth, reducing the explosion to little more than a cough. But it was enough.

"Who's there?"

She shrank back further into her corner, her heart beating fast. She heard him rise from his chair and cross to the cabinet. He opened it, then closed it again. Then he peered round the side.

At once Lisa hugged her breasts, her other hand placed flat over her crotch as she stared back at him.

"What the hell are you doing in here?"

Lisa recognised him at once. His name was Conrad Lang, and he was the company's sales director. He was tall, with dark hair and a strikingly handsome face, tanned by numerous visits to sunny climes.

"Answer me," he ordered.

"I.., I'm sorry, Sir," she stammered. "I was taking a shower."

"In my office?"

"There was no towel Sir. I was looking for one. Then I heard you, so I hid in here."

"But you're naked."

"My clothes are in the bathroom Sir."

Which bathroom?"

She lowered her eyes. "The executive bathroom, Sir."

He frowned. "Well young lady, you'd better come out of there."

He stood back whilst Lisa slid out of her hiding place. Her face was bright red as she stepped into the room, her hands still covering her nudity.

The man returned to his chair, settling into it and swivelling it around to face her as she stood trembling before him.

"Now tell me, who are you?

"My name is Lisa Carling Sir."

"What are you doing in this building?"

"I work in the Data Processing department Sir. I'm a computer programmer."

"Then what on earth are you doing up here?"

"I wanted a shower. It's so hot with the air conditioning

broken."

"But the shower is in the executive washroom. That's for directors only."

"I know. I'm sorry Sir. I thought there was nobody about."

"That's no excuse."

"I know. I'm sorry," she repeated lamely.

"Naturally I shall have to report this. It's a serious offence. Who's your supervisor?"

"Miss Larkin, Sir."

"And what will she say when I tell her I found you naked in my office?"

Lisa couldn't imagine what Miss Larkin would say. A spinster in her early fifties, she was a strict disciplinarian and something of a prude. Only the day before she had berated one of Lisa's colleagues for reading a tabloid newspaper during his lunch hour that contained photographs of topless girls. What she would think of Lisa's actions was hard to imagine. It was doubtful that she would be allowed to keep her job.

"Well?"

"I think she'd sack me Sir."

"Precisely and..." he broke off suddenly, staring at her. "What did you say your job was?"

"I'm a computer programmer Sir."

"Then you'll know how to get into this damned system."

"Which one?" she asked, confused.

"The weapons design system. The one that holds the plans for the design of our products."

"Don't you have a password?"

"No. I'm supposed to, but someone's screwed up."

"I'm not allowed to issue passwords Sir."

"Nevertheless, you can get into the system, can't you?"

"I'm not supposed..."

"Listen Miss Carling," he said. "You're already in enough trouble. I would remind you I'm a director of this company.

12

I can dismiss you myself if necessary. Now, are you going to help me?"

Lisa sighed. She really had no choice, and she knew it. Her position was impossible. Here she was, stark naked, having just been caught in a part of the company where she knew she shouldn't be. The man held all the cards.

"I can get you in Sir," she said quietly.

He pushed back his chair and indicated the screen. "Go on then."

"Couldn't I go and get my clothes please Sir?"

"No. I want access to that system now."

Reluctantly Lisa moved round behind the desk. She stared down at the keyboard, her hands still covering her body.

"Come on."

Blushing brightly, Lisa lowered her hands, exposing her luscious body to the man. As she did so she hung her head. Lang had no way of knowing it, but no man had ever seen her naked before that moment, and she was doubly embarrassed by the fact that he made no pretence of his interest, his eyes roving over her breasts and sex.

What would become of her now, she wondered.

Chapter 2

Lisa Carling was a solitary girl, with no real close friends. She had never known her parents, who had died when she was a child, leaving her to be brought up in a series of children's homes. There she had been a quiet, withdrawn girl, and had made little impact on either those who taught her, or her companions in the homes. But at the age of sixteen a slightly awkward child had suddenly blossomed into an extraordinarily beautiful young woman, though at first she had been barely aware of the fact.

Something else happened to her as well. Something that was ultimately to change her life completely. It happened soon after she turned eighteen and went to live in a hostel for young women.

Lisa was forced to discover her sexuality.

It had all taken place late one evening. At the time Lisa was at college, studying computers, and had been up late completing a homework assignment. She had been on her way from the bathroom to her bedroom when she had heard a commotion coming from one of the other girls' rooms. She had paused outside for a second, and just at that fateful moment, the door had opened and a girl had come out. On seeing Lisa she had stopped short, an indignant expression on her face.

"What the hell are you doing here?" she demanded.

The girl's name was Angela. Lisa recognised her as a worker at the local factory. She was a tall girl, with coarse manners, and Lisa had scarcely exchanged a word with her since she had entered the hostel. Now, as she confronted the woman, she found herself at a loss for words.

"I'm sorry," she stammered. "I was just passing."

"Spying more like."

"No. I was on my way to bed. Honestly!"

Then why had you stopped?"

"No reason. I just heard the voices and..."

"Come in here, you nosey bitch."

"No I..."

"Come in, I said!"

Lisa was given no choice. Suddenly she was grasped roughly by the arm and pulled inside. The room was thick with cigarette smoke, and two empty wine bottles stood on the bedside table. Both smoking and drinking were forbidden in the hostel, and Lisa realised at once that she had stumbled on an illegal party. Besides Angela there were two other women in the room. Lisa knew them only by name.

Trudy was a loud woman with large breasts and a propensity for lewd jokes. The third one, known as Dot, was rumoured to be a prostitute, though Lisa had never actually seen her with a man.

"What the hell's going on, Angela?" asked Trudy.

"I caught this little bitch listening at the door."

"Oh, her. Little Miss Goody-Two-Shoes," snorted Dot. "Going to turn us in, were you darling?"

"No. I'm sorry. I didn't mean..."

"Shut up," barked Angela. "Bitch is probably a spy for the warden." She grabbed Lisa by the hair. "Isn't that right?"

"No. Please I..."

"I said quiet!" Angela tugged at her hair again. "What do you think girls?"

"I think this little spy deserves teaching a lesson," said Trudy.

Lisa looked from one to the other of the three women. She was shaking slightly as she stared from face to face. She wished that she had gone straight back to bed. It was clear to her now that she would have to undergo some kind of ordeal at the women's hands before that would be allowed.

"What about the belt?" said Angela. "Do you reckon she's ever had her arse tanned?"

"I doubt it," said Dot. "Let's take a look. Strip her."

Lisa tried to back away, but Angela was just behind her, and grabbed her by the arms.

"Get that nightie off."

All Lisa wore was a nightgown. A modest garment that fastened up to her neck and hung down to her knees. Now Dot took hold of it and simply pulled it over her head, tossing it to one side.

Lisa blushed crimson as she stood naked before the three women, who hooted with laughter at her discomfort.

"Scared to flash your tits and cunt are you?" said Dot.

"Mind you, they're nice ones. You ever been fucked dar-

15

ling?" asked Angela.

Lisa shook her head.

"Little bitch is a virgin," said Trudy.

"So's her arse by the look of it," replied Angela. "I think a taste of leather is what's called for here. Get her on the bed."

They grabbed Lisa's arms and pulled her up onto the bed, making her kneel and face the wall. Then a piece of rope was produced. Lisa tried to struggle free when she saw it, but they held her down whilst Angela tied her wrists together and secured them to the bars at the end of the bed. Lisa was left, on her knees, naked and helpless before the three of them.

"Lift up your backside," ordered Angela. "Let's get a good look at you."

Lisa hesitated. Then, seeing the look in Angela's eye, shuffled backwards onto all fours, raising her behind to the watching trio as she did so. She felt a hand on the bare flesh of her behind, giving a little start as she did so.

"Spread your knees apart," ordered Angela. "Let's see that little virgin cunt of yours."

Scarlet with shame, Lisa did as she was told, presenting what she knew to be a perfect view of her sex and anus to the onlookers. The hand on her backside stroked the tight flesh.

"This'll look better with a few stripes across it," said Trudy, and the others laughed their agreement.

Trudy crossed to a wardrobe by the door and took something from it. She carried it across and held it under the hapless Lisa's nose. It was a leather belt, no more than an inch thick. She doubled it over and swished it through the air a couple of times.

"What do you think girls?" she said. "Six strokes?"

"Make it ten," said Angela. "I want to see the hoity-toity little bitch squirm."

"Please..." said Lisa softly.

"Quiet you," ordered Dot. "One more word and we up it to twenty. And don't scream either, or we'll have to gag you."

Lisa closed her mouth. It was obvious that pleading with them would have no effect. They were determined to have their fun, and they needed a victim. But did they really have to strip her naked? And tie her in such a degrading way? She looked round at the three of them. They were all grinning broadly, clearly enjoying what they were watching. Lisa's colour deepened and she turned to face the wall.

Trudy raised the belt.

Thwack!

She brought it down across Lisa's backside with tremendous force, the blow stinging the tethered girl terribly as the hard leather bit into her tender young flesh. Lisa gritted her teeth, her eyes firmly closed.

Thwack!

Down came the belt again, delivering another stripe across Lisa's behind and sending another shock of pain through her helpless body.

Thwack!

It fell for a third time, this time wrapping about her bottom cheeks, the end delivering an excruciating blow to her thigh. Lisa bit her lip hard, trying desperately not to cry out as the cruel blows rained down on her.

Thwack!

Trudy's accuracy was deadly, each stroke finding a new area of virgin flesh and planting a burning weal across it. A sweat had broken out on Lisa's body now, and each lash with the belt raised a small spray of wetness.

Thwack!

"Ah!"

This time Lisa had been quite unable to suppress a cry, since the blow had been delivered vertically, and the end had wrapped itself round and slapped hard against the lips

17

of her sex, making her jab her hips forward. Her flesh stung dreadfully with the blow.

But it had another effect as well.

Suddenly Lisa realised that the throbbing between her legs was not exclusively caused by the pain. The blow had aroused something else inside her; something she wouldn't have believed possible.

Even as she awaited the next stroke from the belt, Lisa felt her clitoris harden as a sudden spasm of lust ran through her, bringing an unexpected wetness to her vagina. It took her completely by surprise. She had never experienced anything like it before, but she knew at once what it was, and it shocked her deeply.

She was becoming sexually aroused.

Thwack!

This time, when the blow fell, it had a totally different effect on her. It stung, certainly. In fact the pain was abominable, but compared to the lust that was rising within her, it seemed paltry.

Thwack!

"Oh!"

Lisa's love bud was fairly throbbing now as her juices flowed freely. All of a sudden the beating stopped.

"Well I'll be damned," said Trudy.

"What?"

"Look at her cunt. The little slut's getting a thrill out of this."

"What?"

"Here, let me check," said Angela. She reached forward and thrust two fingers into Lisa's vagina.

"Ahhh!"

The cry that escaped Lisa's lips this time could not possibly be mistaken for one of pain. There was no doubting the lust in her tone, nor the way her hips thrust downwards onto Angela's fingers as she attempted to pleasure herself on them, little whimpers coming from her as she did so.

"My god, you're right," said Angela wonderingly. "She's like a bitch on heat. Just look at my fingers."

She held them up, and all could see how they glistened with moisture.

Dot laughed. "Shit, I never saw a dame get horny from a thrashing," she chuckled. "Finish it off, Trudy, I wanna watch this."

Thwack!

The belt fell across Lisa's backside for the eighth time, then the woman stood back to watch Lisa's hips pumping back and forth against the empty air, the lips of her sex expanding and contracting, as if wrapped round an invisible cock.

Thwack!

Lisa's backside was red now, the stripes merging together into an angry mass of pain. Yet she seemed barely to notice the belt now, her entire body undulating back and forth whilst moans escaped from her lips.

Thwack!

The final blow descended with all the force of the first, the crack of leather against bare flesh echoing about the room. Then there was silence, broken only by the panting of the naked girl and the creaking of the bed springs as she continued to thrust her hips back and forth.

Angela reached beneath her and caressed her breast. The nipple was already rock hard and Lisa's moans doubled in volume as the woman massaged the soft flesh.

"Shit, we've got to bring this little slut off," she said. "You still got that dildo, Trudy?"

"Sure. It's in that drawer.

Lisa watched with trepidation as Angela went to the drawer and opened it. The woman withdrew something long and pink. Something Lisa did not recognise. Angela brought it over and held it under her nose.

19

The young captive's eyes widened when she saw what it was, It was a perfect model of a man's penis, complete in every detail, the rough surface bulging with veins,

"That's right, little virgin," said Angela. "That's what a cock looks like."

She turned a knob at the base and the object began to hum quietly. Then she held it against Lisa's cheek, so that the girl could feel the vibrations that ran through it. It was an extraordinary sensation, and when she moved it down to rub against Lisa's nipples, the young captive gave a sudden gasp of pleasure.

Angela ran the humming phallus over Lisa's body, sliding it down her stomach then bringing it round to her back. She rubbed it against the burning flesh of her behind, tracing out the cruel stripes thereon. Then she found the crack of her backside, moving it ever lower towards her still undulating sex lips.

"Ahhh!"

Once again Lisa was quite unable to suppress a cry of pleasure as the dildo slid down her slit and found her swollen clitoris. Never before had she been touched so intimately, and the sensation made her begin thrusting her hips forward once more as her lust was renewed. It was as if her cunt had become the centre of her being.

Suddenly Lisa realised that she wanted the dildo inside her desperately. It was a sensation she had never felt before. A primeval animal lust that seemed to have taken over from all her other instincts. Whimpering quietly, she pressed back urgently with her behind, urging Angela to penetrate her.

"Christ the slut wants it bad," exclaimed Dot. "She's positively panting for it."

"Yeah," put in Lucy. "Give it to her Angela."

With a shudder Lisa felt the bulbous end of the imitation cock seek out the entrance to her vagina. Then Angela began to press, twisting it as she did so.

There was a moment of resistance and a sudden pain. Then it was in, sliding deep inside her, pressing all the way home until she felt it come up against the deepest part of her vagina.

It was the most extraordinary sensation imaginable to Lisa, the thick object humming inside her, causing a sudden gush of love juice into her hole as she cried out with the sheer pleasure of it. Her hips were pumping back and forth with vigour now, so that Angela had simply to hold onto the end of the knob whilst her own actions forced it to slide in and out.

Lisa knew she must make a sight, naked and tethered, her striped backside high in the air as she fucked the dildo with all the strength she could muster. Beneath her she could feel her breasts shaking back and forth with every jab of her hips, and she knew the three women were amused by her arousal. But she was beyond caring now, simply lost in the exquisite sensation of penetration and, whilst she had never before experienced orgasm, she knew instinctively that something wonderful was about to happen.

"Ah! Ah! Ah!"

Her cries rang through the room as the glorious relief of a climax swept over her. She closed her eyes tight, her entire being consumed by the pleasure the dildo was giving her. The orgasm went on and on, her cries gradually dying to moans as she came down from her high.

At last, though, she was spent, collapsing forward onto the bed and burying her head in the pillow, suddenly overcome with the shame of what the three women had witnessed.

"Well," said Angela, dragging the now dripping dildo from inside her. "You're a proper little dark horse, aren't you young lady?"

Chapter 3

The extraordinary encounter with the three women had happened two years ago, and Lisa had left the hostel soon afterwards, unable to face the other women once word of her exploits had got round. She had moved into a small bedsit where she could live alone, and complete her studies, and was now a qualified computer programmer with a good job.

But she had never forgotten that evening with the three women. She would lie in bed at night, turning it over in her mind, trying to make sense of what had happened and the recalcitrant way in which her body had behaved.

Then would come the dreams, vivid images in which large, broad-chested men would strip her, tie her to a tree and whip her whilst a cheering crowd looked on. Or others where she would find herself stark naked amongst a group of fully-clad strangers and would expose her body shamelessly to them. Such dreams would inevitably end with her waking up suddenly, her sex running with moisture. She would slide her hand down between her legs and seek out her love bud, feeling it harden as the memory of the nudity, the beating and what had followed filled her mind. But then she would withdraw her fingers, afraid of the power of her sensuality, and of the behaviour it might invoke.

And since that day she had been careful to steer clear of men, keeping them at arms length, refusing any contact and earning for herself the reputation of being a prude.

Until tonight, that was.

Standing as she was, naked and helpless before this powerful man, the memories of those erotic dreams suddenly flooded back, and with a shock she realised that with the recollection was also returning the sense of arousal. She couldn't fully understand why it was that being in this man's power gave her such a thrill. All she knew was the aching sensation in her sex as his eyes took her in.

"Come on, then," he ordered. "The computer."

Lisa shook her head, as if awakening from a reverie. She turned to the machine. There was no chair, so she was forced to lean forward over the desk in order to use the keyboard. This served to emphasise the shape of her breasts and she was aware of the way they shook with every keystroke. She tried hard to concentrate on the visual display unit in front of her and to blot from her mind the sight she knew she was making to him.

The weapons planning system was protected by a sophisticated password system, but this posed no problem to Lisa, who knew it well. In no time she had the main menu up on the screen in front of her. Lang sat close to her, barking commands as she steered her way through the system. Soon she had accessed some of the more complex weapons plans.

"Print them," he said.

She tapped in the appropriate codes. His closeness was having an effect on her, the smell of his expensive aftershave filling her nostrils and increasing the desires that were welling up inside her. When he leant forward to study the screen and casually placed his hand on her backside a tremor ran through her whole body and she sensed her nipples hardening despite the fact that she hadn't even been touched there.

The printer began to whirr and he momentarily left her side, crossing to the machine and picking up the sheets as they came off. Lisa remained where she was, not daring to move, her heart thumping against her chest.

"This isn't the one," he said. "Try the next. And do hurry, girl. We don't have all night."

Lisa turned her attention back to the keyboard, her fingers flying over the keys. He moved close again and his hand reached for her breast.

23

"Oh!"

The touch was so unexpected and so intimate that she gave an exclamation, her concentration momentarily broken.

"Your nipples are hard," he remarked, taking the knob of flesh between his fingers. "Why is that?"

"I... I don't know."

"In my experience of women, hard nipples mean she's either cold or turned on. It's not cold in here, is it?"

She reddened. "No Sir," she said quietly.

"Where's that data then?" he said, suddenly seeming to lose interest in her body.

Lisa hurriedly typed out the appropriate code, trying to shut from her mind the exquisite sensation as he casually fondled her breast. The required files appeared on the screen and once more she was ordered to print them. This time he seemed more satisfied with the output. He spread the papers out on his desk and pulled up his chair. Then he began to study them closely. Lisa stood beside him, her hands dangling at her side, waiting for orders. The nipple he had been caressing was positively tingling and she longed to touch it herself, but dared not. Instead she simply remained where she was, a thrill running through her every time he raised his eyes from the document and let them rove over her body.

Suddenly he spoke again.

"There seem to be a couple of formulae missing from these papers. Come here and see."

Lisa approached him and looked questioningly at the sheets before her.

"Look here," he said, pointing to one of the sheets in the centre of the desk.

Lisa leaned forward, suddenly aware once again of the way this made her breasts more prominent. Her nipples were still erect, the hard little protrusions in stark contrast to the whiteness of her flesh.

She studied the area to which he was pointing. "That's an encryption code Sir," she said. "Some parts of these documents have a secondary protection on them, a sort of double safety device."

"You mean I can't see all the data?"

"Not without the right security code."

"Do you have such a code?"

"No Sir."

"Can you get one?"

"But you're a director Sir. Surely you..."

"Never mind that. I asked if you could get one."

"I'm not supposed to Sir."

"Nevertheless you know this system. Can you get hold of one?"

"Not from here."

"What do you mean?"

"Security is controlled from the main terminal in the computer room. And that's locked."

"But you can get in there during the day?"

"Yes Sir."

"Good. Lie forward over the desk."

"I beg your pardon?"

"I think the order was simple enough. Lie forward over the desk."

Lisa hesitated for a second, then complied, leaning forward and prostrating herself over the desk's surface. The wood felt hard and cold against her bare skin and she shivered slightly as she lay her cheek against it.

"Open your legs."

Once again the order took her by surprise, but this time the shiver was one of excitement as she spread her thighs apart, aware that in doing so she was opening the pink folds of her sex to his gaze.

She gave a little start as she felt him grasp the cheeks of her backside, forcing them apart and revealing the small dark star of her anus.

"Do you have a boyfriend, Miss Carling?" he asked.

"N-no Sir."

You have a lovely body. Do you usually show it off so blatantly?"

Lisa closed her eyes. "No Sir. I.., Ah!"

A cry escaped her lips as he slid his fingers around and ran them down her slit.

"Look at this."

She craned her neck around. He was holding up his hand for her to see. His fingers were shiny with moisture.

"It's giving you a kick, isn't it?"

Lisa didn't answer.

"It seems to me that you have two choices, Miss Carling." His fingers were back at her sex, and she felt her whole body lurch as he found her clitoris. "Would you like to hear them?"

"Y-yes please Sir." She was panting slightly now, her hips beginning to writhe as he toyed with her love bud.

"Either I report your behaviour tonight to Miss Larkin. And believe me I'd have to tell her every detail, including how you reacted just now. Or you can co-operate with me. What do you think?"

"I'll..." Lisa broke off as a spasm of pleasure ran through her, making her gasp. "I'll do whatever you say, Sir."

"Good. Stand up."

He took his hand from her sex. Slowly she rose to her feet. She looked down at the desk. Her body had left a mark where she had been lying, the round globes of her breasts clearly outlined. What was more embarrassing to her, though, was the pool of moisture where her crotch had been. She dropped her eyes and realised with a shock that there were drops of wetness on her inner thighs.

He moved close to her, taking her chin in his hand and pulling her face up to stare into his eyes. His other hand dropped to her breast, kneading it between his fingers.

"I need someone to assist me, Miss Carling," he said. "Someone I can trust to be discreet. Someone who can get me the information I require. Do you understand?"

"I think so Sir."

"There is information I require from the system. Information that must be obtained covertly."

"But surely, as a director, you have access to any information you require?"

"Not necessarily. Some data is kept secret even from me. But this is something different."

"Sir?"

"We believe somebody is tampering with the data. Someone very senior indeed. Only the Chairman and I are aware of this sabotage. We need to be able to get the data and pass it on to some experts without anyone else in the company knowing. That's why we need someone who understands the system. Do you think you could do it?"

"I think so Sir."

"Good. This is very important to your career. Co-operate with me and you will go far. Do you follow?"

"Yes Sir."

Suddenly a faint smile came to his lips.

"There are other duties I'll be calling on you for as well, Miss Carling." He said. "Duties of a more personal nature."

"Sir?"

"This body of yours. I shall expect you to use it to entertain some of those experts."

"Entertain them Sir?"

"Exactly. These are very important men and it's vital that we keep them happy. And, being men, they naturally have their desires. Do you understand me?"

"But I..," she made as if to protest, then gazed down at her nakedness and her voice trailed away. "Yes Sir," she said meekly.

27

Lisa couldn't believe what he was asking. What was more she couldn't believe her own reaction. On hearing his demands a spasm of excitement had shaken her small frame, and she felt another drop of moisture escape onto her thigh as her sex lips convulsed momentarily.

"Good. Now some of these experts will be visiting in the next couple of weeks. There is some information I need you to get for them. We will discuss your other duties later. Meanwhile you should expect some instructions in the next few days. Is that clear?"

"Yes Sir."

"Right. And now, Miss Carling, I intend to fuck you."

The words were spoken casually, as if he was suggesting something perfectly ordinary. Yet the effect they had on Lisa was electric, and a gasp escaped her lips as his grip tightened on her breast. She was astounded at her own reaction. She knew she should object, show outrage even. But she was too far gone for that now.

It was then that the revelation hit her. For the first time she realised how she craved a man who would dominate her. A man who would force her to disport herself naked before him, who would manoeuvre her and touch her as casually as he would some domestic animal, and who would demand her submission without a thought for her own consent. Lang was just such a man

"On the desk. On your back this time."

Lisa's reaction was almost eager. She turned her back to the desk, and pressing her backside against the edge, leaned backward, prostrating her body before him, her breasts flattening slightly and falling to the sides as she did so, leaving her gazing down at him through a valley of soft flesh. She didn't wait to be asked to spread her legs, opening them wide so that the lips parted for him, allowing him to see into the entrance to her vagina.

He unzipped his fly and pulled out his cock. Lisa stared

in fascination at it. She wondered what he would say if he knew it was her first. It was larger than she had expected, thick and swollen, the end purple and shiny with lubrication. As she watched he took the shaft in his fist and worked the foreskin back and forth a few times. She wriggled her backside forward so that it projected slightly over the edge of the desk. Then she waited, her sex lips still twitching slightly.

"Ahhh!"

When the end of his knob touched her love bud she almost shouted with lust. She wanted him badly now, so badly that she lifted her backside up and thrust her cunt at him, willing him to penetrate her.

He moved his glans up and down her slit, coating the tip with her juices. Then he positioned it at the entrance to her love hole and began to press.

"Oh!"

Suddenly her lips parted and he was inside her. Just the tip at first, but as he pressed harder, his cock slid deeper and deeper. She gasped at the sensation, spreading her legs still wider in order to accommodate him. Then, just as she felt she could take no more, she felt the hardness of his zipper pressing against her pubis.

He started to fuck her, his movements smooth and even as he worked his cock in and out. Lisa writhed and moaned beneath him, her whole body alive with pleasure. She had had no idea it could be like this. The dildo had been fantastic, but the feel of a real live throbbing cock in her vagina was something else. She gazed at her ravisher. He was standing, looking down on her, his face expressionless, his hands gripping her thighs as he pumped his hips back and forth. It was as if she was no more than an inflatable doll. A toy to give him relief from his needs, rather than the hot-blooded young nymph that she was.

Would it have made him feel any different if he knew he

was deflowering her? She thought not, nor did she care. This was how she wanted to be taken, without emotion or tender words. Simply fucked for the pleasure of it.

He increased the force of his thrusts and she whimpered softly, raising her hips and pressing back at him, her breasts shaking back and forth with every stroke. Inside her she could feel her orgasm building, but she wanted to hold back and wait for him, to witness a male climax for the very first time. Her sex lips were convulsing uncontrollably now and she could feel the juices leaking round the side of his rampant weapon and flowing down her legs.

All at once a glazed look came over his face and she felt his body stiffen. Instinctively she knew he was about to ejaculate and she tightened the muscles inside her sex.

He came with a hoarse grunt, and suddenly Lisa's vagina was filling with semen. The sensation was incredible, spurt after spurt of thick, hot fluid gushing into her and triggering her own orgasm almost at once.

Lisa's cries echoed about the room as her climax overcame her. Her head shook from side to side, her backside banging down against the surface of the desk as she abandoned herself to the passion of her lust. She had never imagined fucking could be as good as this, and she wondered momentarily why she had avoided it for so long. Even as she came, thought of the liaisons Lang had planned for her with his guests flashed through her mind, taking her to new heights as they did so.

Suddenly he withdrew, and she gave a cry of disappointment, gazing pleadingly at him as he tucked his cock back into his trousers. He gave a little frown, and then stuck two fingers crudely into her vagina. She groaned with gratitude, her writhing hips pressing down on his hand and wringing the last ounces of pleasure from his coarse digits.

Gradually she came down, the gyrations of her crotch decreasing as the passion ebbed from her. At last she was still, her breasts rising and falling as she struggled to regain her breath. He paused for a moment, then grasped her arm and pulled her into a sitting position.

Lisa felt a mess, her body shiny with sweat, her hair hanging in lank strands, her thighs splattered with semen. She gazed up at Lang wearily as he placed his fingers up to her face. They were running with his spunk.

"Lick them clean," he ordered.

She leant forward, taking them into her mouth and sucking at them. The taste of his seed was alien to her, as was the taste of her own desires, but she swallowed it down hungrily, licking the remnants from her lips. When his hand was clean he yanked her to her feet, then indicated the desk, where a pool of wetness had formed and was trickling down the wood.

"Clean that too."

Lisa dropped to her knees, licking from the bottom of the desk upwards, swallowing down yet more of his come, working feverishly until her tongue had removed every trace. Then she rose to her feet and stood before him, hands held at her side, a picture of naked submission.

"Good," he said. "You will be hearing from me soon. Now get out of here, and don't trespass on this floor again without permission. Is that clear?"

"Yes Sir."

Lisa turned and walked toward the door, slipping through and closing it carefully behind her. She made her way back to the washroom as if in a dream, oblivious to the sight she must make. When she re-entered the changing room her clothes were just where she had left them. But she ignored them. Instead she lay down on the hard wooden bench and spread her legs.

Then, for the first time in her life, Lisa Carling began to masturbate.

31

For the following week Lisa moved almost as if in a dream. No matter what she did, she couldn't rid her mind of the incident with Lang. At first her reaction was one of disgust with herself and contempt for his behaviour. She told herself that her response to the director had been a freak, and that nice girls like her simply didn't behave like that. But the longer it took for him to contact her, the more she found herself wondering whether she would ever hear from him again. Before long the incident was dominating her thoughts, and every morning she would scan her doorstep for mail, as she would her pigeon hole at work. But in vain.

She tried to rationalise her emotions, telling herself that she was being stupid, and that no normal girl would have subjected herself to the humiliations he had heaped on her. But every time she was alone the memories came flooding back and the wetness returned to her crotch. Then she would be forced to slide her hand down between he legs and bring herself relief, an action which would fill her with shame the moment her orgasm had subsided.

At the same time she knew her work was suffering. On more than one occasion she had incurred the wrath of Miss Larkin for being inattentive, something that had never happened before. The thought of Conrad Lang was becoming an obsession with her, and there seemed nothing she could do about it.

It was almost two weeks later that the note appeared on her doormat. It bore no address or stamp, and had been delivered during the day whilst she was at work. She found herself shaking as she picked it up and studied it. It was in a plain brown envelope that simply bore the word 'Carling' on the outside. She carried it into the kitchen and slit it open with a knife. The note was typewritten and unsigned. She read it carefully.

'You are to obtain the encrypted information on the M271 and L360. You will receive further instructions on delivery tomorrow. Destroy this note.'

She turned the paper over. That was it. There was nothing else. She wasn't sure whether to be excited or disappointed. It wasn't exactly what she had expected, but it was, at least, a development, and it meant that Lang had been serious when he had disclosed his intention to use her further. She lit the gas stove and burned the note. Then, picking up her brief-case, she headed for the front door again.

She had no difficulty obtaining the information he had asked for. She had taken the trouble some days before to obtain a key to the computer room and, with the rest of the staff having gone home for the night, it was easy to gain access to it. Employing her computer skills, it took only a short time to discover the passwords required to the encryption system, and shortly afterwards the data she needed was spewing from the printer. She studied the pages as they came off, wondering what it was about them that was suspect. Then, realising that the formulae they contained was beyond her understanding, she simply clipped them together. Within half an hour of arriving back at work she was tucking the papers into her briefcase and heading home once more.

That night Lisa could hardly eat a thing, and the following day she found it more difficult than ever to concentrate on her work. Her stomach was churning with excitement and she couldn't help consulting her watch every few minutes. The day seemed endless, the program on which she was working suddenly trivial, and she barely wrote twenty lines of code before the hands on her watch finally crawled around to five-thirty and she felt free to pick up her bags and hurry for the train home.

When she arrived at her flat she hardly dared open the door for fear of an anticlimax. Gingerly she inserted the key in the lock and turned it, almost unwilling to look down as she pushed the door open. She need not have worried, though, for there on the mat she found a large envelope. Like the previous one it was completely unmarked apart from her surname printed in block capitals. She picked it up at once and tore it open with trembling fingers. Inside was a smaller package and another typed sheet. The message was, once again, a short one.

'You are to wear the clothes in this package and nothing else. A car will collect you at seven fifteen. Bring the papers.'

She read it through twice before burning it. Then she picked up the package and headed for the bedroom.

An hour later she was standing before the mirror contemplating her reflection with dismay. The words in the note had been quite clear. She was to wear the clothes in the package and nothing else. Yet, as she studied the reflection that confronted her, her heart sank. How could she possibly dare to go out like this? Her eyes travelled down her body, an expression of anguish on her face.

The parcel had contained a pair of black hold-up stockings, an apron and a pair of impossibly high stiletto heels.

And that was all.

She had turned it inside out, searching for something else, but without success. The discovery had appalled her. How could she possibly leave the house dressed in those? It was more than could be asked of any decent girl. She could have wept with the ignominy of her position. Even a simple pair of panties would have been something. But that was all there was.

Reluctantly she had donned the garments. The stockings came up to about six inches below her crotch, the high heels

34

making her legs look even longer and more slender than usual. The apron was like that of a parlour maid, with a pair of strings that tied behind her neck and two more at the waist. Its tunic was small and square and quite inadequate to contain her breasts; brown half-moons of her aureoles showing on either side and a valley of cleavage at the top. Its skirt too was tiny, like a small bib that scarcely reached her crotch. When she turned sideways the slightest movement revealed her breasts and pubic thatch, and from behind she was, to all intents and purposes, entirely nude, the full contours of her pert backside completely uncovered.

She trembled slightly as she regarded herself. She even felt embarrassed wearing the outfit in the privacy of her bedroom. She could scarcely contemplate going out in this state of undress. Yet, at the same time, that odd, unaccountable thrill had come back, as she had known it would, and she couldn't help running her finger down between her legs and toying briefly with her clitoris.

The ring of the doorbell made her jump, and she snatched her hand away from her crotch guiltily, almost as if she had been caught in the act of masturbating. She stood, rooted to the spot, still staring at herself in the mirror. For a moment she almost lost her nerve. Then she thought of Lang's cruel features and she knew she had to obey. She picked up the sheaf of papers that lay on the table, and with one last vain effort to tuck her breasts into the tiny tunic, she went to the door.

"Blimey!"

The taxi driver was a large, heavily-built man wearing jeans and a sweatshirt. Two days of stubble grew on his chin. He eyed his prospective passenger with undisguised interest, his eyes wide. Lisa felt her cheeks glow red under his scrutiny.

"Haven't you got a coat or something?" he asked with a grin.

She shook her head, her eyes still downcast.

"Well I guess we'd better go, then, although I recommend you avoid any draughts,"

Stepping into the road in front of the house was yet another ordeal. Two youths lounging on the corner spotted her immediately and their wolf whistles rang out as she tried hard to walk in the tiny apron without exposing her breasts and sex. The cab driver walked behind her, his perfect view of her backside bringing a broad grin to his face.

It was a minicab, and Lisa was obliged to stoop low to climb inside, so that the apron hung down away from her body, leaving nothing to the onlookers' imagination. Once she had settled, the plastic of the seat feeling hard and uncomfortable against her behind, the driver paused, peering down the front of the tunic at her protruding nipples, the grin still fixed on his face. Then he slammed her door and climbed into the driving seat.

Lisa stared out of the window at the two youths, who had by now approached the car and were making lewd gestures to her through the window. For a moment she feared that they might reach inside and grope her vulnerable body. Then, with a sigh of relief, she heard the driver engage gear with a crunch and the car lurched forward, carrying the hapless girl off to new ordeals, the nature of which were beyond her wildest dreams.

Or nightmares.

Chapter 5

The journey was a long one. Lisa sat in the back of the cab, saying nothing, thankful that the cabbie kept his silence, restricting himself to the occasional sly glance in the mirror at his scantily clad passenger. When, at last, the car drew to a halt outside a large, important looking house in one of the more salubrious residential areas of the city, the driver turned in his seat.

"This is the place, darling," he said. "Time to get out."

Lisa fumbled with the doorhandle, but by the time she had mastered it he was out of the car and standing beside it. Once again it was an awkward and embarrassing struggle to clamber out of the vehicle, and by the time she had done so there was no part of her anatomy that hadn't come under his leering gaze. The cabbie was determined to get his money's worth though, and when at last she had straightened and patted the apron into position he pointed to her papers, still lying on the seat beside where she had been sitting. Lisa was then obliged to bend back into the car and give him a further delightful view of her bare behind as she picked them up. At the same time she felt him grasp the smooth flesh of her backside in his large, rough hand. His index finger pressed against her anus. By the time she was upright again she was very flustered indeed.

He grinned at her, his hand still caressing her behind.

"Good luck in there," he said. "Any time you want fucking by a real man, give me a call."

Then he gave her a wink and climbed back into his cab, before disappearing down the street in a cloud of exhaust fumes.

Lisa stood, staring after him, forgetting for a moment her exposed position as she tried to calm her nerves. She turned to look at the house. It was a modern two-storey building with a wide, sweeping drive. She pushed the gate open, stepped through, and then made her way up to the door, glancing over her shoulder as awareness of her near-nudity returned.

She pressed the doorbell. From within she heard footsteps approaching and for a second her instincts made her want to turn and run. But run where? She couldn't possibly be seen in public as she was, and even if she found another cab, how would she pay for it? There was nothing for it but to stand where she was, her heart pounding in her chest as she waited for the door to open.

In a way that she couldn't possibly understand at the time, this was Lisa's last opportunity to escape the dreadful fate that awaited her as a result of her encounter with Lang. Had she turned and run away at that moment, she would have faced no more than the ignominy of an indecent exposure charge. In waiting for the door to open, she set in motion a series of events that would end in her taking on a new role in life as a slave, a slut and a whore.

"What on earth?" The woman who opened the door made no secret of her surprise and distaste as she surveyed the barely clad youngster in front of her. She was a large woman in early middle age. For a second it struck Lisa as amusing that the only similarity between the two of them was that both were wearing aprons. Though the woman's, she reflected bitterly, was of a far more practical design than hers.

"Are you the new waitress then?" the woman demanded in a harsh voice.

"I-I'm not sure," stammered Lisa. "I was told to come here."

"What, dressed like that?"

She dropped her gaze. "Yes."

"Well I suppose you'd better come inside then before somebody sees you. Though what the boys will think I've no idea."

She stood aside and allowed Lisa to enter, closing the door behind her. Then she led her down a long hallway to a room at the end.

It was a kitchen, with a large table in the centre. Laid out upon the table were cutlery and crockery. A pot was steaming on the stove, being stirred by a young man about her own age. His jaw dropped when he saw her, as did the spoon into the pot.

"Don't stare, young man," snapped the woman. "There's work to do here, and we have to be out in five minutes."

As she spoke a second man of a similar age to the first entered carrying a vase of flowers. He too stopped in astonishment at the sight before him.

"Come on," said the woman impatiently, "get those in the dining room and lay the table."

Obediently the man headed for the other door, almost colliding with the doorpost as he stole a last look at Lisa.

"Thank goodness I don't have to put up with your sort too often," sniffed the woman. "Now, come with me and I'll show you what's to be done."

Obediently Lisa followed her through to the dining room. The table was large, and set for three people.

"This is the dining room," the woman said unnecessarily. "The meal is due to start at eight precisely. The wine is in the chiller and there are spirits and liqueurs in the cabinet there."

She showed Lisa about the house, and slowly the girl began to understand the extent of her duties. She was to act as waitress and maid to the men, serving a three course meal which the woman and her helpers had already prepared. As to what was to follow, she could only imagine what would be required of her.

The woman finished her tour and began to pack her bags, with the assistance of her two helpers. The pair of them were unable to tear their eyes from the blushing girl, who stood in the corner of the kitchen wishing they would leave. At last they were ready and, collecting their bags together, they headed for the door, the woman casting a final disdainful look at Lisa before closing it behind her.

Lisa was relieved to be alone at last, even though she knew it would not be for long. She found a mirror and checked her appearance, patting her hair into place and straightening her stockings, trying once again to conceal her breasts inside the inadequate top. Then all she could do was wait. She dare not sit down, for fear of the chair leaving a mark on her bottom. With so much of her body on display she wanted her skin to appear flawless. So instead she wandered through the rooms, making minute adjustments to the ornaments and pictures in an attempt to keep her mind occupied.

The ringing of the doorbell made her jump, and at once her heart began beating hard as she realised that the main part of the evening was about to begin. She took a final look into the mirror, trying for the umpteenth time to cover her breasts. She then headed for the front door.

There were three of them, all much older than her, probably in their mid-forties. Immediately facing her was a thin and cunning looking man with dark, evil eyes that darted about him.

"My name is Bulcher," he said in a low voice. "I believe you are expecting me and my companions.

Lisa eyed the companions. One was short and balding, with something of a paunch. The second was taller, heavily built with a wide, muscular chest. Like Bulcher, both had tanned skin, indicating that they came from a tropical country. When they spoke their voices held an accent Lisa couldn't place. All eyed their hostess appreciatively as she opened the door for them.

Lisa showed them into a drawing room, where a tray of drinks had been prepared. She served the drinks in silence whilst the men spoke together in a language she didn't understand.

When finished, she made to leave, but the weasel faced man grasped her arm.

"I believe you have some papers for us?"

"Oh. Yes Sir. I'll get them."

In her confusion and embarrassment Lisa had almost forgotten the chief purpose of their visit. She hurried to the kitchen where she had left the sheaf of papers, returning with them and handing them to Bulcher. Once again she turned to go, and once again he stopped her.

She froze, staring questioningly at him. He said nothing. He simply placed a hand on the bare flesh of her flank, and then ran it down over her hip and reached behind to squeeze her backside. Lisa remained motionless all the while, not trusting herself to move or to speak as he felt her soft skin. Her breath shortened, however, when he brought his hand round and under her apron, his fingers sliding through her pubic hairs, and then on to the lips of her sex itself.

Lisa gasped as he found her clitoris and ran his finger about it. It was as hard as a nut, and she knew he would notice this, as well as the warm moistness that had invaded her crotch. Indeed, when he removed his hand, he held it up for the others to see the moisture, and they nodded approvingly.

"You may go," Bulcher said suddenly, and turned his back on her, spreading the plans out on a side table.

Lisa returned gratefully to the kitchen. There she busied herself ladling the soup into bowls before loading them onto a tray and carrying them through to the table. Once the steaming dishes were placed, she struck a gong that stood beside the door and retired to a corner to watch as the men came in.

For the next hour Lisa was fully occupied in serving the meal, dashing back and forth from the dining room to the kitchen carrying trays of food and crockery. The men worked her hard, barking orders at her and taking advantage when she had her hands full, caressing and squeezing her breasts and backside and making her flesh tingle with their ministrations.

At last the meal was complete, and she handed round the brandy and cigars before carrying back the last of the plates. She sat down on a stool in the kitchen, grateful for the chance to rest. It wasn't long, though, before she was summoned back to the dining room.

They made her stand in the centre of the room, then all turned their chairs around to face her. Lisa felt suddenly very alone, and she glanced from face to face with some apprehension.

"What is your name?" asked Bulcher, who had dominated the dinner conversation and appeared to be the senior member of the trio.

"Lisa, Sir."

"Well Lisa. I presume you are aware that we expect your duties to extend beyond simply serving our meal."

Lisa felt a sinking sensation in the pit of her stomach. "Yes Sir," she said quietly.

"Good. Take off your apron."

Lisa hesitated. The apron wasn't much, but it was at least some concession to modesty. Without it her situation would be completely unambiguous. Then she saw the impatience in Bulcher's eyes and, her fingers trembling slightly, she reached behind her back and grasped the ends of the tie that circled her waist. She pulled, and the bow came undone, the cords dropping down to her sides. She looked up at the three men, then took hold of the apron and pulled it over her head. For a moment she held it against her body, taking comfort from the minimal cover it gave her. Then the thin-faced man caught her eye again and, her face red, she tossed the garment aside and let her hands drop to her sides.

Behind the men was a mirror, and Lisa studied her reflection. She still wore the high heels and hold-up stockings, but these, of course, hid nothing. In fact they seemed somehow to enhance her nudity, drawing attention to her bare crotch, where even now she could detect a hint of the wetness that coated her outer lips. Letting her eyes travel up to her breasts she noted that her nipples too were betraying her arousal, hardened into solid brown nuts that rose and fell with her breathing.

"Come here."

Slowly Lisa moved forward, her mind whirling. On the one hand she felt repulsed by the trio of strangers who sat before her, forcing her to abandon her modesty in this fashion. Yet her body was alive with arousal, the very treatment that repulsed her sending thrill after thrill through her lovely young frame as she approached the men.

She stopped just in front of Bulcher, planting her feet about fifteen inches apart and once again allowing her hands to fall to her sides, leaving her body open and unprotected. He stretched out a hand and placed it on her inner thigh, making her jump as if an electric shock had passed through her. He began to move his hand, letting it drift up the silky flesh, his touch sending a shudder through her. Every movement brought him closer to the centre of her desire, and she felt her breath shorten as his fingers drifted higher.

"Oh!"

His hand had only brushed against her sex, but the effect had been extraordinary. Her outer lips twitched violently at the contact. She saw the man smile at his two companions, who returned the look. Lisa closed her eyes, ashamed of the blatancy of her desires.

The man slid a finger along the length of her slit, bringing a new shudder of pleasure to her slight frame. She knew her sex was swollen now, and that her clitoris was visible between the glistening pink lips. She knew too that she should stop what he was doing and hide her nakedness. But she couldn't. Her body simply wouldn't allow her to, and instead she found herself thrusting her hips forward at him, bending her knees slightly and offering him her open cunt in a lewd gesture of desire.

"Ahhh!"

Suddenly the man slipped two fingers into her and she felt her knees go weak, until she thought she might collapse onto the floor. It was only with the utmost willpower that she steadied herself. His fingers probed her deeply, making odd slurping sounds as her juices flowed over them. Lisa found herself breathing hard, suddenly more turned on than she dared admit. It was all she could do not to come then and there, such was her arousal.

"You like that, don't you Lisa?" he said softly.

She was too embarrassed to speak.

"Ah!" She gave a cry, half of pain, half of lust as he suddenly rammed his fingers hard into her.

"Don't you?" he asked, his voice insistent.

"Y-yes, Sir."

"Now you must give us pleasure. Do you understand?"

"Yes Sir."

"My colleague has need of your services. Look, Lisa."

Lisa realised that her eyes were tightly shut. She opened them now, and saw with a shock that the stocky, balding man was on his feet. He had taken his cock out of his trousers and was masturbating as he watched her. She looked questioningly at her tormentor, and he nodded.

Lisa turned, giving a slight cry of disappointment as she felt Bulcher's fingers slip from within her. She stood hesitantly in front of the masturbating man, her eyes looking questioningly into his.

"On your knees."

Obediently Lisa dropped to a kneeling position just in front of him. At once he grasped hold of her hair and, still working his foreskin back and forth, guided his cock toward her mouth. Lisa resisted for a moment. She had never had a penis in her mouth before, and the idea had always disgusted her. Somehow, though, in her current state of arousal, she found herself strangely attracted to the notion. All at once she had the urge to taste his rampant rod, and as he pulled her head forward she opened her mouth for it.

She took him inside, and closed her lips about his thick

44

shaft. The smell and taste of his organ were like nothing she had previously experienced. They had an oddly primeval effect on the wanton young girl, actually increasing her excitement. She brushed his hand away and wrapped her own about his erection, dragging the foreskin back and forth in the same way he had been doing. She was rewarded by a sudden twitch and a gasp from the man.

She began to suck greedily on his penis, her other hand reaching up and cupping his balls, which seemed to have a life of their own, the sac expanding and contracting as she worked him. So intent was she on fellating him that she momentarily forgot the presence of the other two men in the room.

Not for long, though. All at once she felt hands wrap about her body and grasp hold of her breasts.

"Get up on all fours," someone hissed.

It was the tall, muscular man. He had hardly spoken since their arrival, being apparently content simply to watch and listen whilst she had served them. Now, though, he evidently wanted her, and as she obeyed his command, moving her body back and raising her behind, she gave a gasp of pleasure at the sensation of his hand closing over her sex.

He found her clitoris, teasing it out from between her thick nether lips and running the rough tip of his finger over it, causing yet more convulsions inside her vagina as a delicious sensation coursed through her body. She pressed herself back against his hand whilst her own hands and mouth continued to pleasure the balding man in front of her.

When she felt the hard, swollen tip of his knob press against her, she wanted to cry aloud with excitement, but the sound was muffled by the mouthful of cock on which she was sucking so enthusiastically. Her backside quivered as he placed his manhood at the very portals of her pleasure hole and pushed.

He slid easily into her; her wetness saw to that.

45

Lisa wanted to turn and watch; to catch a glimpse of the meaty shaft that was violating her so freely. But the man in front of her was jabbing his hips against her face now, his urgency increasing with every stroke and she knew she must give him all the attention she could.

She did manage to glance out of the corner of her eye at the mirror though, and what she saw added new impetus to her desires. There she was, looking pink and exposed amidst the men in suits, crouched like a dog on the floor, her mouth and sex filled with cock. Both men were thrusting hard against her and her body rocked back and forth with every stroke, her breasts swinging free beneath her. It was the most extraordinarily erotic thing she had ever seen, and she stared at her reflection, scarcely able to believe that the naked young wanton she was watching was herself.

Her attention was drawn back by a loud grunt from the man whose member she was sucking. At that moment she felt his body stiffen, then the first jet of semen suddenly unleashed itself from the end of his cock.

The ejaculation took her by surprise and she drew back instinctively so that the next spurt caught her full in the face. The man grabbed her hair and yanked her face forward onto him once again and she found herself sucking hard and gulping down the hot, viscous fluid that filled her mouth.

He seemed to come and come, the semen escaping from her lips and dribbling down her chin as she struggled to swallow it all. The spurts were becoming less frequent now, but still every twitch of his manhood sent a fresh helping into the back of her throat. And all the time the man behind was pounding his hips against her, shaking her small frame with every thrust as his motions became more frenzied.

Then, all of a sudden, he was coming too, his spunk squirting into the deepest recesses of her vagina in great gobs. The sensation was too much for Lisa, and her entire body shook as a violent orgasm swept through it. Wave after wave of intense pleasure washed over her as she let herself go, allowing the cock in her mouth to slip free again as she screamed aloud with the release of her climax.

Lisa's orgasm was long and loud. Her body thrashed about uncontrollably whilst the man behind her continued to pump his sperm into her love hole, each spurt sending her into new paroxysms of lustful joy. Everything around her was forgotten in that moment, her entire being taken up with the pleasure his cock was giving her. It was as if she had been born for this, and shudder after shudder ran through her small body as she came and came.

At last, though, the violence of his motions began to decrease, and she sensed his ardour was spent. She stayed as she was, her hips still moving back and forth, her tongue licking the last dregs from her first ravisher's tool whilst the man behind her finally slowed to a stop. Only then did he withdraw, his cock making a wet sound as it slid from within her.

Lisa collapsed onto the carpet, quite exhausted. She gazed up at the three of them. The two who had had her were looking slightly sheepish now as they tucked their cocks back into their trousers, but the thin-faced man was still watching her with interest as she writhed about on the floor, her face and thighs splattered with sperm.

"Get the bitch up on the table," he barked to his companions suddenly.

The other two acted at once. Grabbing the astonished girl by the arms, they pulled her to her feet and frogmarched her across to the dining table, scattering the crockery and cutlery as they shoved her onto it on her back. Before she knew what was happening she found her wrists being bound with cords and secured to the table legs on the far side. More cords were produced and her ankles were bound in a similar manner, leaving her spreadeagled and helpless across the cold, hard wood. It all happened so fast that she scarcely had time to think before she realised the vulnerability of her position, her limbs spread taut, her sex open and unprotected.

The thin faced man sauntered over to her, gazing down at her trapped body, a faint smile on his face.

"That's better," he said. "Now you really are in my power. How does it feel, slut?"

Lisa, staring fearfully at him, didn't answer. Her mind was in a whirl. What had she let herself in for? For the first time she saw the cruelty in the man's eyes, and she trembled under his fearsome gaze. She tried to struggle, but the bonds held her still, biting into her wrists and ankles. She was held fast, and entirely at Bulcher's mercy.

He crossed to the fireplace and took a poker from the hearth. He returned and stood between her wide open thighs, holding the weapon in one hand and slapping it against his other palm. Lisa shuffled uncomfortably under his gaze as his eyes seemed to bore into her flesh. When he took the end of the poker in his hand and stretched out his arm, a tremor of fear shook her whole body.

The handle of the poker was made of heavy brass, and depicted some kind of figurine in an elaborate carving. It was about an inch in diameter and seven inches long, and when Lisa saw where he was placing it she bit her lip and tensed herself.

The brass felt very cold as it pressed up against her sex lips. Lisa's first instinct was to close her legs and keep it out, but she was quite unable to do so due to the way her legs were tied. Instead, all she could do was raise her head and watch in horror as the thick metallic object invaded her most private place.

"Ah!"

The exclamation escaped her lips as she felt the poker penetrate her; the cold, hard metal unwelcome after the vibrant warmth of the cock that had been inside her only minutes before. And yet, despite the unfriendliness of the object, she felt her sex contract about it and a gasp escaped her lips as the man began to move it back and forth.

He smiled again, although there was no humour in his eyes.

"I see that even this cold object can arouse your desires," he said. "Although, how you'll react when it's heated up a bit will be more amusing. First of all though, I think a whipping is in order. A little slut like you needs whipping to bring her into line."

Lisa stared at him, realising for the first time that his intentions went well beyond simply fucking her. This was clearly a man whose pleasures came from cruelty. She struggled vainly in her bonds as he began to remove his jacket, the cold smile still spread across his features.

Then, all of a sudden there was a loud banging on the door, and a loud voice shouted:

"Security Police! Open this door!"

Chapter 6

At the sound of the banging, the three men all froze and stared at each other.

"What the hell..."

"Where did they come from?"

"Quick. We've got to get out."

"You fucking little slut!" Bulcher's expression had contorted into a snarl as he dropped the poker and moved forward, grabbing Lisa by the hair. "You set us up!" He pulled a stiletto knife from his pocket and held it against the soft flesh of her breast.

"No! I didn't! You must believe me!"

"Then who the hell did?"

There was a crash from the direction of the front door.

"Come on, Bulcher!" shouted one of the men. "There's no time for that! Leave the bitch!"

Bulcher hesitated. A second crash sounded, accompanied by the splintering of wood. Clearly someone was knocking the door down.

"I'll see you suffer for this," he hissed at the frightened girl. "We'll meet again, make no mistake."

He remained where he was for a second, his eyes gleaming with malice. Then he withdrew the knife. From where the point had been pressing against her breast a tiny bead of blood bubbled up and trickled down her creamy white skin. Then they were gone, slipping silently out of the room and leaving Lisa alone.

Crash!

The door finally gave way with a noise that echoed about the house. Once again Lisa fought against her bonds, desperate not to be discovered as she was. But her wrists and ankles had been tied by experts, and there was no escape.

The door to the dining room crashed open and two men ran in. They were both dressed in dark blue uniforms, with white crash helmets on their heads. They both carried thick truncheons. They glanced about, scarcely registering the naked girl, then dashed out through the door the three men had gone through a short time earlier.

The next few minutes were pandemonium, with uniformed men running in and out of the room and a good deal of shouting taking place between them. From the garden Lisa heard voices calling out and the sound of a car starting up. An engine was gunned, and then there was squeal of tyres.

The two security men ran back into the room.

"They had a getaway car out the back, dammit!" shouted one of them. "Quick, get after them!"

More running feet. More engines starting. Then silence.

For a few seconds Lisa thought she had been left alone,

and wasn't sure whether to be relieved or concerned, since she had no way of escaping from her bonds. Then the door swung open and two more men entered. These two were dressed in plain clothes, both wearing long grey raincoats. Both were tall and muscular. One had the face of a pugilist, with a heavy brow and broken nose. The other was quite pale, with a long scar running down one cheek. They strode across to the table and stared down at the girl.

Lisa wondered at the sight she must make, stretched out before them, naked but for her dark stockings, her sex still penetrated by the thick poker handle. Sperm ran from her sex and over her thighs, more was splattered on her face and hair. There could be no doubting what she had been doing.

"Miss Carling, I presume?"

Lisa was shocked to discover that they knew her name. She stared at them.

"My, what a dance you've been leading us," the man went on. "Fortunately someone remembered seeing you getting into that cab. Mind you, it's scarcely surprising he remembered, if what he said about the way you were dressed was true. Now, where are the papers?"

"Papers..?"

"Don't play games with me, Miss Carling. It took us a while to discover it was you that hacked into the computer yesterday and accessed the encrypted information. Fortunately the machine has its own monitoring software, and we soon had it down to three suspects. The other two had alibis. From what I've seen this evening, I'm prepared to bet you haven't."

"I-I don't know what you're talking about. I..."

Her voice trailed off as she realised that the second man was holding something up for her to see.

It was the papers.

Clearly the three men had left in such a hurry that they had forgotten to take them. And now here they were, the most damning evidence possible. She stared dumbly at the two men.

"Right Miss Carling," the man spoke again. "We want to know precisely who the men were that you met tonight."

"I don't know who they were."

The man scowled. "Don't play games with us, Miss Carling. Just give us the names."

"But I tell you I don't know."

At this point they were distracted as two of the uniformed men entered the room. Lisa recognised them as the two who had entered the house first of all. Then they had barely glanced at her, but now they took a good deal more interest, their eyes fixed on her open crotch and the ugly metal tool that protruded from it.

"What news?!" barked scarface.

"Bastards gave our guys the slip. Seems they were well prepared Mr Dawson."

"The mystery is that they left the papers behind," replied the scarfaced man, now identified to Lisa as Dawson. "I think this little slut must have proved too much of a distraction."

"She'd distract anyone," grinned the guard. "Gorgeous pair of tits on her."

Lisa averted her gaze. "Do you think you could untie me please?" she asked quietly. The exposure before the men was getting too much for her now, and she longed to have the poker removed from her vagina.

"You'll stay there until I'm ready to release you," replied Dawson.

"Well could you at least cover me?"

"If you start co-operating, then maybe I'll think about it. Now who were those men?"

"I don't know. I swear I don't."

"Then how did you contact them?"

"I didn't. I was told to just come here with the papers."

"What, almost naked? That cab driver's eyes were popping out of their sockets."

She reddened. "I was told to come like that. I had to deliver the papers, then serve the meal."

"And then let those bastards fuck you rigid?"

Lisa said nothing.

"All right then. If you were told to come, who sent you?"

"I can't tell you."

"Because it was all your own doing."

"No."

Dawson turned to the two guards.

"It seems we'll have to be a little more persuasive," he said. "Turn her over and fetch my stick."

The two guards exchanged grins, then set to work undoing Lisa's bonds, untying the ropes that held her ankles, then her wrists. But there was to be no respite for the unfortunate girl. The moment she was free she found herself hoisted to the floor, the poker sliding from her sex and clattering to the ground. Then they turned her to face the table and bent her forward over it, so that her upper body was pressed hard against the surface. At once they set to work with the rope again, one man securing her ankles to the table legs whilst the other pulled her arms across the table, tying her wrists together then yanking the end of the rope down to secure it below the level of the table top.

Once again Lisa was helpless, this time with her backside protruding over the edge of the table and her legs trapped wide apart. She tried not to imagine how she must look in such a position, her sex lips spread wide, the spunk still leaking from inside her and trickling down her leg.

She watched in trepidation as one of the guards left the room.

Two minutes later he was back, bearing a thin bamboo cane. He passed this to Dawson, who flexed it in his hands, demonstrating how whippy it was. Then he gave it back to the guard, who wielded it with some strength, making it whistle through the air.

"Right, Miss Carling," said Dawson quietly. "I shall ask you once more. Who were the men you met tonight?"

"I tell you I don't know," cried Lisa despairingly.

"Right," he said. "We'll see if the cane can loosen your tongue. Three strokes."

Lisa stared at the weapon, then back at Dawson. Surely he couldn't mean it. Surely he was just trying to scare her. After all, the police weren't allowed to use corporal punishment, were they? But then again, the uniforms the men wore weren't police uniforms. She watched, trembling, as the guard drew back his arm.

Swish! Whack!

The cane descended with devastating force, the thin bamboo cutting cruelly into Lisa's behind and sending a stinging pain through her body. Tears leapt to her eyes at the agony that seared through her backside.

Swish! Whack!

Before she had time to draw breath he struck her again, the blow catching the underside of her behind and laying a stripe across the back of her legs that quickly darkened to an angry red colour.

Swish! Whack!

The third blow landed right across her nether cheeks, bringing a cry of pain from her lips as her body was rocked forward by the force of the stroke.

The man paused, gazing down at the writhing form of the girl.

"Now, Miss Carling," said Dawson. "I'll ask the question again. "Who were they?"

"I don't know. Really I don't," gasped Lisa. "You must believe me."

"Six more strokes," he said.

"No! No more!" cried Lisa. But Dawson simply ignored

her.

Swish! Whack!

Once again the cane crashed down onto her bare buttocks, finding yet another patch of virgin white flesh to decorate with a slash of red.

Swish! Whack!

Lisa was struggling madly with her bonds now, making vain efforts to get out of the way of the rain of blows. But she was caught fast, and her feeble efforts made no difference whatsoever as the cane continued to find its target.

Swish! Whack!
Swish! Whack!
Swish! Whack!

A sheen of sweat covered Lisa's naked body. Small rivulets ran down her spine and trickled down the wide open crack of her backside.

But there was another wetness that she found less easy to explain.

Deep inside her a perverse sense of arousal was beginning to surface. If she was honest with herself, she had to admit that having her naked body spread open before the gaze of all these men had thrilled her from the start, though her initial fear had suppressed those feelings. Now though, the strokes of the cane on her bare skin had awakened the same desires as had the belt that had been used on her behind all that time ago, and suddenly she was aware of the hardening of her nipples and the swelling of her clitoris as her body began to respond.

Swish! Whack!

If her punisher was aware of the effect that the beating was having on her, he showed no sign of it. The blows continued with unabated force, leaving a criss-cross of welts across her behind, each one stinging like the attack of a thousand wasps. But Lisa's mind was beginning to blot out the pain, as her lust began to get the better of her other emotions.

Swish! Whack!

Once again the beating stopped. For a few moments the room was silent apart from the panting of the tethered girl. Then Dawson spoke again:

"Well? You going to talk, or do you want some more?"

"I don't know who they were," gasped Lisa through clenched teeth.

"Listen," said the burly man with the broken nose. "This doesn't seem to be getting us anywhere. We'd better take her in."

"A few more strokes should do it. Give her another six."

"No!" But this time Lisa's protests were more feeble, and she clenched her fists as the man raised his arm once more.

Swish! Whack!
Swish! Whack!
Swish! Whack!

Each cut of the vicious cane made Lisa scream aloud. There was no part of her backside that was unmarked now, so that every stroke fell onto a part of her behind that was already stinging. But the pain had done its job, and it was lust that filled Lisa's mind now. She could scarcely believe the way her body was reacting. Her breasts felt as if they were swollen to twice their size, the nipples intensely sensitive as they pressed down against the wood. But the real centre of her desire was her clitoris, which felt harder than she had ever known it, and she found herself grinding her hips against the table top in an attempt to rub it against the surface and obtain some kind of relief from the sexual tension that continued to build inside her.

Swish! Whack!
Swish! Whack!
Swish! Whack!

Lisa scarcely noticed the last three blows. It was as if her backside had gone numb, and all the nerve ends had been transferred to her cunt. She was barely in control now, her hips pumping back and forth as if she was fucking the very table.

"What the..."

"Holy shit!"

Lisa knew then that the two plain clothes men had realised what was happening to her and she cursed the recalcitrance of her body as she fought to control her emotions. But it was no good. Try as she might, she couldn't keep her hips still, and the image in her mind of how she must look - her bright red behind jerking back and forth whilst the men watched - served only to spur her on in her desperate efforts to gain stimulation from the table top.

"My, God, she's turned on," said Dawson.

"I think you're right. Here, give me that poker."

Lisa gazed behind in consternation as she saw the guard lift the poker from where it had fallen and hand it to Dawson's companion. Then, without warning, he thrust the handle between her thighs.

"Ahhh!"

The cry that escaped Lisa's lips was one of pure lust as she felt the cold roughness of the metal make contact with her rampant love bud. Suddenly she was grinding her hips down upon it, revelling in the sensation its gnarled surface gave her. To her delight the man began to press it firmly against her, moving it back and forth in a sawing motion over her dripping slit.

"Ah! Ah! Ah!"

Lisa's shrill cries rang through the room as a delicious orgasm swept through her body, finally giving her the relief she craved so badly. Suddenly the pent-up tensions caused by the exposure, the mistreatment and the beatings were released in a glorious gush of pure pleasure, her hips jabbing down at the handle as she came, her body slapping wetly against the table top.

At last, though, she could come no more, and with a final gasp, her body slumped down with exhaustion. The rise and fall of her bare shoulders was now the only motion from her exhausted body.

"My God, she's something," said Dawson quietly. "I think we'd better get the bitch down to headquarters straight away."

Chapter 7

When Lisa awoke she had no idea where she was. She gazed up at the harsh spotlight above her head, blinking uncertainly. She tried to lift herself into a sitting position, but found herself strangely unable to do so. She tried to move her legs, with equal lack of success. Alarmed, she glanced across at her arm and saw that a chain ran around her wrist, securing it to the head of the bed. She tugged hard at it, but it was too strong for her and held fast.

She glanced down at herself and gave a cry of dismay on discovering that she was still completely naked. What was more, her ankles were chained in the same way as her wrists, leaving her spreadeagled on the small bed. She raised her head, wincing slightly at the dull pain at her temples. There was another pain too, an altogether more acute one in her backside. It was that pain which brought back the memory of the beating she had received at the hands of the security men, and she winced as she recalled the wantonness of her behaviour in front of them.

She glanced about her. She was in a small, featureless room with white walls and ceiling. The only object of furniture was the bed to which she was chained. There were no windows, just a heavy metal door with a small hole about two thirds of the way up, which was covered by a metal shutter.

She racked her brains to try to remember how she had arrived here, and slowly the memories began to return.

They had drugged her in some way. She recalled the hypodermic needle that had been jabbed into her arm whilst she was still tied down over the table. From then on everything had been dreamlike, though she had remained semiconscious throughout.

They had untied her and half walked, half dragged her out of the house. There, in the driveway, a van had been parked and they had bundled her inside. There had followed a long journey, during which she had been secured by her wrists to a ring in the van's roof, so that her body rocked back and forth every time the van lurched round a bend or drew up sharply.

When they finally came to a halt she had been led from the vehicle into another building. She vaguely recognised it as the one in which she worked, but the entrance through which they took her, set at the back of the building, was unfamiliar. They had led her downstairs into the very bowels of the place, and she had a vague recollection of stout doors being unlocked.

Next she remembered a shower room, where they had removed her stockings and stood her under a cold jet of water, one guard holding her upright whilst the other ran a soapy cloth over her body, cleaning her all over, even in the most intimate of places.

Finally she had been brought into this room and the shackles fitted to her. She had protested, but once her head had touched the pillow she had fallen into a deep sleep. And now here she was, awake, but totally helpless, and quite unaware into whose clutches she had fallen and what fate would befall her.

She shook her head, trying to clear her mind and make sense of what had happened the night before. She cursed herself for her stupidity in thinking she could access the encrypted data on the system without being discovered. She might have known there would be software monitoring on the main terminal. Narrowing down the search to her would have been easy.

But who on earth were they, the men in uniform and their mysterious plain clothed superiors? They weren't ordinary policemen, she was sure of that, yet they clearly wielded a great deal of power. She had heard once before of a secret police force that operated underground for the company. After all, such a large weapons company was certain to attract the attention of espionage agents from all kinds of places. But wasn't that precisely why Conrad Lang had put her up to the whole thing? To trap anyone trying to access computer files illegally. Yet if he was conducting such an operation, surely the security guards would have known about it. Unless they were the ones being checked.

Of course! That must be it. It was all a test to ensure that the security men were on their toes. But if that were the case, why had Lang not already contacted them? It was too bad of him to have left her in their power for so long. Particularly considering the state she was in. How long were they intending to keep her in this exposed and vulnerable condition? And how many of them had already feasted their eyes on her naked body? The thought sent a shiver of excitement through her as she thought of all those men able to ogle her breasts and sex, and she began to feel that odd arousal stir within her as she contemplated the idea.

A sudden scrape of metal made her look up. The plate over the hole in the door had been drawn back and a pair of eyes were gazing in. A man's eyes. Lisa shifted uncomfortably under their steely stare. Then the plate slid shut again.

"Wait!" she called. But there was no further sound. Lisa lay back and stared at the light above her head. Clearly her ordeal was not yet over.

It was some time before the spy hole suddenly opened

again. In that period Lisa's thoughts had run wild. A number of scenarios filled her head, many of them extremely erotic, despite her efforts to rid her mind of such thoughts. Now she was forced to snap back to reality as once again she felt a man's eyes roving over her nakedness.

There was the clang of a bolt being shot back, then the door opened. Two men stood in the doorway, both dressed in the same blue uniform as the men who had brought her there the night before. One of them remained standing by the door whilst the other came inside.

"Shit, nobody told me she was so sexy," he remarked to his companion as he studied the tethered girl.

"And pretty randy from what I hear," replied the other man. "Apparently the bastards who she tried to sell the papers to gave her a damned good fucking before our guys arrived."

"I wouldn't mind a bit of that myself. Look at those tits."

"Better not touch. Besides, Dawson's waiting for her."

Lisa had remained silent whilst they had been discussing her so casually. Now she spoke out:

"Please, what's going on?" she asked. "Why am I being held like this? And who are you?"

"Better keep your mouth shut darling," the guard replied, dropping to his knees and beginning to remove the shackles from her arms and legs.

"But can't I just have some clothes? Even a bathrobe or something?"

"They told us you were like that when they picked you up."

"Yes but..."

"I thought I told you to be quiet!" There was a menacing tone in the man's voice now. "If you wanna go about flashing your tits and cunt that's your problem. Now get up."

Lisa sat up and swung her legs over the side of the bed. Then she rose unsteadily to her feet. She still felt a little groggy from the drug they had administered on the previous evening and her limbs were stiff and sore from their prolonged immobilization.

"Jeez, they sure whacked your arse for you," said the man, grinning. "Take a look at this, Pete."

He turned her round so that her back was to the door, and the man outside laughed.

"More stripes than a bloody sergeant major," he said. "I'd liked to have watched that."

Lisa was swung round again, then felt something cold and hard close about her wrists. It was a pair of handcuffs, and they trapped her arms behind her.

"Right," said the man. "Let's go," and he shoved her out of the cell.

They made their way down a corridor, the walls plain white like the cell. There was no carpet, simply a stone floor, which felt cold under the naked girl's feet as she padded along. They climbed a flight of stairs, at the top of which was an elevator. The guard pressed a button and the doors slid open. Lisa was pushed inside and the doors closed behind her.

The walls of the lift were formed entirely of mirrors, and to her intense embarrassment Lisa was confronted by images of herself on all sides, with reflections of reflections within these, so that her pale body seemed to be everywhere, the images disappearing into infinity as if down long, brightly-lit passages. She could see herself from in front, from behind and from the side, as well as from above and below. No part of her body could be hidden in this small, reflecting box. She examined the marks on her backside. The worst of the inflammation had subsided now, leaving a series of clear red stripes that criss-crossed the tender flesh of her behind. She ran a tentative finger along one of the stripes and winced at the pain.

The lift started to move upwards, though Lisa had not

pressed any buttons. She stood in the centre, regarding her reflection and wishing desperately she had some way of covering herself. The ascent seemed to last a very long time. Lisa searched for an indicator to show what floor she was on, but there was none. Then she felt the machine begin to slow and a cold fear gripped her as she contemplated what she might find.

With a slight bump the elevator came to a stop. Lisa watched the doors. They seemed to take an age to open, but at last there was a click and they slid silently back. Lisa stood, staring out uncertainly. She could see nobody. Then an unseen voice crackled from a speaker hidden somewhere above her.

"Step out and wait in the lobby."

For a moment Lisa wasn't even sure if the words were directed at her, but glancing about she could see nobody else, so she obeyed, stepping uncertainly through the doors. Almost at once the doors closed behind her and she heard the whirr of machinery as the lift descended. Then silence.

Lisa felt trapped and isolated. The room she was in was simply a lobby, devoid of furniture. It was like the lobby to be found in any office building. Somehow its very ordinariness made her feel even more exposed. The clinical nature of the cell block below had made her nudity somehow less outrageous. Here, in this normal, everyday environment it brought back memories of her dreams, in which she found herself naked amongst fully-clothed strangers who stared at her body as she moved amongst them. But this was no dream. And worse, her hands were trapped behind her, leaving her unable to cover herself or defend herself against anyone wishing to ravish her.

Suddenly, a door behind swung open. She turned to see a young man carrying a sheaf of papers. He paused, his eyes taking in every inch of her body. The blood rose immediately to Lisa's cheeks as he studied her. She lowered her eyes, waiting for him to speak, but he said nothing. He simply grinned and moved past her, before disappearing through another pair of doors on the far side of the room.

Lisa didn't know how long she waited there. She estimated it was about fifteen minutes, and all the time people were passing through as they went about their daily tasks. Most were young men, apparently office messengers. There were one or two women as well, who generally came in pairs and giggled at the sight of the naked girl.

At last another of the uniformed men appeared.

"Come with me," he said shortly, and held open the door.

Lisa stepped through, finding herself in another corridor. On either side were offices in which she was able to glimpse people working at computer screens. Once again the incongruity of her situation struck her, walking through an apparently normal office environment totally naked. She wondered if she should pinch herself to make sure that this wasn't just another strange dream. But the pain in her backside told her that this whole experience was only too real.

At the end of the corridor was a door marked 'Private' and it was to this that she was led. The man rapped twice on the door, and then paused.

"Come!"

He opened the door and pushed Lisa inside, closing it behind her. The room was in darkness, and she stopped, blinking as she tried to orient herself. Then, suddenly, a light came on. It was a bright light, blinding almost, and it shone directly into her eyes. Beyond it she could just discern three shadowy figures who sat behind a desk facing her.

"Come here."

The voice was Dawson's, and she guessed the man beside him was his companion of the night before. She had no idea who the third man was.

Lisa moved forward, stepping carefully in her blindness. She stopped just infront of the desk.

"I trust you slept well?" asked Dawson.

Lisa didn't reply.

Bang!

The man crashed something down onto the desk in front of him, making Lisa jump with the suddenness of the noise.

"Answer me when I ask a question!" he barked.

"What do you want?"

Bang!

Again the object descended. It appeared to Lisa to be a heavy stick, and the noise it made was quite frighteningly loud.

"Answer!"

"I-I can't remember the question."

"Never mind. Tell me what you were doing at that house last night."

"I was delivering those papers."

"Naked?"

"I.., I had something on..."

The man snorted. "If that's your idea of what to wear for a night out."

"I was told to wear it."

Dawson sat up. "By whom?"

"I-I can't tell you."

Bang!

The sound of the stick on the desk top was unnerving Lisa, as was Dawson's questioning. She wished they would turn the light out too. But most of all she wished they would give her something to wear. The enforced nudity was becoming too much for her and she longed to cover herself. She struggled to concentrate on what the man was saying.

"Who told you?" he demanded.

"I was told not to say. It's for security."

Dawson rose to his feet, the sound of his chair scraping back sounding unnaturally loud in the silent room, He skirted the desk and approached Lisa.

"Listen, bitch," he snarled. "I'm security around here. Now tell me who told you!"

"I'm afraid to."

Whack!

This time the stick contacted Lisa's bare behind, making her cry out with pain.

"I'm the one you should be afraid of," he said. "Tell me the name."

"It.., it was Conrad Lang."

For a few seconds there was silence. Then:

Whack!

Dawson brought the stick down on her behind again, making her almost dance with the intense pain.

"Get real, slut," he said. "Who was it?"

"It's true," she gasped. "He told me it was a test of security."

"And the whoring?"

Lisa dropped her eyes. "That was his idea too," she said quietly.

Dawson sniffed. "All right then," he said. "Tell us the whole story."

Chapter 8

Lisa was asleep when they came for her. It was the crash of the cell door swinging open that woke her, and she blinked up into the bright lights above her as the guard entered the room.

This time there was no discussion. He simply released her arms, which had been chained together to the head of the bed, and dragged her to her feet. There was a moment's delay while he snapped the cuffs onto her wrists, then the still naked girl was hustled off down the corridor.

Lisa was barely awake as she stumbled along, her mind trying to grasp what was happening to her. She wondered how long she had been allowed to sleep. Down here, in this windowless basement, it was impossible to tell what time of day or night it was, since the lights seemed to be kept on all the time.

She had no idea where they were taking her, but she suspected that she was about to encounter Dawson once more, and the idea did not fill her with enthusiasm. On the previous occasion, under the bright lights, he had interrogated her for more than two hours, extracting every detail of what had occurred between herself and Conrad Lang. She had told him of her visit to the shower, and how she had ended up naked in Lang's office. She even had to relate how he'd fucked her across his desk. Then she had been forced to go step by step through her encounter with the three men at the house. And all the time Dawson had barked questions at her whilst the other two had sat silently taking notes.

At last, though, they had heard enough, and Lisa had been led back down the office corridor, watched by the sniggering staff, and taken below once more. There she was given a meal, standing in the corner of a canteen full of guards and plain clothes security men, before being taken back to her cell, chained to the bed, and left there alone.

Until now. And as they led her down the sterile, white corridors, she felt her apprehension growing with every step.

This time they took her, not to the elevator, but to another part of the basement. It was a large room, decorated in the same plain white as the rest on that floor. On one side was a row of high backed chairs, and in the centre a set of gleaming chains hung from the ceiling. It was to these that she was led. On the ends of the chains were manacles of equally shiny metal and these were affixed to her wrists, after which the chains were tightened, dragging her arms up above her head. Her ankles were then secured to shackles attached to rings set in the stone floor, spreading her legs wide apart. Finally the guards tightened the chains above her head still further, so that she was forced to stand on tiptoe, her body stretched taut, facing the chairs.

On the wall behind was a mirror, clearly placed there deliberately to allow the captive to see herself. Lisa gazed at her body, once again wishing they would give her some clothes. Even a pair of panties would make a difference, she thought bitterly. As it was, the way her legs were forced open gave anyone seeing her a perfect and unrestricted view of her gaping sex, the lips pulled apart to expose the pink petals of her labia within. She glanced at her breasts. They were stretched slightly oval by the tension in her arms and body, but still jutted forward, inviting the caresses she was powerless to prevent.

She realised that the guards were watching her and her face reddened. One of them moved close to her so that his face was only inches from hers.

"Is it true what they say about you?" he asked. "That you enjoy flaunting that gorgeous little body of yours? That's why you were looking in the mirror, wasn't it? To make sure we had a good view of your cunt."

Lisa dropped her eyes. It was true, her enforced nudity did arouse her, though she was at a loss to understand why. Even here, confused and apprehensive as she was, she could feel the warm wetness inside her sex which she knew must soon be visible to her captors.

The man raised a hand and placed it over her breast, taking the nipple between finger and thumb and rolling it back and forth. Lisa gave a little moan as he did so and the man grinned.

"Look at that," he said to his companion. "She just can't resist a bit of rough. Let's cop a feel of her cunt."

"No!" said Lisa, shaking her head. But of course there was nothing she could do but watch herself in the mirror as the man's hand slid down her rib cage, over her belly, and down to the dark triangle beneath.

She gave a gasp as his strong fingers came into contact with the hard little nut of her clitoris. She tried to pull away from him, but she was held fast and was forced to endure his crude probing, her gasp turning to a low moan as he slid a finger into her gaping vagina.

The guard began to move his hand back and forth, winking to his friend as they watched Lisa's reaction. She closed her eyes with shame at the way her body responded; her hips pressing forward against his hand; her striped backside gyrating as his ministrations stirred the lust of the wanton young girl.

Lisa both hated and loved what the guard was doing to her. Hated it because of the humiliation of her helplessness, and of the treachery of her young body, and loved it because of the delicious sensation of his hard fingers which penetrated her so deeply, bringing her the most exquisite pleasure imaginable. And somehow the bondage added to her pleasure, the pain of the shackles and the way they rendered her helpless bringing her a perverse kick that she was unable to explain.

The man inserted a second digit into her throbbing sex, bringing a fresh cry from her as he began to frig her hard. His companion had moved round behind her meanwhile and was mauling her breasts, and pinching her nipples until they ached. This simply served to spur the young girl on, causing her to thrust her hips forward with renewed vigour.

Once again she glanced up at her reflection in the mirror, and was shocked at what she saw. Was that really her? That naked, slut whose face was a picture of undisguised passion as the two heavies groped her young body? She could scarcely believe what she was seeing, yet the spectacle simply served to spur her on as she ground her hips down on the guard's hand.

She came with a cry. A shout of lust that rang around the room, her body thrashing back and forth in her chains, her unrestrained breasts bouncing up and down as the wonderful climax overcame her. The man kept his fingers embedded in her, extracting every ounce of pleasure from the girl, keeping her at her peak for what seemed ages before slowing his movements and allowing her to come down again.

When he slid his fingers out of her vagina, Lisa slumped in her chains, her breasts rising and falling as she fought for breath. The two men stood back to watch as the exhausted girl struggled to regain her composure. It was fully five minutes before her breathing slowed and she raised her scarlet face to look at her captors.

"Enjoy that, did you, slut?" said the guard who had brought her off. "They said you were randy, but I had no idea."

Lisa said nothing, cursing herself for her wantonness.

The two guards, having had their fun, wandered off to stand either side of the door as sentries, and the room fell quiet. Lisa was left to her own thoughts, and to contemplate what would happen next.

Her musings were interrupted by the sound of a door being opened. She glanced across to see that Dawson had just entered the room. He seemed scarcely to notice her, though, walking across and taking one of the seats. Lisa wanted to ask him what was going on, but she dared not. She stood in silence, waiting to see what would happen.

The door opened again and more people entered. With a gasp she recognised the chairman of the corporation and two other board members. They were soon joined by more people, some of whom Lisa recognised from the photographs of board members that stood in the lobby where she worked.

But the final person to enter gave her the biggest shock of all.

It was Conrad Lang!

They all took their seats. There were about a dozen of them, two of them women. All were expensively dressed, and they chatted quietly together. Lisa felt very uncomfortable indeed, trussed and naked as she was, and her eyes couldn't help wandering to the reflection in the mirror behind the small audience.

Suddenly Dawson rose to his feet and the assembly fell silent. He walked across to stand by Lisa, then began to talk.

"Ladies and gentlemen. Thank you for coming here at such short notice. I appreciate that many of you have come quite long distances to attend this meeting. Let me assure you that it was absolutely necessary. As head of security for Bellco I have to tell you this is the most potentially dangerous case of espionage I have encountered since you gave me the job."

There was a general nodding of heads about the room.

"The basic facts are undisputed. The young woman you see before you, Miss Lisa Carling, used her position as a member of the Data Processing department to obtain top secret information on two of our most important weapons. These she took to a neutral house, where she handed them to three military attaches from an extreme right wing government based in southern Africa. At the same time she prostituted herself, allowing the men sexual favours. When we found her she bore all the evidence of having given oral and vaginal sex to at least two of the men."

A murmur went round the room, and Lisa hung her head, unable to meet the eyes of any of those present.

"Next," went on Dawson, "she proceeded to give us the most extraordinary statement. She claimed that a member of this board had put her up to the whole thing, on the pretext of a security check. I shall read you her statement."

Dawson then read out a full account of what had happened between Lisa and Lang in precisely the way she had described it. When he had finished, a silence descended on the room as the rest of the board turned to look at Lang. Lisa looked at him too, and was surprised by his relaxed demeanour. Then the chairman spoke for the first time.

"These charges are very grave, Conrad," he said. "What have you to say?"

Conrad Lang rose to his feet, a slight smile on his face.

"I say they are completely ridiculous Mr Chairman," he said. "A total fabrication from beginning to end."

"But why should this girl have made up such a tale?"

"I believe she has an obsession with me," he said. "When I said the charges were a total fabrication that wasn't quite true. I did find her in my office one night. She was as naked as she is now, and she threw herself at me. It was all I could do to stop her advances. Naturally I sent her packing and since then she's had a grudge against me."

Lisa gasped. "That's not true!" she shouted. "He's lying, can't you see that?!"

Whack!

Dawson's stick found its mark as it always did, delivering a stinging blow to her backside.

"Quiet!" he thundered.

Lisa glared at him, but said nothing.

If this is the case," said the chairman to Lang, "why did you not report it at once?"

"To be honest, I didn't want to get the girl into trouble. I assumed it was just a harmless phase she was going through."

"But you had been placed in a very compromising position. What if she had accused you of rape?"

"I took the precaution of recording everything that happened that night in my desk diary. I'll show you if you want."

"That won't be necessary," said the chairman.

"But surely you're not going to believe him?" gasped Lisa.

"Why shouldn't we?"

"Because he's lying."

"Do you deny you were in Mr Lang's office?" asked

72

Dawson.

"No, but..."

"And you were naked?"

"Yes, but I told you why that was. And it was him that seduced me. Not the other way round."

Lang shook his head. "The girl's disturbed," he said.

"What about the note you sent me?" demanded Lisa. "And the outfit? Then there was the cab, and the house, and the caterers and..."

"That's enough," snapped Dawson. "Mr Chairman, we have investigated all these."

"And?"

"And all were booked anonymously by telephone. By a woman."

"That doesn't mean it was me," said Lisa. "He could have got anyone to do it."

"Nevertheless, it was a woman's voice," said Dawson.

"So what are you saying?" asked the chairman.

"That this girl is indeed obsessed with Mr Lang. And that when he spurned her advances, she planned this whole thing as revenge against him and the company."

"But I didn't!"

Whack!

Once again Lisa was quieted with a blow to her backside.

The chairman turned to his fellow board members.

"I'm inclined to believe Dawson," he said. "After all, the girl's behaviour has been unreasonable from the start. Just look at her now, the brazen hussy."

The other board members nodded their assent.

"No need for a vote then," said the chairman. "Sorry you had to go through all this, Conrad, but it was necessary to hear your side. Right, this meeting is ended."

The board members rose to leave. Lisa stared at them in disbelief. Was that it? Was that all the hearing she was to get? She, who had been stripped, fucked, beaten and humiliated and now forced to appear before this kangaroo court? She opened her mouth to protest, then caught Dawson's eye and closed it again. She watched in silence as the board filed from the room, leaving her on her own to contemplate her fate.

Chapter 9

If Lisa had been privy to the conversation that followed, she would no doubt have been even more apprehensive about her fate. As they filed out of the room, Dawson and the chairman took their leave of the other members of the board, then took the lift up to Dawson's office. Dawson closed the door behind them, turning the key in the lock. Then he gestured to the chairman to sit down. He took his own seat and glanced across at his companion. The chairman spoke first.

"What do you think about Lang, then?" he asked.

"Difficult to say. He has an alibi, and we've got no reason to believe he'd pass on secrets."

"It's just that the girl sounded so convincing. It's difficult to imagine she's lying."

"If she isn't we've got a bigger problem on our hands than we thought. Lang's been with the company a long time. Do you really think he'd betray us?"

"Until today my answer to that would have been an emphatic no. Nevertheless I'd like you to keep an eye on him for the time being."

"How do you mean?"

"Check his movements. See when he uses the computer. Find out who he's telephoning, both from home and the office."

"Okay. That should be easy enough."

"And find out how he spends his spare time. Make sure

he's not open to compromise."

"You mean like running up gambling debts, or making use of ladies of ill repute? Certainly."

"Now, what about the girl?"

"She'll be dismissed, naturally."

"Of course. But that's not enough, is it?"

"How do you mean?" asked Dawson.

"Those plans she stole. They were absolutely vital to the success of the most important products the company produces. And the most controversial. Those things are designed to kill and maim indiscriminately. They're completely contra to the Geneva Convention. If those plans fell into the wrong hands it would mean total disaster for Bellco, both politically and financially."

"So you don't think she chose them at random?"

"Definitely not. She knew exactly what she was doing. And that means we can't afford just to dismiss her. She needs silencing completely."

"I see."

"Do you? Do you really see what I'm getting at?"

"You want her killed?"

"I don't want it. This is a dirty enough business as it is, without murdering our own employees."

"I think I know another way."

"What other way?

"A means of ensuring that Miss Lisa Carling doesn't bother us, or anybody else, again."

"I don't understand."

"Are you sure you want to?"

The chairman stared at him for a moment, then shook his head.

"No. No I don't think I do. Just see to it that she ceases to be a problem to me. I don't want to see or hear of the little slut again. Do you understand?"

"Perfectly."

"Good." The chairman rose to his feet. "I'll leave it in your capable hands then."

Dawson unlocked the door and let the chairman out, closing it behind him. Then he returned to his desk and slumped down behind it deep in thought. After a while he unlocked the bottom drawer of his desk and pulled out a small black book. He rifled through the pages until his finger came to rest on an entry. He picked up his phone and began to tap out a number.

"Yes?" The voice on the other end sounded crackly and distant.

"Get me Mr Hameer," he said quietly.

Chapter 10

They came for Lisa in the middle of the night. One minute she had been sleeping peacefully, her graceful young body spread-eagled across her bunk, the next she was blinking into the rays of the spotlight above her as her cell door crashed back against the wall.

"W-what is it?" she mumbled, trying to force her eyes open.

"Time to go," said the guard.

He undid her shackles swiftly and hauled her to her feet. Then the cuffs were snapped onto her wrists and she was being half led, half dragged down the corridor.

"Where are we going?" she asked in alarm.

"Never you mind," snapped the guard. "Just keep your mouth shut or I'll gag you."

They took her up a short staircase and into another part of the basement. This appeared to be some kind of warehouse, with boxes and crates stacked on all sides. At the end was a huge pair of doors, like those found on an aircraft hangar. They were open about ten feet, and outside Lisa could see the night sky. In the gap was parked a van, its rear doors open. It was toward this that she was being taken.

Lisa tried to hang back, suddenly afraid of what was about to happen to her, but her guards simply took hold of her arms and frogmarched her forward. As they came closer she could discern a man standing beside the van. He was tall and dark skinned, with black hair and a foreign appearance. For the umpteenth time Lisa wished she had something to wear as she saw his eyes travel over her naked body.

As they reached the van , Lisa realised that there was another man inside, sitting watching their approach. As the guards brought her to a halt the man climbed out. Like his companion he was tall and foreign looking, with a dark droopy moustache and glittering black eyes.

"This the merchandise?" he said.

"This is it," replied one of the guards.

"Very nice." He cast his eyes over Lisa's body. "Very nice indeed. Even better than I expected. And is it true she's a randy little bitch?"

"Loves it. She's probably horny already. She gets a real kick out of flaunting her tits and cunt."

Lisa opened her mouth to protest, but suddenly her eyes detected a movement to her left and, turning her head, she saw a figure emerged from the shadows. It was Dawson. The two guards stiffened to attention when they saw him, but still kept their grip on her arms.

"Mr Hameer," said Dawson. "It's a pleasure to meet you again."

The man who had emerged from the van gave a slight bow. "Mr Dawson," he said. "This is something of a departure from the usual products I buy from you."

"I trust the guns have proved reliable?" said Dawson.

"Perfectly. But this young lady. I'm intrigued."

"Don't be," said Dawson. "It's just a business deal, like

77

any other."

"But such a fine piece of merchandise." The man moved close to the captive, his eyes drinking in her beauty.

"Turn round!" he ordered.

Lisa glanced at Dawson, who nodded. The guards let go of her hands and she slowly revolved until her back was to Hameer.

"Stop."

Lisa stood stock-still, aware that she would incur Dawson's wrath if she disobeyed. She shivered slightly as she felt the man's hands close about the soft globes of her behind. He pulled them apart and she imagined him studying her anus.

"I see they have beaten you," he mused. "That is good. A woman needs beating on a regular basis. It increases her sensuality."

"I don't think you'll find that a problem with this one," said Dawson. "I believe her to be a true masochist."

"And I'm told she enjoys being fucked?"

"A real nymphomaniac. I never saw a woman so quickly turned on, or so free with her favours. That's why she should be kept naked. It turns her on like nothing else."

Lisa listened to the conversation in silence. It was as if she wasn't there. As if they were discussing a piece of livestock at a cattle auction. She thought about the words Dawson had used to describe her. A masochist and a nymphomaniac. Perhaps it was true. That at least would explain the true sexual pleasure she derived from the beatings she had been subjected to, as well as the arousal she felt at the rough treatment she had received at the hands of her captors.

"Turn again."

Obediently she turned to face the man once more. He reached out for her breasts, closing a hand about each, and she blushed as she felt her large brown teats pucker to hardness.

"Hmm, very nice," he said. "Very nice indeed. So firm,

yet soft. Spread your legs."

For a second Lisa wasn't sure if she had heard correctly. She stared at him.

"Spread your legs I said!" he barked. "I can see some training in obedience will be necessary."

Reluctantly Lisa widened her stance.

The man stretched out his hand, his arm angled down, his palm upwards. "Push your cunt forward. Offer it to me."

"Why are you doing this?" she asked.

Whack!

Dawson's ubiquitous stick was put to use once more, delivering a stinging blow to Lisa's backside.

"Just do as you're told."

Lisa hesitated for a second. Then, her face crimson, she pressed her hips forward, bending her knees slightly as she deliberately thrust her sex toward the man's open hand.

"Pleasure yourself on my fingers."

Lisa looked to Dawson, an expression of pleading in her eyes, but he was stony faced. Averting her gaze from the man's she pressed forward further until her open sex came in contact with his fingers.

A shudder ran through her body as she felt his fingertips brush against her most private place and the desire began to burn within her. Why was it that she was so sensitive? What was it made her want to rub all the harder against his hand, despite the fact they were being watched by others? Lisa couldn't say. All she knew was that, ever since being deprived of her clothes and her modesty she was like a hair trigger, the slightest touch being enough to start the juices flowing within her.

The man withdrew his hand, smiling at the gasp of disappointment this brought from the girl, and at the way her sex lips twitched closed as an involuntary convulsion shook her.

"Hmm," he said. "You are right Mr Dawson. She does seem eminently suitable. In need of a little training perhaps, but otherwise quite a find."

"What's going on?" said Lisa. "Why am I here? And who are these men?"

Dawson shook his head. "All in good time, young lady," he said. "Now Mr Hameer. Do we have a deal?"

Hameer smiled. "We certainly do, Mr Dawson." He turned to the man standing by the van door.

"Prepare her."

Before Lisa knew what was happening her arms were seized by her guards and they dragged her over to the doors of the vehicle. There was a clink of chains, and something cold and hard snapped round her arm just above the elbow. Then another on the other side, pinning her arms back and rendering them completely useless. Then a pair of shackles were placed round her ankles, the chain between them no more than nine inches long. As soon as this was in place she felt herself lifted bodily and placed face down in the back of the van. At once her ankles were pulled up behind her and the chain between the shackles was snapped onto the one between her elbows.

In seconds Lisa had been totally incapacitated, so that now she was quite incapable of using her limbs. She lay helpless on the hard floor of the van, her breasts thrust forward, her eyes wide with consternation. But they hadn't finished yet. The dark skinned man produced something from his pocket and offered it up to her face.

"Open your mouth."

Lisa stared at the thing. It was a large rubber ball with straps dangling from it.

"Open your mouth!"

The man grabbed her by the chin and forced her jaws apart, jamming the ball between her teeth and fastening the strap behind her head. If Lisa had intended to protest, her chance had now gone. With the ball gag in her mouth she could manage no more than a muffled mumbling sound.

Then she saw that the man had a strip of black cloth in his hand and, before she knew what was happening, he placed it over her eyes, plunging her into total darkness.

Lisa had never felt so helpless. Previously they had only prevented her from using her limbs. Now she was totally in their power, deprived of movement, speech and sight. For a second she was engulfed by panic, and she tugged at her bonds. But there was no escape and she knew it.

Once again powerful arms were gathering her up, taking her further inside the van. The guard placed her down on her side, on what felt like a piece of carpet. Then she heard another rattle of chains and a tug at her wrists and realised that she was being chained to the floor of the van. Thus her bondage was complete, and she knew at last what it was to be totally in another's power.

And with that knowledge she felt another sudden surge of arousal.

The doors of the van slammed. She wondered if she was alone in there, or whether the man was riding with her. She thought of his eyes on her body and felt a tingle of excitement. Her legs were slightly apart, but she made no attempt to close them, suddenly wanting the man to see her sex, and perhaps detect the wetness therein.

There was the chatter of a starter motor, followed by the roar of the van's engine coming to life. She heard a few words shouted, then the vehicle lurched forward and they were moving.

The journey was a long one. More than an hour, Lisa calculated. And all the time she was left in darkness with her thoughts. Thoughts that became hard to control, given her sensory deprivation.

She found her mind filled with the most erotic imaginings. She saw herself thrown from the van by the dark skinned men and left by the wayside, where a passing gang of youths found her, dragging her off into the bushes and taking it in turns to fuck her. She imagined the men taking her naked through he streets, where the people pointed at her and laughed at her nakedness. And she imagined being trussed up and whipped until her body was a mass of angry red stripes. And all the time she longed to be able to touch her sex and to bring herself the relief that she suddenly desired so much.

She was jerked back to reality by the sound of the vehicle slowing down. All at once she felt it pull to the left onto an unmetalled surface, the wheels bumping along what was clearly quite a rough track.

This went on for a further five minutes, then suddenly, a new sound reached Lisa's ears. It was a kind of whistling, though she couldn't place exactly what it was. It grew louder, and she guessed the van was taking them closer to its source They seemed to be on smoother ground now, though they still bumped and rocked more than it had on the main road.

By the time they stopped the whistle had swelled to a low roar, which increased still further as the doors were opened. It was then that Lisa realised what it was.

It was the sound of jet engines.

Lisa's heart jumped. An aeroplane! And clearly it was to that she was being taken. But what could they possibly want with an aeroplane? She knew, though, that the question was a pointless one. The answer was simple. They were taking her somewhere. Somewhere a long distance away.

At that moment she felt the presence of someone close to her, and a hand grasped her wrist. Then came the unmistakable click of a lock being unfastened, and she was scooped up in the person's arms and carried from the aircraft. Outside the air was cold, chilling her bare skin and making her shiver. The noise was considerably louder here, and she could hear men shouting above it, though she couldn't discern the words. Then they were ascending some steps and the noise level dropped once more.

The man dropped her onto the floor of the aircraft which, like the van, was carpeted. Then she heard a door close and suddenly the note of the engines rose. The machine must have been waiting at the end of the runway, for it started its takeoff run immediately, the force of the acceleration almost rolling the girl over as they bumped along the runway.

All of a sudden, their ride was smooth and Lisa knew they were airborne, though where they were going she had no idea.

Chapter 11

Lisa didn't know how long she had slept. She was woken by the sensation of hands fiddling with the chains that held her. She opened her eyes, but could see nothing, since she was still blindfold. She lay where she was, without moving, whilst the chains were removed one by one. First her legs were detached from her wrists, then the shackles that held her arms and hands together were undone. She sat up, and the gag was taken from her mouth. Then the blindfold was pulled off, and she blinked into the light, her focus temporarily impaired by the pressure that the blindfold had applied.

"Get up."

She rose to her feet, using a seat beside her for support. Her limbs ached terribly with their prolonged immobilisation and her jaw too was extremely painful. She raised her arms above her head, stretching her lovely young body, her breasts standing out proudly as she arched her back. Then she remembered her nudity and went to cover herself with her hands, only to have them brushed aside.

"Your modesty does you credit."

Lisa squeezed her eyes shut and opened them again, and gradually the features of Hameer took shape.

Unwilling to meet his eyes she looked about her, seeing the inside of the aircraft for the first time. It was not a large one, the cylindrical fuselage having two sets of four seats facing one another on one side. At the rear was a small galley, where the Hameer's companion was standing over a stove. At the front end a pair of curtains had been pulled across and she guessed that was where the cockpit was.

The smell from the stove reached her nostrils, and all of a sudden she realised that she was ravenously hungry. She stared back at the galley, and Hameer read her thoughts.

"The meal will be ready in a moment," he said. "Go forward and sit down."

Lisa took a step and nearly fell headlong, grasping at the seat for support. She had forgotten the shackles that were still attached to her ankles. Steadying herself she shuffled forward to the seat Hameer had indicated.

She sat down at the table. Suddenly it seemed very strange to be as she was, preparing to eat with her bare breasts jutting forward over the table top. She considered covering them with her hands, but thought better of it. She looked up as the man approached with a plate piled high with steaming stew, a glass of beer in his other hand. He placed them down in front of her and nodded.

"Eat."

Lisa didn't need to be asked twice. She positively fell on the food, devouring it in great forkfuls and swigging at the beer, which the man kept topped up for her. By the time she had finished, both plate and glass were empty and she was feeling a good deal better.

The man cleared the plates and she moved across and gazed out the window. It was dawn, the orange rays of the sun just poking through the great snowfield of cloud below them. There was no possible way of knowing where they were. She turned back to see Hameer standing over her.

"Where are we?" she asked. "Where am I being taken?"

He frowned. "You will soon learn not to ask questions," he said. "You are not to speak at all except when spoken to. That is the first rule. Do you understand?"

"Yes but..."

Bang! He hammered his fist down on the table. "Do you understand?"

Lisa lowered her eyes. "Yes."

"There are many rules you must learn, little English bitch," he said. "But most important is total obedience. Any misdemeanours and you will be thrashed like you have never been before. What am I telling you?"

"That I must be totally obedient Sir," mumbled Lisa quietly.

"Good. All will be revealed to you in due course. Meanwhile you take your orders from me and Karam here. Just understand that you are no longer an individual. Your life is now controlled by others, and you must do exactly as they say. Understand?"

"Yes Sir."

Lisa's mind was confused. What could he mean? What could lie in store for her at the end of this journey? One thing was for certain, her life was about to undergo a fundamental change. She stared at Hameer, then at Karam. Both were strong and handsome men, with undeniable appeal. And for the time being she knew she had to obey them. Then she glanced down at her own body, and the vulnerability of her position sent a shiver through her.

"Right," said Hameer. "Have you ever heard of the Mile High Club?"

She shook her head. "No Sir."

"Then I'll tell you. In order to join this club you need only do one thing. You need to fuck more than one mile above the earth's surface."

Lisa felt a strange lurching feeling in her stomach as he spoke the words. "Sir?"

85

"The pilots inform me that we are at precisely such a height. Therefore it is time for you to perform your first duty for me."

She stared at him, her heart beating hard. The words were spoken so casually. As if he was suggesting she perform some menial task. Yet what he proposed was the most intimate thing that could take place between a man and a woman. And she knew she had no choice but to comply. She felt her nipples stiffen to hardness at the thought. As they did so his eyes dropped to her breasts and she knew he had seen it happen.

"Go to the back of the aircraft and lie down," he ordered.

Lisa hesitated, and his brow furrowed.

"We can do this two ways," he said. "Either you can comply and show me your talents at giving pleasure to a man, or I can have you tied down and gagged, and fuck you against your will. I have no special preference. Either way will do."

Lisa listened to the words in silence, but inside her they set in motion a storm of conflicting emotions. On the one hand there was indignation at the way in which he addressed her, as if she were simply a chattel for his own pleasure. On the other a huge surge of excitement swept through her body as she realised the inevitability of the fucking she was to receive. She rose to her feet and shuffled unsteadily to the rear of the aircraft.

At the back was a wide expanse of carpet, and she lowered herself onto it, prostrating herself on her back. Then she spread her legs as wide as the shackles would allow and reached her arms up above her head, mimicking the spread-eagled position in which they had tied her to her bunk in her cell.

Hameer strolled down the fuselage and smiled when he saw her.

"Hmm. Perhaps I will have you tied anyway," he said. "From what Dawson tells me, a slut like you isn't going to

86

object to that. You might get even more pleasure from it that way,."

Lisa did not reply, but the surge of wetness inside her that the remark triggered must have transmitted itself to the expression on her face, because Hameer turned and shouted something to Karam.

The man moved up to Hameer's side, his eyes taking in the position of surrender into which Lisa had arranged her limbs. A few words passed between the two men, then he picked up Lisa's chains, which had been lying on one of the seats.

She offered no resistance as he chained her, holding out her wrists to be secured to the bulkhead of the aircraft above her head about three feet apart. Once this was done, he undid the shackles on her ankles and spread her legs still wider, attaching them to the opposite wall. Then he straightened up and stared down at his captive.

Lisa was completely helpless once again, and the thought sent a spasm of excitement through her. Somehow it was easier this way. Like this she had abrogated all responsibility for what was about to occur, and had surrendered control totally to her captors. Whatever they did now was beyond her control. She raised her head and stared down between her swelling breasts, imagining the sight her pink nether lips must make, forced apart so that the men were able to feast their eyes on the dampness within. She could barely suppress a moan as Hameer stepped between her thighs and began undoing his trousers.

His cock was long and thick, hanging down before a large, pendulous scrotum. As he kicked his pants aside and stood before her clad only in his shirt, she licked her lips in anticipation. He saw this and stepped forward, straddling her body, then dropped to his knees.

Lisa opened her mouth, understanding at once that he wanted her to take him inside, and aware that she had no choice in the matter. As she looked at his penis hanging in front of her face she found herself almost wishing that her hands were free too allow her to stroke his beautiful organ, but she knew she had to perform for him with her mouth alone. He pressed his hips forward and she took him between his lips and began to suck. At the same time she wormed her tongue under his foreskin, running it over the smooth skin of his glans and seeking out the tiny eye in the centre. At once she was rewarded by the sensation of him thickening inside her mouth.

She sucked harder, beginning to move her head back and forth as she did so, the smell and taste of his arousal spurring her on. And with every second he became more and more erect, his tool beginning to completely fill her mouth.

She continued moving her head back and forth. It wasn't easy, given her restricted position, and almost at once her neck began to ache, but she had ceased to care. All of a sudden the most important thing to her was Hameer's cock, and the fact that she was being taken against her will only seemed to enhance the wanton pleasure she was taking in fellating him.

But Hameer wanted more than her mouth, and when he pulled his now engorged penis from her lips she knew her honour was lost. Yet her only reaction was to press her pubis forward, lifting her backside from the floor in an unambiguous gesture of surrender.

He slid his cock straight into her, bringing a strangled moan from her lips as he filled her with his meaty truncheon. He lay over her, his face close to hers, staring into her eyes, his weight bearing down on her.

Then he started to move.

"Ahhh!"

Lisa cried aloud as Hameer's cock began to pump back and forth. He moved slowly at first, as if he was savouring the sensation of taking the gorgeous young girl so easily.

And Lisa was something to savour, her exquisite body spread open for the taking, her nipples like hard brown buds standing proud from the soft globes of her breasts, her hot, wet sex enveloping his penis, the muscles tightening suddenly as if to embrace and welcome it inside.

Lisa too found it a moment to savour. Ever since she had been taken into captivity she had become like a hungry animal, except that it was not food in her stomach she craved, but a man's thick rod sliding into her cunt. The nudity, bondage and ill-treatment simply seemed to exacerbate this desire, and for the first time it occurred to her that one of the functions of the chains in which she had been held was to prevent her from masturbating. Such a prohibition made the fucking she was getting from Hameer seem almost like a reward, and the skill of her captors in playing on her desires began to dawn on her.

Hameer's motions were increasing now, the gentle movement of his hips turning to thrusts as his own passion increased. Lisa too was thrusting, pressing her pubis up against him and urging him ever deeper inside. Her body was rocked back and forth by his actions, making her breasts shake in a delightful way, and the thought of the effect this was having on her seducer seemed to redouble her own pleasure.

All at once, something made Lisa tear her eyes from Hameer's and look across to one side. It was then that she realised that Karam was standing, watching her debauchment, his long brown cock projecting from his fly as he wanked himself slowly. The sight of him so close gave her a shock. Suddenly it occurred to her that, no sooner had Hameer finished with her, than Karam intended to ravish her too. From that moment her desires had a new impetus. Her sex muscles tightened and brought a gasp from the man who was already enjoying her.

Hameer's cock was pumping in and out of her like a piston now, each stroke bringing a grunt of pleasure from her lips. Lisa knew she couldn't withhold her orgasm much longer, but she wanted to feel his spunk inside her before she abandoned herself to it.

The sudden tensioning of his muscles told her that the moment had come, and seconds later she was rewarded by the sensation of a gush of hot semen escaping from his rampant tool.

"Ah! Ah! Ah! Ahhh!"

Lisa came with a scream, her body jerking like a marionette on elastic strings as the pleasure engulfed her. It was a glorious orgasm, the sensation of Hameer's cock pumping spurt after spurt of his seed deep inside her vagina bringing waves of indescribable pleasure to her hot little body. Her entire being was concentrated in her cunt at that moment, and the shrieks and moans that escaped her lips were more like the cries of an animal than of the decorous young girl that she had so recently been.

Hameer pulled out suddenly, his cock still dribbling spunk from the tip, which trickled down the length of his shaft and ran down his balls. He moved forward until his glistening pole was right in front of her face. She didn't need asking. She raised her head from the carpet and protruded her tongue, catching the drip of sperm that was forming under his scrotum and swallowing it. She worked her way over his balls and up the length of his penis, licking greedily and devouring all traces of his spunk and her juices. Only when he was completely clean did she lower her head to the floor once more.

Hameer rose to his feet and turned away, saying nothing. Somehow Lisa didn't care. Soft words and sweet nothings were for lovers. What had just happened had nothing to do with love. It was simply a man relieving his sexual tensions and using her as the instrument of that relief. Lisa was no more than a living cunt to him, an object to satisfy his desires. And if, at the same time, hers were satisfied as well, then so be it.

Her musings were interrupted by the sudden invasion of a second penis into her open sex, and all at once her arousal was renewed. Her vagina enclosed Karam's cock with the same enthusiasm as it had Hameer's.

Karam's love making was less refined than was Hameer's. From the start he was thrusting hard, his face screwed into a mask of concentration as he rammed his cock into her. His raw desire was infectious and Lisa responded in like manner, her backside banging up and down on the floor of the aircraft as she matched his rhythm.

His orgasm came quickly, yet still Lisa responded with her own, her cries of pleasure no less urgent as her lust overcame her. By the time Karam withdrew she was panting with exertion, and her sex was brimming with come, which leaked from her and ran down the crack of her backside, where it formed a pool on the floor between her legs.

Her body ached now, and the stiffness was beginning to creep into her limbs once more. She looked up to see where Hameer had got to, hoping for relief.

All she saw was a man in a blue uniform staring down at her and beginning to undo his trousers.

She had forgotten the pilots.

Chapter 12

Lisa gazed out of the window as the aircraft banked steeply over the rough terrain. They were flying alongside a range of hills which, to the girl, seemed dangerously close to their wing-tips. She searched the landscape below, looking for any sign of life, but without success. The earth was an unusually red colour with a meandering brown river running through it. The vegetation was sparse, with a few copses beside the water and one or two patches of green. All the rest was barren.

They had been at this low altitude for nearly fifteen minutes, having descended soon after the cloud below them had dispersed. Now they sped on down the valleys at what seemed a very precarious height.

Lisa was sitting in the seat at which she had eaten earlier. The handcuffs that held her arms behind her and the shackles on her legs seeming almost comfortable after the discomfort of her earlier bondage. At the other end of the aircraft sat Hameer and Karam, deep in conversation. Since her ravishment, which had included both the pilots, followed by second helpings for her two guards, she had been released and allowed to sleep once more. She had woken to discover it was daylight, and soon afterwards the engine note had dropped and they had begun to descend. Now, as she sat alone, staring from the window, the apprehension was beginning to return.

She thought back over what had happened earlier in the flight, and of her disgraceful behaviour. She could scarcely believe the way she had reacted. It was as if the modest young girl of just a few weeks before had been replaced by a completely different person. Even now, as she glanced down at her nakedness, she couldn't suppress the thrill that she felt, knowing that the two men could see her.

She wondered what would happen when they landed. She had already been given an inkling. Since she had heard them, Hameer's words about obedience had been ringing round in her head. It was clear that her life was about to change totally, but what would her new one be like? For how long would she be kept like this, bound and denied the simple modesty of clothes? And how many more men would take her in the way these four had done, without thought for consent?

Suddenly the aircraft's engine note dropped and it banked

again. Then a gleam of reflected sunlight caught Lisa's eye. She squinted. There, some way below, she could discern a long grey strip with white markings on it. The flash of light had come from the centre and, as the aircraft dropped lower, she realised that there was a vehicle parked beside the strip. It was a landing ground, and as the nose of the plane came round she realised that that was where they were headed. The clunk and rumble of the lowering undercarriage confirmed this.

Lower and lower they dropped, The patches of green turning to trees as they came closer. The aircraft was descending fast now, and Lisa pressed her cheek to the window, searching ahead for the runway.

So near the ground were they that she was certain they would miss the strip altogether. But the pilot was clearly an expert and, the moment the white stripes at the end of the runway passed beneath the wings, they were down and bumping along the ground. The engines roared briefly, slowing them almost to a walking pace. Then they swung round and taxied back up the length of the strip.

Lisa could see the vehicle clearly now. It was a Land Rover. It appeared to be an old one, and was covered in the red dust that seemed to be everywhere. There were figures standing beside it and she shrank down in her seat for fear of being seen. As they came closer the figures revealed themselves to be four men. One was a Negro, small and wiry and aged about forty. Next to him was a huge man with olive coloured skin similar to Hameer's. He was well over six foot tall, with a girth to match. His head was completely shaven and he wore a large gold ring in one ear. He was naked from the waist up, his chest broad but hairless. From his belt hung a long, thin horse whip. His two other companions were also of Arabic appearance, both dressed identically to him, but lacking his size and presence.

Lisa looked round to see Hameer standing beside her.

"This is as far as you go," he said. "Time to get off."

Lisa rose uncertainly to her feet. Hameer must have seen the apprehension in her face, for he smiled, not unkindly.

"Don't be afraid, little English rose," he said. "Remember, always to be obedient. That man is called Pakat. He is well versed in the training of young slaves like yourself."

Slave? Lisa opened her mouth to exclaim, but stopped herself just in time. She stared at Hameer in disbelief.

"Surely you have guessed the nature of your new existence?" he said. "You are to be trained in total obedience, then sold in the slave market to a wealthy man. Your duties will be to keep him happy in any way he demands. It's as simple as that."

Lisa shook her head. Despite the fact that she had already begun to suspect that some kind of servitude lay before her, the knowledge still came as a shock. Now, as she looked across to where Karam was unlocking the door of the aircraft, a strange sense of finality settled upon her. It was as if the fuselage of the aircraft was a final link with the life and civilisation she had known thus far. Beyond it lay the unknown. She turned her eyes back to Hameer.

"You wish to ask me something?" he asked.

"Yes Sir."

"Go ahead."

"Where am I Sir? And where am I going?"

"Suffice to say you are in Africa. The name of the country is unimportant. It is a convenient entry point for girls such as you who come from the West."

Africa! Of course! The colour of the soil, the barrenness of the earth. It all tied in with what she had seen and heard of the Dark Continent. Lisa felt suddenly very alone.

"As to where you are going," he went on. "From here you will be transported by road to a training camp. It will take a number of days, and you will pass through some dangerous country on the way."

"Dangerous?" Lisa had not meant to speak, but the word had escaped her lips before she had time to stop it. Hameer ignored the slip, however.

"There are dangers, certainly," he said. "Many of these lands are ruled by despots, and in the bush are bands of armed rebels. But don't worry. The men who will transport you are experienced, and nobody has yet been lost to the rebels."

The door to the aircraft was open now, and Karam beckoned to her. Lisa shuffled forward toward the opening, then turned for a last time to Hameer. She had known him only a few hours, and in that time he had bound her and fucked her. But he had also showed some compassion, and somehow his presence seemed almost benign compared to the men who awaited her outside.

He moved across to her, taking her by the shoulders and pinning her to the wall of the aircraft. One hand went to her breast, caressing it gently whilst the other slid down between her legs.

"Oh!"

She gave a start as he slipped two fingers into her vagina, pressing them deep inside her and bringing a gasp of surprise to her lips. He worked his hand back and forth a few times, and at once she felt the familiar lust rise within her.

He slid his fingers out again and stood back. Lisa was already starting to pant, and her hips were moving slightly.

"You will make a good slave," he said. "You are so sensuous, any man who sees you will want to fuck you. And I know you will want it too. Now go."

Lisa dropped her eyes, trying to quell the lustful thoughts that were rising within her. Then she turned and stepped through the door.

The sun was blinding. In normal circumstances Lisa would have welcomed its warm rays caressing her bare skin. This was different, though. Today her nakedness was enforced, and the men who looked upon her were strangers with unfamiliar foreign faces. If her hands had been free she would have used them to cover her breasts and sex. But they weren't, and she was forced to endure the frank stares of the four men as she made her way awkwardly down the steps of the aircraft to where they were standing.

Her feet touched the earth. It was hot and stony, but she remained erect, determined not to show discomfort or fear before her new captors. Still hobbled by the shackles on her legs she made her way across to where the men were standing and stopped in front of them.

For a few seconds they faced one another. Then the big man, who Hameer had called Pakat, barked an order. His two similarly dressed companions stepped forward, each grasping one of Lisa's arms. They bent down, and placing a hand behind her thigh, lifted her into a sitting position, at the same time spreading her thighs apart to reveal the pink petals of her sex to the other two.

They carried her to the vehicle. It was a fairly battered machine that had clearly seen better days. The back end was open, with a metal frame over the top that was clearly designed to support a canvas roof. The tailgate was down, and the two men lifted her over this and onto the floor. Then they vaulted up beside her. One of them reached for the cuffs at her wrists and undid one of them. Then they pulled her arms above her head, so that her hands closed about the bar that ran down the centre of the vehicle. At once the cuff was snapped back into place, leaving her standing, facing backwards.

The Negro pushed up the tailgate and fastened it on both sides, then he turned to Pakat and gave a kind of salute. The big man nodded. The two guards settled down on padded seats on either side of their captive. Then Pakat and the black man went around to the front, the larger man climbing into the passenger seat. The doors slammed and the engine started, a plume of black smoke emitting from the exhaust. Then there was a grinding of gears and the vehicle moved forward with a lurch that threw Lisa off balance. She staggered sideways, clutching onto the bar above her head for dear life as they bumped and rocked along the track before swinging right onto a narrow dirt road and heading off through the bush.

A sudden roar reached Lisa's ears and she turned to see the aircraft accelerating along the runway. She watched it as it rose into the air. To her it seemed to represent the freedom she was leaving behind. Ahead lay the prospect of slavery, submission and punishment. She kept her eyes on the speeding aircraft until it disappeared over the hills. Then she turned her gaze toward the road ahead as the Land Rover carried her away to a new life.

Chapter 13

The Land Rover sped on through the afternoon, the sun continuing to beat down on its occupants. Lisa soon realised that she was in danger of sunstroke in the searing heat of the African sun. Even despite the wind that blew over her naked body she was beginning to sweat, and she knew her skin would burn unless they found some shade.

She needn't have worried, however. Before they had been travelling for half an hour, one of the men pulled a bag from under his seat and reached inside. He pulled out a bottle. It was unmarked, and contained a viscous white fluid. He uncorked the top and poured a quantity onto his hand, then rose to his feet, grasping onto the bars above him. He held out a hand and Lisa shrank back momentarily. Then he began wiping streaks of the fluid onto her skin, beginning with her forehead, then a dab each on her breasts and another on her shoulders.

Once most of the fluid had been deposited, he returned to her face, working the lotion into her skin with circular motions. He covered the whole of her visage, caressing her cheeks, chin and neck. The substance had a scent like coconut, which Lisa found not unpleasant, and the motion of his fingers felt good to her.

Then his hands dropped to her shoulders, again massaging her gently as he worked the fluid into her pores, covering her upper back and working down to the base of her spine.

He turned her round to face him and her eyes dropped to her full breasts, both of which bore a blob of the lotion which had, in the heat of the sun, trickled downwards, so that both her nipples had a shiny stripe running over them. She tensed herself as he reached for her, his hands closing over her jutting mammaries, and began to rub the warm liquid into her soft, pliable flesh.

"Mmmm"

Lisa was quite unable to suppress the moan of pleasure as his hands began to stroke and squeeze her breasts. At once her nipples swelled into hard little points under his touch and she threw back her head, her eyes closed, her body tingling with the delicious feel of his hands.

He moved lower, his fingers sliding over the undulations of her rib cage, then her belly, all the time massaging the fluid into her pores with a gentleness and sensuality that belied the man's stern appearance. He worked all the way down to her pubic hair, his fingers brushing it lightly and sending new waves of desire through her as he touched her so close to her most private place. Then he removed his fingers, eliciting a sigh from the tethered girl.

He picked up the bottle, applying more to his palm. This time he deposited it on the swelling globes of her backside, down her thighs and on her lower legs. Then the massage began again.

He started with her bottom, his hands showing the same gentleness as they had on her breasts as he kneaded the pliant flesh. He was very thorough, sliding his fingers down right into the crack of her behind, the sensation of his touch on her anus bringing another gasp of pleasure to her lips.

Next he dropped to his knees, taking her right foot in his hand and spreading the lotion over it. He moved to her ankle, then her calf, and finally up to her knee, taking care that every inch was covered. He did the same with her left leg, working with meticulous care until the only place left untouched was the area between her knees and her crotch.

When he started working up the inside of her thighs, one hand on each, Lisa was suddenly afraid she might lose control. His hands had such a gentle touch that every caress sent a new surge of desire through her. She looked down at him. His face was level with her pubis, his eyes able to drink in the soft petals of her nether lips as his hands moved higher and higher up her thighs. She made to close her legs, but he wouldn't let her, slapping the sensitive flesh on the inside of her leg and barking an order at her. Lisa closed her eyes and gritted her teeth as his hand came closer to her sex.

The first time his hand brushed her there, she gave a little gasp. His fingers felt wonderful to her as they glided over her skin, each stroke ending with the back of his hand running along her slit and sending delicious sensations through her body. When he finally closed his hand about her sex, his index finger tracing the length of her nether lips and lingering on the hard, wet little nodule at the top, she very nearly came.

Then his hands left her, and she gave a little moan of disappointment. She opened her eyes and saw the grin on his face, then looked down at her body. She was shocked to see that her hips were gyrating in the lewdest possible manner and she fought to bring her recalcitrant body under control as the two men sat back to watch her.

The vehicle rumbled on over the hot, dusty track, every now and again striking a pothole that made it lurch sideways, throwing its reluctant passenger off balance as she clung grimly to the bar above her head. The terrain remained unchanged; mile after mile of scrubland punctuated by the occasional tree. Every now and again she would spot small herds of gazelle or an occasional brightly coloured bird. There were a few humans too, their houses like small brown mounds, only identifiable by the plumes of blue smoke that rose from holes in the top. The people were the darkest black, tall and haughty looking. They would hear the vehicle approaching from afar, jumping to their feet and lining the road to stare at the passing Land Rover. When they caught sight of the naked white girl who stood in the back they would point at her and laugh aloud at the sight she made.

The two guards chatted to one another as they went along. Lisa could understand nothing of what was said, but it was clear to her that it was her that they were talking about. Every now and again they would raise their whips, running them down her flank or up her inner thigh, watching her body react as the rough leather sought out her sex and slid along it, bringing fresh moans from their captive. Soon the flesh about her sex was covered in shiny streaks where they had rubbed her wetness from the end of their whips.

After about three hours Lisa spotted a village ahead. It was larger than any they had seen all day, with a few brick-built buildings as well as the traditional huts. Lisa hoped desperately that they would bypass this small outpost of civilisation, but to her dismay she saw they were heading toward the centre. Her dismay increased when she saw the filling station and realised they were about to stop.

The Land Rover drew up in front of the single petrol pump and sounded its horn. A man emerged from a small shed. He was of Arabic appearance, like her captors, and his face creased into a grin when he spotted the girl. He pulled a lever on the ancient petrol pump and it whirred into life. Then he removed the petrol cap from the vehicle and began to fill it up, his eyes remaining fixed on Lisa's breasts and sex. At the same time a crowd of locals was forming, all gazing in fascination at the lovely young captive so delightfully displayed to them. Lisa's face glowed scarlet as they chatted and laughed, and she longed for the Rover to be on its way again.

Suddenly she heard a voice, and looked down to see Pakat standing beside the vehicle. It was the first time he had shown his face since the airfield. As he spoke the two guards climbed to their feet, and to Lisa's surprise, began to undo her cuffs.

The guards lowered the tailgate and the crowd parted as the red-faced girl was taken to the edge and lifted down. At once they fastened her wrists behind her back, then Pakat took her arm and led her through the chattering mob toward a building opposite. He pushed open the door and shoved her inside, allowing it to close behind them, much to Lisa's relief. Inside, the building was cool after the heat of the African sun, the only light coming through a barred window at the side.

Lisa stared about her. It appeared to be some kind of shop, the shelves stacked with all kinds of diverse goods from tinned food to pots and pans. The walls were covered with advertisements and the place had a spicy smell which was by no means unpleasant. The establishment seemed deserted, but no sooner had the door closed than there was a noise from the back and a man emerged. He too had the lighter skin that distinguished him from the locals and his small eyes gleamed as they alighted on Lisa's naked body.

A conversation began between him and Pakat, and once again Lisa felt sure she was the subject. She stood by quietly, her eyes cast down, while the pair laughed and joked together like old friends. When Pakat finally addressed her she was, at first, unaware that it was to her he was speaking.

"The gentleman wishes to measure your neck."

The words startled the girl. Pakat's English was perfect, the accent reminding her of old wartime newsreels in which the vowels were exaggerated to the extent of sounding false. Somehow the voice didn't seem to fit the gruff looking foreigner from whose mouth they came. It was almost like seeing a film badly dubbed into English.

"I-I beg your pardon Sir?"

"I said, the gentleman wishes to measure your neck. And kindly refer to me as Master."

"Master?"

His hands went to the whip at his belt. "I am not accustomed to having to repeat myself."

"I'm sorry... Master," she muttered, eyeing the weapon with trepidation.

She turned to the shopkeeper, who had produced a tape measure and was holding it up. She stepped forward, wishing her hands were free.

He placed the measure about her neck, pulling it snugly around her throat and checking the reading. He nodded and let go, allowing his hand to drop to her breast, which he fondled gently. Lisa closed her eyes, embarrassed by the way her nipples hardened under his touch.

The two men exchanged a few more words, then the shopkeeper turned away and opened a drawer behind him. He rummaged inside for a short time, then pulled out something and laid it on the counter.

Lisa stared down at it. It resembled a dog's collar, being a strip of brown leather set with pointed studs. In the centre was a ring made of the same material as the studs. The collar itself was about two inches thick, and at each end was a strap, about half that width, one end of which sported a buckle.

The man placed his hand under Lisa's chin, raising her

102

head. Then he picked up the collar and placed it about her neck. It was lined on the inside with a sort of velvet, which felt soft against her skin. He pulled the strap through the buckle and fastened it.

The collar was a snug fit. Very snug. It hugged her neck closely, almost, but not quite, restricting her breathing. Pakat ran his finger round it, nodding his approval while the man again fondled Lisa's breasts.

"This is your collar," said Pakat. "It is a symbol of your slavery. When you are bought by your new owner it will display his name. It is an honour to wear such a thing."

Lisa said nothing. There was nothing to say. Every step of this journey seemed to be taking her further and further from the girl she had been previously, and the fitting of the collar was yet another indication of how her free will was being taken from her.

"It is made of the most expensive leather," went on Pakat. "This gentleman is a master craftsman at such things. For a male slave he would ask a good deal of money. However, he wishes for you to pay in a different way."

Lisa turned to him. Her heart beating hard as she digested his words. Meanwhile the man continued to fondle her breasts.

"You are to use your mouth to give him relief."

The words rang in Lisa's ears. There was no emotion in Pakat's voice. He might as well have been asking her to make the man a cup of tea. She stared at him, then at the man, who was smiling as he kneaded the soft flesh of her mammaries.

Suddenly Pakat grasped her wrists, and there was a snapping sound as he removed her cuffs. Lisa's immediate instinct was to cover herself, but she resisted the temptation, knowing it would anger her captor. Instead she let her arms drop to her sides while the shopkeeper continued to caress her.

"On your knees," ordered Pakat.

Lisa obeyed at once, dropping down into a submissive position before the shopkeeper. She stared at the bulge in his trousers, a strange feeling at the pit of her stomach as she contemplated what she was about to do.

"Now," said Pakat. "Show us how you service your Masters."

Lisa hesitated, unable for a second to believe what was being asked of her. She looked about her at the dingy shop, then up at the man in front of her. Her eye was caught by a mirror on the wall beside the counter and she contemplated her reflection, kneeling pale and naked before the shop owner, her breasts jutting forward so that the long brown nipples brushed against his trousers. Could this really be happening to her? Was that brazen slut in the mirror really her, baring her all to some squalid shopkeeper and paying for his goods with her body like a common prostitute? A shudder ran through her small frame, but it wasn't fear or cold that caused it. To Lisa's chagrin she realised it was a shudder of pure lustful desire.

She reached up and ran her hand over the swelling at the man's crotch. It felt very hard indeed and as she squeezed she felt it move slightly. She took hold of his belt, undoing it and then fumbling with the waistband of his trousers. Next she slid down the zipper, and the garment dropped away. His cock was straining so hard against the thin material of his briefs she felt sure they must soon split. She reached inside the gap at his waistband and her hand closed about a hot, thick rod of flesh. The pants snapped downwards and all of a sudden his cock sprang to attention.

To Lisa it was a beautiful sight, long and thick with a great vein up the centre, the purple head bobbing up and down as his tight scrotum contracted rhythmically beneath. She ran her fingers up and down the solid flesh, sliding his foreskin back to uncover yet more of his shining glans. She looked up into his eyes, and he nodded to her.

Lisa licked her lips. She opened her mouth and took him inside.

His cock was even bigger than she had thought. The glans alone seemed to fill her mouth completely. Yet even after she had closed her lips about it he continued to press forward. More and more of his shaft rammed into her face until she feared she might gag. His balls were almost brushing her chin now and she could feel the throbbing power of his knob as he began to thrust it against her.

Lisa sucked for all she was worth, one hand gently caressing the man's testicles while the other worked up and down his shaft. Now that she had him inside her mouth, all thoughts of shame deserted her as she concentrated on giving him pleasure. She began to bob her head up and down. Loud slurping noises came from her lips as she devoured him hungrily, her breasts bouncing with every jab of his hips.

Suddenly there was a loud bang as the shop door was flung open. Lisa's eyes darted sideways, though she dare not stop what she was doing for fear of incurring Pakat's wrath. A man stood in the doorway, staring at the scene before him. He was black, dressed in shabby trousers and an old white shirt. He stared contemptuously at the naked white girl, then looked up at the shopkeeper and shouted something. The man replied with a shake of his head, waving the newcomer away.

Once again the man shouted, pointing to something behind the counter, and Lisa realised he was asking to buy a pack of cigarettes. The shopkeeper was too preoccupied with the wanton girl who was fellating him, though, and simply turned away.

All of a sudden Lisa felt her hair grasped from behind and yanked backwards, so that the shopkeeper's shaft slipped from her lips. Her head was dragged round and she found herself staring into the eyes of the newcomer. They were cold eyes, filled with hatred. His lip curled back in a snarl, and she tried to cower back, suddenly afraid. The man was speaking to her. She couldn't understand a word he was saying, but she knew he was berating her. On his cheek was a mark. A long serpent that had been literally cut into the flesh of his face. It seemed almost alive as he spat out the insults, writhing back and forth with every word he spoke.

Whack!

Pakat's whip flashed down, cutting across the man's wrist and making him suddenly scream with pain. He dropped Lisa's hair at once and she cowered back against the counter.

Whack!

The whip descended again, this time across the man's face, the thin stripe that it left seeming to slice the dreadful serpent in two.

Whack!

By now the man was backing toward the door, still shouting abuse as the whip slashed across his chest. Pakat raised his arm again, but the man had had enough and fled through the door, slamming it behind him.

The incident had lasted no more than a few seconds, yet Lisa found her heart was thumping like a hammer. She looked up at Pakat, who was sliding the whip back into his belt.

"Damned upstart," he said. "These people need a lesson in manners." He looked down at the girl. "They hate us you know, because they see us as having all the wealth. But not half as much as they hate your people. They see the white man as the thief of their lands. That's why some of them rebel. Damned savages."

Lisa stared at the door. She couldn't get the man's eyes out of her mind, nor the image of that dreadful serpent on his cheek.

Suddenly she felt her head being pulled round, and she

was confronted by the shopkeeper's erection once more, now wet and shiny with her saliva. She grasped it in her fist and lowered her head over it, sucking hard.

It didn't take much longer. She knew it wouldn't. His cock was already twitching violently and the grunts that emitted from his throat as he thrust his hips against her face were becoming louder by the second.

He came suddenly, his thick semen pumping into the back of her throat, threatening to drown her so copious was the flow. She choked and gagged, trying hard to swallow every drop as spurt after spurt flew from the end of his penis into her open mouth. Despite her best efforts, though, the viscous fluid began leaking from the corners of her mouth and dribbling down her chin, dripping onto the white swellings of her breasts.

The man continued to pump his hips back and forth until every last drop of his semen had either disappeared down Lisa's throat or onto her body. Only then did he release his grip on her head and ease his still twitching member from between her lips. Lisa remained where she was, kneeling before him as the spunk ran down her, turning colder as it did so. She watched as he pulled up his pants and trousers, then turned and nodded his approval to Pakat. The large man tapped Lisa on the cheek with his whip.

"Come along, little one," he said. "Time to move on."

Chapter 14

The next morning they were on the road early, before the sun was fully up. The air felt cool against Lisa's naked flesh as the vehicle began to gather speed along the track, but she didn't mind, aware that the day would soon be hot enough.

The night had been spent at a small oasis at the side of

the road. The two guards had erected a bivouac whilst the driver had prepared a meal, leaving Lisa still tied to her spot in the back of the Land Rover. Once everything was prepared Pakat had allowed her down, shackling her by one leg to a nearby tree. Then she had been allowed to bathe in the small pool and to wash the grime and the mens' dried discharge from her body.

She had been given a bowl of stew and a bottle of beer for her supper, after which the guards hammered stakes into the earth and spread-eagled her on top of an old blanket. She had half expected to be ravished by the four of them, but they paid her scant attention, the three lighter skinned men sitting round the fire and chatting animatedly together whilst the Negro sat alone, his back against the tree, contemplating the naked beauty. Lisa had lain for some time gazing up at the night sky before finally falling into a troubled sleep, in which evil men with snakes in their hair chased her across endless miles of wasteland.

She awoke feeling stiff and cold, to find Pakat undoing her bonds. A bowl of oatmeal followed, after which she was ordered to assist the guards in striking camp. She complied willingly, glad to have something to do to pass the time. When everything was finally packed away she was manacled in position once more and they were on their way again.

The road seemed endless, with very little to take the girl's attention as the sun rose higher into the sky. The state of the surface did not improve, and the prolonged standing, accompanied by the constant buffeting, soon made her weary. The guards too seemed to be feeling the effects, lapsing into silence, their heads nodding down onto their chests.

In fact, when the ambush came, nobody was in the least prepared for it.

It started with a single shot. At first Lisa thought the vehicle had backfired, but then was alarmed by the way they suddenly slid sideways across the road. A second crack rang

108

out and they swung back the other way. It was then that she realised that both front tyres had been punctured.

The vehicle's momentum continued to carry it forward as it slewed crazily from side to side, the driver wrestling desperately with the wheel. Lisa hung on as tightly as she was able, her knuckles white whilst the guards threw themselves onto the floor.

In the end, the crash was quite gentle, the Rover sliding towards the edge of a ditch and almost stopping before the wheels slipped into it and it dropped down onto its side, depositing Lisa and the two guards into the dust. At the same time a second volley of shots rang out, the bullets clanging against the underside of the vehicle.

Lisa lay where she had fallen. She was completely unhurt, not even a graze on her bare flesh. But she was still manacled to the vehicle and quite unable to do anything than flatten her body against the earth as the bullets whistled overhead.

There was a crash as Pakat kicked out the windscreen. Then, showing a surprising agility for one so bulky, he scrambled through the gap, closely followed by the driver, both throwing themselves down behind the vehicle. The guards, meanwhile, were scrabbling in the luggage. They came up with a pair of ancient looking rifles that, even to Lisa's inexperienced eye, looked to be little use against the automatic fire that was striking the vehicle.

One of the guards cocked his rifle, then peered cautiously round the side of the overturned Rover. At once a volley of shots rang out and he darted back. Lisa looked at the mens' faces, and saw nothing but fear.

Pakat barked an urgent command to the other three, but the two men with rifles simply shook their heads. It was clear that the small party was outgunned by their ambushers, and neither of the men was willing to risk his neck by trying anything silly.

The gunfire stopped, and an uneasy silence fell over the scene. Lisa raised herself to her knees, hugging her body against the bar to which she was still manacled. The three men remained where they were, huddled behind the overturned vehicle.

A conversation ensued between Pakat and the two guards. Voices were raised and arms waved, and there was much shaking of heads. The driver was called in, and he too argued with some gusto. It became clear to Lisa that Pakat was making a lone stand against the other three, and that he was losing the argument. At last he simply turned away from the others, shaking his head, clearly defeated. A brief conversation followed between the other three, then one of the men reached into his pocket and pulled out a large white handkerchief, which he tied to the barrel of his gun,

The other four watched with trepidation as he slowly raised the flag above the side of the vehicle. Lisa tensed herself for a barrage of shots, but none came. Then a shout rang out from their attackers.

The man with the flag shouted a reply, and a dialogue began. Lisa was frustrated by her inability to understand a word that was being said. She turned to Pakat, but he remained stony faced, like a child in a sulk.

More shouting, then the man with the white flag slowly rose to his feet, so that he could see over the vehicle. Once again Lisa tensed, but there was no shooting. With slow, deliberate steps the man walked out of the shelter of the crashed Rover and disappeared in the direction from which the gunfire had come.

Another silence fell. The tension amongst the three men was palpable and Lisa found that she too was trembling as the minutes passed.

At last she could bear the suspense no longer. Slowly, cautiously, she raised her body into a crouching position, then peered over the side of the vehicle. The guard was standing about a hundred yards away in the middle of an open space. He was face to face with a black man, standing about ten feet from him. The two were conferring, though not a sound of their conversation was audible from where Lisa was. Beyond them was a small rocky outcrop, and as she watched she saw a glint of metal catch the sun, indicating where the rest of the ambushers were concealed. At that moment the guard turned away from the other man, and the two of them made their way back to their respective positions.

When the guard stepped round the side of the vehicle and lowered himself beside his friends his face was grim. They began to talk in earnest, occasionally casting a glance toward their naked captive, who watched them silently. Pakat soon joined in again, but this time he seemed less inclined to argue, and at last gave a shrug and a nod and reverted to silence once more.

The guard who had done the parleying crawled across to where Lisa crouched in the dust. He reached into his pocket and pulled out a key. Then he undid her manacles and the shackles on her legs. It was the first time she had been completely without bondage for some time, and she felt suddenly very nervous. It was almost as if the chains had been a sign of the men's protection of her. Now they were gone she felt very alone and isolated.

The guard looked at Pakat, who scowled, then turned to Lisa.

"Go to them," he said shortly.

Lisa stared at him.

"What..?"

"Go. It's you they want. This scum has just traded our lives for you. Now get out there. You're theirs now."

"But I can't..."

"Do not speak without permission," he thundered. "Now go!"

Lisa looked at the faces of the four men, but each dropped his eyes when they caught hers, and she sensed that none was happy with what was happening. She hesitated, then a shot rang out from the other side.

"Go now!" ordered Pakat. "Before they start firing again."

"Couldn't I have some clothes?"

"What's the point? They'd strip you naked in the first minute. Now get a move on."

Slowly Lisa rose to her feet. Now that her manacles had been removed she was able to raise her head completely clear of the side of the vehicle, giving her an unrestricted view across to where she knew their ambushers to be concealed. The idea of handing herself over to these strangers filled her with foreboding, the thought of doing it naked doubling that fear. She turned to give a last despairing look at the four men. Then, hugging her arm across her breasts and placing her palm flat across her pubis, she stepped out from behind the Rover.

She started to walk across to the outcrop where she had seen the gleam of sunlight earlier. At first she could see nobody, but as she drew closer she could discern faces peering between the rocks, watching her as she approached. She wished desperately that she was clothed, feeling pink and vulnerable in this open, exposed place, with eyes on her from both in front and behind. She was very apprehensive indeed, her footsteps faltering the closer she came to the men in whose power she was about to fall.

Suddenly she heard a shout. One of the ambushers was waving his gun, beckoning her to approach him. He was over to the right of the mound behind which the attackers were concealed and she turned reluctantly toward him.

As she came up to him she was able to see his face for the first time. Like so many of the locals his skin was a very dark black, his features Negroid, with flaring nostrils and a wide mouth. He was wearing a tattered combat jacket, a sub machine gun cradled in his arms. He said something to her and pointed behind him, indicating that she should go round behind the rocks. She did so, glancing behind her as the crashed vehicle disappeared from her view.

Once behind them she could see the ambush party for the first time. There were five of them, all dressed in a motley assortment of combat gear, and each carrying one of the deadly looking automatic weapons. Lisa stopped, staring uncertainly at them, her hands still trying desperately to preserve her modesty as their eyes took her in. And what a sight she knew she must make, her small, shapely body devoid of clothes, only her hands covering her most private places as she tried desperately to hide her swelling breasts and dark pubic thatch from their eyes.

One of the rebels rose to his feet and walked towards her, and Lisa's jaw dropped as she saw his face for the first time.

On his right cheek was carved a depiction of a snake, with a cruel looking whip mark across the centre of its body.

Chapter 15

Lisa couldn't believe her eyes as she stared at the cruel-eyed man who Pakat had driven off so brutally in the shop the day before. Then he had seemed intimidating enough, but to be confronted by him alone like this was another matter altogether, and she found herself cowering away as he walked toward her. Her rearward progress was stopped, however, by a pair of hands which grasped her arms from behind and she swung her head round to see one of the rebels standing behind her.

The man with the snake mark moved closer, an evil grin on his face as he surveyed his captive. He barked an order to the one that was holding her and he yanked her arms back, exposing her charms to all. Lisa cast her eyes down as the man moved to no more than a foot in front of her, but he grasped her chin and pulled her face up to stare into his.

He spoke a few words and Lisa shook her head, indicating that she did not understand.

"You make slave of my people," he said in a low voice. "Now white woman is my slave. Obey me, Okama, the general of the rebels. What your name?"

"Lisa."

"Ha!" he laughed, but there was no humour in his eyes. "Lisa! Lisa who walks about shamelessly naked amongst men. Lisa who gives pleasure to mere shopkeepers with her mouth in front of others. Lisa not your name. Now your name Slut. That good name eh? Tell me your name."

"Slut."

Smack!

He brought the flat of his hand down onto the soft swelling of her breast, making her cry out with pain and leaving a red mark in the shape of his hand across her skin.

"You call me Master!" he roared. "Too long my people have to call yours master. Now things changed. On your knees, Slut."

The man behind her released her arms and Lisa dropped to her knees at once. She allowed her hands to dangle by her side, afraid to cover her nakedness and incur his wrath still further. It was rapidly becoming clear to her that Okama had a pathological hatred of her kind, and she did not wish to upset him further. She wondered what it was that left him hating her so much. She had read of the exploits of the colonials in Africa, and some of the cruelty of their ways, as well as of the lawlessness that prevailed in some of their countries. Now she felt a pang of fear as she contemplated her situation. Obviously Okama saw her as some kind of scapegoat. Someone who personified those settlers who had subdued his people in the past. And she suspected he wasn't

114

about to treat her lightly, a suspicion that was confirmed by his next words.

"Tell me why I should not have you whipped," he said.

"M-Master?"

"You are my slave now. Tell me why I should not whip you, Slut."

"I have done nothing wrong, Master."

"Your people took my land. They took my cattle. They took my dignity."

"That was not me, Master."

"Hmm," he cocked his head on one side. "You are right of course. It was not you. I cannot beat you for your kinsmen's crimes."

"Thank you Master."

"So I shall beat you as an example to your friends cowering behind the vehicle."

"Master?"

"They shall see what happens when they practice their trading in my country. And how we treat their merchandise." He took hold of her hair and pulled her head back. "And you will see what it is to be maltreated simply because of the colour of your skin, Slut."

He shouted a few words, and the man behind her dragged her to her feet. Another man joined him, and together they began dragging her up the mound behind which they had been hiding. Lisa struggled with them, entreating them to spare her, but her words fell on deaf ears, and they were more than a match for her feeble efforts at escape. At the top of the slope was a tree, weathered and twisted with age, and it was to this that she found herself being dragged.

As they came over the brow she could see the Land Rover once more, and could discern the mens' eyes as they peered across at the scene before them. She wondered that the rebels had the audacity to show themselves to their foe so openly, but she guessed that Pakat's men wouldn't risk taking a shot at the rebels as long as they had her. Besides, these men held all the cards. They were on home territory, and could stay where they were for days, whilst the men behind the vehicle were exposed on three flanks and an easy target should the rebels decide to attack once more.

The men took her up to the tree and pushed her against it. The bark was dry and rough, and chafed against her bare skin as they made her hug it close. The trunk was about fifteen inches in diameter, and was an odd shape, rising vertically for about three feet, then bending over at an angle. A branch had long ago snapped off at the point where it bent, leaving a knobbly protrusion, and it was against this that she found her crotch resting as the men pulled her ankles apart and began to wrap rope about them.

They tied her fast, her arms wrapped about the trunk, fastened at the wrist and then pulled upward, the end of the rope secured to a branch above her on the opposite side. Stakes were banged into the ground about a yard apart at the foot of the tree and her ankles roped to them. Finally a length of rope was wrapped twice round the trunk and her waist, then pulled tight, holding her body fast against the tree's surface.

Lisa craned her neck round to stare at her captors. They were standing back and admiring her body, trapped as it was, slightly bent over, her backside pressed back by the lump in the surface so that its naked curves were beautifully presented to them. She wondered at the sight she must make from behind, her legs spread so wide that she knew her sex would be visible to them, and that she was helpless to prevent them caressing her in that most intimate place should the mood take them.

And it was that thought that began the first stirrings within her.

It was an odd sensation. She was afraid, certainly. Terrified almost. After all she was completely nude, brutally tied

116

and in the control of Okama, and it was he who had decreed she was to be bound like this. But it was the very presence of the bonds that gave the spark to her arousal and started her too fertile imagination speculating on what might happen to her. She tried to shift her position, and succeeded only in rubbing her nipples against the bark, sending a sudden sensation of pleasure through her body and causing them to pucker into brown protruding knobs that were at once twice as sensitive.

Then she became aware of the hard lump that was in direct contact with her clitoris. The spread of her thighs forced her already hard bud out from the folds of her sex lips and caused it to rub against the protrusion. It was almost as if the tree had been designed to give pleasure to one such as herself, and she bit her lip to suppress a moan as ripples of pleasure began to emanate from this centre of her desire and spread through her naked body.

Then she saw the whip.

The handle was thick, so that it fitted snugly into the man's hand. It was made of some kind of horn, probably cut from one of the antelopes she had seen on the plains. From it sprouted a number of thin leather cords, starting about the thickness of a pencil and tapering off along its twenty or twenty-five inches of length to a knotted end, each knot about the size of a pea.

The man draped the whip over her shoulder, and she discovered that the ends were weighted, hanging down almost vertically despite the thickness of each strand. She shivered as the smooth leather travelled down her spine and over her backside. One of the weights brushed against her anus, then slipped down the crack and rested against her sex lips, causing the muscles to contract and trapping it momentarily in the entrance to her vagina. She glanced across at Okama, who was watching, and her face reddened as she realised he had seen this evidence of her arousal.

Then he barked out an order, and the man drew back his arm.

Crack!

The leather came down high on her back, the strands cutting into her flesh whilst the ends struck her flank with amazing force, like a dozen sudden beestings in her tender skin. The pain was excruciating, and she clenched her teeth in an effort to suppress the cry of pain that had sprung to her lips.

Crack!

This time the man had moved back slightly, so that the fierce little knobs beat a tattoo of agony across the centre of her back. The whip had been cunningly designed so that no strand was of precisely the same length as any of the others, meaning that the ends spread in a pattern across her flesh, each one a separate source of pain.

Crack!

Once again he had shifted his position and had found another patch of virgin skin on which to inflict a criss-cross of stripes. His aim was clearly deliberate, the blows striking just below her shoulders so that her upper body began to be infused with a flush of redness.

Crack!

Crack!

Crack!

He worked with a steady rhythm, each stroke falling on white flesh that immediately reddened under the searing impact. The pain was agonising. Tears flowed down Lisa's cheeks as she hugged the tree. She pressed her body harder and harder against it as if she wanted it to open and swallow her up, protecting her from her cruel tormentors.

Crack!

Crack!

Crack!

He had moved down to the small of her back now, the ends of the whip catching her just above the swell of her

118

behind. Her whole back felt as if it was on fire, as if a million sharp points were being pressed into her flesh, their ends glowing red hot.

Crack!

He had moved on yet again, this time targeting the tops of her legs, the shorter strands whipping round and burning into her upper thighs. The man was clearly an expert at what he was doing, the anticipation of where the next blow would fall almost as agonising as the dreadful pain when it did.

Crack!

Crack!

Crack!

Even her calves and ankles did not escape the lash as he laid down the stripes with meticulous care. Lisa knew that only her backside was untouched now, and she imagined how it must look, the whiteness of her rear globes in stark contrast to the bright red of her upper and lower body. Then he touched her behind with the strands.

Crack!

This time the blow fell squarely across the cheeks of her arse, the ends wrapping round and peppering her thigh.

Crack!

He had moved no more than an inch further over, so that the marks overlapped, doubling the pain that coursed through the agonised girl. The force of these blows was tremendous, much more than those on her back and legs, thrusting her body forward against the tree.

And that was when Lisa was reminded of the knobbly protrusion against which her crotch was pressed.

Until now she had almost forgotten the stirrings in her body. But now that the punishment was suddenly concentrated on her bare behind, she was again reminded of her lack of modesty, and of the eyes that were on her naked flesh.

Crack!

Suddenly her mind became concentrated on the small, pink bud of flesh between her legs as it rubbed against the rough wood, and at once she felt her juices flow anew at the delicious stimulation this contact brought. A soft moan escaped her lips, the first sound she had made since the beating had begun.

Crack!

Crack!

Crack!

Each blow brought a new charge of lust as her crotch ground down against the protrusion. Her breasts too were being wonderfully stimulated by the bark against which they were pressed. And somehow the stinging of her raw backside seemed to redouble the pleasure that the contact was giving, so that every lash of the whip heightened her arousal still further.

Crack!

Crack!

Crack!

The relentless rain of blows continued, as did Lisa's perverse pleasure. Her clitoris felt twice its size, and she knew that the wetness that welled inside her was leaking onto the tree so that her slit was able to slide back and forth more easily.

Crack!

Crack!

Crack!

"Stop!"

Lisa barely heard the order, or realised that her punishment was at an end. She was too taken with her own stimulation, her hips pumping back and forth as she pressed her love bud hard down against the unyielding wood. She glanced sideways at Okama, who stood watching her, a grin splitting his features as the full extent of her arousal became apparent. She wanted to stop then. She wanted to deny them the opportunity of seeing the effect their treatment was having on her. But she couldn't. Her orgasm was too close.

She came with a scream, her red backside jabbing hard against the tree, as if she was impaled upon a thick cock and matching her seducer's strokes with her own. She clung hard to the trunk as her wanton passions took over and she allowed the full passion of her climax to erupt. The whole tree shook back and forth with the force of her gyrations.

It was fully two minutes before she was finally still, hanging panting by her wrists, suddenly completely drained, her face scarlet as she contemplated the exhibition she had made of herself. She barely noticed as the men began to untie her ankles, but when her wrists were freed she found herself staggering as she tried to steady herself on her shaky legs. The pain was returning too, the back of her body stinging agonisingly from neck to ankle, with barely an inch of her naked flesh untouched by the whip.

As she found her balance she glanced down at the tree. There, at the point where it bent forward, was a wide stain of damp; a silver trickle running down almost to the ground. She glanced sideways to see that Okama too was examining the spot. He turned to her and ran his eyes up and down her body.

"I think Slut is a very good name, don't you?" he said

Chapter 16

The rebel party and their lovely young captive slipped away from their vantage point just as dusk was beginning to envelop the countryside. Lisa's hands were secured behind her back with a piece of rope, and another tied to a ring in her collar. One of her captors took hold of the other end, and she was forced to follow as they marched away in single

121

file.

At first they moved from cover to cover, clearly not wishing their adversaries to know that they had quit their vantage point. But, as darkness fell and the distance between them and the crashed vehicle increased, they allowed themselves greater freedom of movement until at last they were following a well worn path through the bush.

They walked in silence, two men in front of the naked girl, two more behind, those behind carrying thin, whippy sticks that they employed freely on Lisa's bare behind whenever she showed any signs of lagging. Meanwhile Okama roved about them, sometimes in the lead, sometimes taking up the rear. Now and again he would give an order in a low voice and some subtle change of course would follow. All about them were the sounds of the African night, the chirping of crickets, the trill of bullfrogs and the occasional distant roar of some much larger animal.

Lisa walked in silence. The pain inflicted by the beating was no more than a dull ache now, though the slightest flick from the sticks carried by the men behind her was enough to remind her of the sting of the lash. Her mind was filled by thoughts of her behaviour that afternoon, and of the exhibition she had made of herself. She thought of Pakat and his band. They must have witnessed the whole thing. What must they think of her now? It was as if her body and her mind were too separate entities, the one retaining the modest decorum of Lisa Carling whilst the other was the naked, wanton young woman that Okama called Slut. And somehow, in this alien environment, kept bound and forcibly naked, it was Slut's character that seemed to be coming to the fore. Even now she knew that her nipples were erect and her sex lubricated by the sheer eroticism of her situation.

They walked for more than two hours before they saw the lights ahead. From a distance they looked no brighter than the stars above, but as they drew nearer, Lisa realised that it was a village they were approaching, not unlike the one in which they had filled-up with fuel the day before. At the sight of it, she tried to hang back, but a couple of hefty whacks across her backside forced her to maintain the same pace as the others.

All of a sudden the path they were on widened and crossed a much larger track. This was rutted with wheel marks and clearly led straight to the village. The group turned left onto the new track and headed directly toward the lights.

The paths along which they had been walking up to now had been worn smooth by countless walkers and had been relatively easy on Lisa's bare feet. This new track was much rougher, however, the vehicles having worn the surface down to the rock beneath, so that Lisa found it much harder going. Her captors were unsympathetic, though, simply tugging harder at her lead every time she stumbled or lost her footing whilst the sticks of the men behind once again found their mark.

They were in sight of the habitation now, and Lisa could discern the buildings. They were almost identical to those she had encountered with Pakat's band the day before; featureless two storey piles with flat roofs surrounded by the huts of the local people. Once again she was filled with trepidation as she drew closer, only too aware of her nudity, and of the marks of her punishment all over her rear.

Suddenly Okama gave an order and the men stopped. He spoke a few more words, and then turned to Lisa.

"Many Arabics in this place," he said. "Not safe to go in by this road. They see you, they tell those bastards back there. We go round side. Understand?"

"Yes Master."

He grinned, his teeth gleaming in the moonlight.

"You learn quick who is boss," he said. "You make good slave I think, Slut."

They turned off the track and plunged into the bush, dragging Lisa with them. She had to be all the more careful as they weaved their way through the undergrowth. With her hands trapped behind her she was obliged to duck and weave to avoid scratching her bare flesh on the branches that overhung their route.

They picked their way through the undergrowth for about ten minutes before joining a narrow path. This wound around the village before taking a turn to the right. A light appeared up ahead and the sound of music reached Lisa's ears. African music, all twanging guitars and male voices in harmony. The more they walked the louder the music became, until they turned a corner in the track and were confronted by a building.

Like all the other buildings she had seen, this one was quite small, only two storeys high. The ground floor was ablaze with lights that shone through the barred windows against which moths were hurling themselves in a suicidal manner. Outside was a small neon sign depicting a bottle of beer and the words 'Ndwenga's Bar' underneath. As they approached a door opened, momentarily increasing the volume of the sound. A man staggered out, clearly drunk, and wove off down the path towards them. At the sight of the naked girl he stopped, staring in amazement before staggering to one side and allowing them through.

Lisa eyed the bar fearfully. Surely they weren't intending to take her in there? Not nude? It was unthinkable. Even from here she could hear the loud, raucous laughter and the tuneless singing from the patrons. It was the sort of place she wouldn't have dreamt of visiting any time, let alone as the naked captive of these men.

She tried to hold back, shaking her head, but a couple of hefty whacks drove her forward.

"What is the matter, Slut?" Okama asked.

"That place. I can't go in there. Not like this."

"Why not?"

"I'm completely naked."

He laughed. "Of course. You are a slave. You have no right to wear clothes."

"Please. Couldn't I have something to cover me?"

He shook his head. "Your ancestors allowed my people to go about naked whilst they wore fine clothes," he said. "Now it is our turn. Besides, you will be an interesting thing for the men in there. Many of them have never seen a naked European woman. Your white breasts and black hair below will be new to them."

He shoved Lisa forward. They were right outside the building now and the light from the window illuminated her body, causing a few figures to emerge from the gloom to stare at her.

"In!"

One of the men held open the door whilst Okama pushed her forward. She staggered in and found herself in a small entrance hall, a bright light shining on her from above. On the wall opposite was a mirror. In better days this had clearly been designed for those arriving to adjust their dress after their journey, though now it was cracked and badly in need of a clean. Lisa stared at her reflection. She looked very small and pale beside the tall black men who escorted her, a fact that simply served to draw attention to her. She glanced down at her full, firm breasts and the hard upturned nipples which, with her hands tied behind her, seemed to invite the caress of any passing man. Her eyes dropped to her crotch, where the lips of her sex showed prominently, and an odd sinking feeling suddenly filled her stomach as she thought of the men in the bar who were about to see her like this. Then the door was opened, and taking a deep breath, she stepped inside.

The atmosphere in the bar was thick with smoke, the smell strangely sweet to Lisa's nostrils. The noise of the music was almost overpowering, made more so by the necessity of the customers to shout above it. At first the patrons continued their chatter, then one by one they spotted the party that had just entered and the conversation died.

Lisa stared about her. The bar's decor, if that was the right word, could only be described as functional. The floor was bare and felt hard and smooth against her feet. The tables were simple metal affairs with Formica tops, and all were laden with beer bottles. The light in the room was provided by a series of strip lights in the ceiling, some of which were flickering where the strip needed replacing. The walls had once been white, but were stained brown by the effects of years of cigarette smoke. They were hung with old advertisements for beer and cigarettes, equally stained and tatty from neglect. The bar itself was at the far end, a spartan affair with a mirror behind and beer crates stacked on the floor. The music came from a pair of speakers set above the bar. As Lisa gazed about her the sound was shut off, leaving the place suddenly silent.

All eyes were upon Lisa and her gun toting companions. Okama stepped forward to a table and gave a gesture. At once the men who had been sitting round it rose to their feet and moved to the other side of the room. Clearly Okama was a man to be reckoned with around here, a fact that gave Lisa a little comfort as she thought of her own total vulnerability.

Okama sat down, along with his cohorts, leaving Lisa standing beside the table. There was an air of tension in the room, and Lisa sensed the others were trying to gauge the rebels' mood. Then Okama pointed a finger at the naked girl and made a remark. At once the room was filled with laughter, the men winking at one another and making lewd gestures that needed no translation.

The music came on again, and the men began to chatter once more. Okama raised a finger in the air, and the barman hurried to him. Okama spoke to the man, whose eyes were fixed on Lisa's crotch as he listened. An astonished look came to his face, then he grinned and nodded vigorously. Okama beckoned to the girl.

"Mr Ndwenga is short of help today," he said. "So you must be waiter."

"Me?"

"Turn and I will take off your ropes. You cannot serve like that."

Lisa stood, momentarily unable to move as she took in what he was suggesting.

"Turn!"

This time there was no mistaking the authority in Okama's voice, and Lisa obeyed at once, turning her back on the crowd and revealing to them the stripes that covered her back and behind, bringing a murmur of interest from those watching.

Okama freed her hands quickly. She stood, rubbing her wrists as he detached the lead from her collar. Then he turned back to Ndwenga and nodded. The man took her arm and led her red-faced to the bar.

He gave her a tray, and at once sent her back to where Okama and his men were awaiting her. Lisa made her way across the room to where the men were sitting, trying hard to avoid the hands that reached out on all sides to grope her behind. She stopped at their table.

"Yes Master?" she said quietly.

"Beers," he said shortly. "And be quick."

She turned and ran the gauntlet back to the bar once more, twisting and turning to stay out of reach of the other drinkers. By the time she arrived the barman already had the bottles and glasses on the bar. Lisa placed her tray on the surface and loaded the drinks onto it. Then she lifted it up and turned back into the room.

It was only then that she realised how vulnerable carrying the tray made her. It was as bad as having her hands tied, as it took all her concentration to keep the tray level. This fact was not lost on the others in the room. Almost at once she felt a hand caress her backside, squeezing the firm flesh. Another ran up the inside of her thigh, brushing against the very lips of her sex and making her gasp as the man's fingers traced the length of her slit.

She squeezed her way between two tables, trying hard to concentrate on not dropping her burden as a large black hand closed over her breast, squeezing it crudely. Another hand was at her crotch now, the fingers trying to force themselves inside her. She broke free with an effort, finally arriving at Okama's table, her face flushed with the ordeal.

She placed the tray on the table top and began to unload the drinks. As she bent forward she felt strong fingers slide down the crack of her behind and seek out her sex. She gave a sharp intake of breath as a single digit pressed its way into her vagina.

Lisa's mind was in confusion. To be naked here in this bar full of dark-skinned strangers was bad enough, but to be forced to parade back and forth at their beck and call was something else. And yet despite her shame she could feel the familiar stirrings within her that always seemed to accompany this public humiliation, and the sensation of the finger sliding into her most intimate place, clearly visible to all, brought a gasp from her as she struggled to keep her backside from pressing down against the intruding digit.

With shaking hands she laid out the last of the drinks, then straightened up, giving a little sigh as the man's hand left her already burning crotch. Then an arm went up on the other side of the room and her ordeal began anew as she pushed her way between the tables.

Lisa worked on for more than two hours in the bar, serving the drinks and enduring the constant attention of the men she was attending. At every table she visited, hands would reach for her naked, unprotected flesh, squeezing her breasts and rubbing her swollen clitoris. And the more she

worked, the more aroused she became, her body fairly alive
with excitement at the treatment she was receiving. It was at
once the most humiliating and the most exciting experience
of her life, to be running about in this scruffy little bar, showing all and allowing the patrons to touch her as and when
they liked. Soon her sex was positively awash with love juice,
her clitoris protruding from the folds of her sex and glistening in the bright light, proof to all of how turned on she was.

There were women in the bar as well. At first she hadn't
noticed, but as she visited each table in turn she started to
notice them. They would glare at her as their men toyed
with her charms, clearly unimpressed with the way the young
white girl flaunted her body before their men. Some would
pinch her viciously when they could get close enough, while
on more than one occasion she was spat upon, much to the
amusement of the men.

At Okama's table the men were clearly beginning to show
the effects of the beer they had drunk, though Okama himself drank a lot less and continued to appear alert. A pack of
cards had been produced from somewhere and a noisy game
commenced, bottle tops being used as chips. Lisa continued
to serve them at regular intervals as the hilarity at the table
grew.

All of a sudden there was a shout and a bang as a hand of
cards was slapped down on the table. Heads turned throughout the room to see that one of the rebels was smiling triumphantly down at a large pile of bottle tops, whilst his friends
looked on with envy. At that point, Okama's voice rang out.

"Slut! Come here."

Lisa laid down the last of the bottles on the table she was
serving and made her way across to the table. She stopped
in front of Okama, expecting an order for more drinks. Instead he sat back and examined her.

His face was level with her crotch, and she knew he could
clearly see the pinkness of her sex lips and the sheen of

moisture that covered them; small droplets gleaming in the dark thatch of her pubic bush. His eyes travelled up to her breasts, the nipples rock hard and projecting upwards. He grinned at her.

"You make good waiter," he said.

"Thank you Master."

"You think you make good whore as well?"

Lisa wasn't sure if she had heard correctly. "Master?"

"That man," he indicated the one who had won the card game. "He has all the chips as you see. Now he wishes to claim his prize. Do you know what the prize is?"

"No Master." Lisa was genuinely puzzled.

"It is you of course, Slut. He has won your body. It is time for you to earn your keep in a new way, but one to which you are suited."

Lisa's jaw dropped, and she stared at Okama, then across at the man, whose grin was unabated. She couldn't believe what she was hearing. She was to prostitute herself for a mere game of cards. Give herself to this strange black man like a common whore. No, not like a common whore, she reflected bitterly. Whores were paid for what they did. She was no more than a slave, and would give herself for nothing.

Give herself for nothing! The very words sent a shudder of excitement through her as she gazed at the man seated opposite her, his eyes fixed on the swell of her firm young breasts. He raised a finger and crooked it. Lisa hesitated for a second. Then, her heart hammering against her chest, she made her way round the table towards him.

By now everyone in the room was aware of what was happening. The music had been turned off once more, leaving a strange silence, and all eyes followed the naked girl as she approached the man to whom she was being given. Lisa kept her eyes cast down, unable to meet those of the grinning men who nudged one another as they watched her. Her face was scarlet as she stopped in front of him, planting her legs slightly apart and allowing her arms to dangle at her sides.

He raised a hand and ran it up the smooth, silky skin of her inner thigh, sending a tremor through her slim frame as it travelled higher toward the very centre of her lust.

"Ah!"

She had meant to remain silent, but when his fingers found her slit and ran over her hard, wet little love bud the reaction was automatic, and she knew that everyone in the room had heard her exclamation and seen the way her hips had thrust forward at his touch. Her entire body seemed to be tingling with anticipation now, and she suddenly realised how badly she wanted to be fucked. Somehow it didn't seem to matter that her ravisher would be this scruffy, dark-skinned man who she barely knew and who simply desired to pleasure himself inside her. All she wanted was to be taken and fucked, though she hoped they at least would be allowed some privacy.

The man rose from his chair and grasped her arm, nodding towards the door. She walked quietly beside him as he took her across the room, still unable to face the people at the tables who nudged and winked at one another, shouting lewd remarks at him which he acknowledged with a grin.

Lisa allowed herself to be led out of the front door of the bar. Outside it was warm and muggy, but it felt good to escape the smoky atmosphere, and she breathed in the air gratefully. As she stepped onto the hard ground she turned to him, her eyebrows raised questioningly, and he pointed to a pile of beer crates that were stacked beside the building.

He led her across to them. They were plastic crates full of empty bottles and they were stacked to a height of about three feet. He took her by the shoulders and turned her round, so that she was facing him. Over her shoulder, Lisa could see the faces that peered from the windows of the bar, and the others who had followed them out and were standing by the door. So she was to be publicly fucked after all. She had hoped that he at least might take her into the bush before ravishing her, but it clearly was not to be.

He pressed her back and she felt the cold hard plastic of the crates against the back of her legs and the cheeks of her backside. He continued to press and she allowed herself to fall backwards so that she was lying across the crates, the cold bottle tops digging into her back. Then he took hold of her knees and dragged them wide apart.

Lisa gazed down between her breasts. She was open to him now, her sex gaping, the pinkness inside visible to him and all the onlookers. She eyed the man. He was tall and strong, with brawny arms and a broad chest. As she watched, his hands dropped to his fly and he began to undo it.

The prostrate girl could barely suppress a gasp as she caught sight of his long, black tool. It seemed huge to her, standing stiffly from his trousers. When he saw her expression the man grinned, grasping it at the base and slapping the insides of her thighs with its heavy end, much to the amusement of the onlookers. Lisa licked her lips as she contemplated what was about to happen to her, a public rogering by this great black stranger, with nobody raising so much as a finger to help her. She caught sight of one of the women amongst the sea of faces, her face twisted in a look of disdain as she watched the scene unfold.

"Oh!"

Lisa's body jumped as the thick bulbous glans slid over her sex, the tip shining with her moisture. He ran his hands up the inside of her thighs, their dark colour contrasting with the milky whiteness of her skin.

She groaned as his thumbs found her sex, forcing the lips apart as they delved inside. Then she felt the end of his tool pressing against the entrance to her vagina.

"Ahhh!"

132

She cried aloud as he slipped inside her, his massive erection ramming deep within, burying itself to the hilt. Lisa had never felt so filled. He seemed to be stretching her to the very limit, and the sensation was delicious.

Then he began to thrust, his backside jabbing forward as he took her. His thrusts were hard, each one shaking her body and rattling the bottles in the crates beneath her.

She came on the fourth stroke. She couldn't help it. All of a sudden the exposure, maltreatment and humiliation that had kept her so completely turned on for the last few hours seemed to combine to force the most exquisite climax as she lay there, spread wide and naked, impaled on the cock of this indifferent stranger, whose name she didn't even know. Screams of pleasure rent the air as she was engulfed by lust, her head shaking from side to side, her breasts bouncing back and forth as he continued to fuck her.

The large dark man's hips worked back and forth with considerable power, each stroke sending a new wave of pleasure through the wanton girl. The intensity of her orgasm had abated now, but she could feel another building, and she pressed her pubis up against his, willing him to climax, no longer caring about her lasciviousness or the sight she must make sprawled across the beer crates.

All of a sudden his rhythm changed. His grip on her thighs stiffened. She glanced at his face. His eyes were closed, his lips drawn back over his teeth, and a hoarse grunting sound came from his throat.

Then he was coming, his cock twitching violently within her as he unleashed his semen deep inside. The sensation was too much for Lisa. Another violent orgasm shook her small frame as she thrashed about beneath him, a long, drawn out wail escaping from her lips.

The climax went on and on. The man's thighs crashed against her own as he emptied his seed into her. She reciprocated every stroke with a jab of her own hips, determined to milk every drop from him. Then, when at last there seemed to be no more, she gradually allowed herself to relax, lowering her backside onto the crates, her breasts rising and falling rapidly as she regained her breath.

He took a step back, his cock slipping from her, and began to tuck himself into his pants. Lisa raised her head and watched as he turned and made his way back into the bar.

Painfully she eased herself off the hard crates and stood up, shivering slightly as she felt a trickle of semen leak from her sex. For a moment she was alone and untethered, and she turned to gaze at the track that led away from the awful bar and into the blackness of the African night. Did she dare take her chance and make a run for it? Then she looked up at the windows and caught Okama's eye, and she knew he was aware of her thoughts.

She gave a sigh, and turned back toward the bar. In front of her, the crowd of grinning men parted, and the red-faced girl made her way up the steps behind her erstwhile lover, back into the custody of her captors.

Chapter 17

Lisa spent that night in a room above the bar, on a small metal bed, her wrists bound together and tied to the bedhead, her ankles secured to the two bottom corners. Okama himself saw to her bonds, checking them carefully, and running a hand over her breasts, smiling as he saw the nipples harden. Then he left her, closing the door and locking it.

Lisa was left alone with her thoughts. The bed was uncomfortable, the old springs making lumps in the thin, dank smelling mattress. She lay for some time, staring at the bars in the window, contemplating her position. Everything seemed to have happened so quickly. Only a few days be-

134

fore she had been a simple programmer, living a day-to-day existence in London. Now here she was, the naked slave of a group of dark-skinned strangers in a country completely foreign to her. She thought of the way she had been forced to behave, and the shameful acts she had been made to perform. She gazed down at her body, her skin glowing white in the pale moonlight, and she thought of the big man's cock violating her. Why was it that her body reacted as it did? Why was she unable to control her desires like other women could? She gave a sigh and lowered her head again, closing her eyes.

She must have dozed off, though she had no idea for how long. All she knew was that a sound had wakened her, and her eyes opened.

For a moment she could see nothing. Then she discerned the figure standing at the foot of the bed. It was a man, tall and dark, clad in a sort of dressing gown. As he came closer she recognised Ndwenga, the bar owner. He was staring down at her, and as he did so his gown fell apart and she saw his massive erection projecting from his groin.

Lisa's mind was a whirl. What was he doing? Did Okama know he was here? She feared punishment if he was to find out she had been allowing this man to touch her without his knowledge. Yet if she cried out or made a fuss she equally risked incurring his wrath. She lay still and quiet as the man settled down on the bed beside her and placed a hand on her stomach.

He ran his fingers up over her ribs and found her breasts, his hands kneading them roughly and pinching the nipples painfully. His other hand went to her crotch, his middle finger worming its way into her vagina, making her moan aloud as he twisted it back and forth.

He stood again and shrugged off the gown. Lisa stared at his silhouette, his rampant tool even more prominent now. He spoke to her, his voice low, but she couldn't understand him. She understood his intentions though as he straddled her waist and began moving up her body, his hand holding his cock as he approached her face.

He grabbed Lisa by the hair, pulling her head up from the mattress. At the same time he guided his erection towards her mouth. For a second she resisted as he pressed it against her pursed lips. Then he tightened his grip on her hair and she surrendered to him, opening her mouth and allowing him to shove his manhood inside.

He pressed it all the way in, until the glans was against the back of her throat, making her choke momentarily. She drew back slightly, and knowing she had no choice, closed her lips about his shaft and began to suck. The man began to fuck her face with vigour, his thick cock sliding in and out of her mouth while the helpless girl sucked hard at it.

Then, unexpectedly, Lisa found herself aroused once more, the presence of the man's erection inside her mouth and the banging of his heavy balls against her chin igniting those desires that never seemed far from the surface since her capture. The taste and smell of him so close seemed to spur her on and she began to lick at him as he pressed ever harder against her. She gave a little groan, her hips starting to gyrate as he thrust himself in and out. She found herself imagining that it was her vagina he was penetrating, not her mouth, and she pressed her pubis forward, the lips of her sex convulsing as if about an actual cock.

But she wasn't to receive the release she required. All at once Ndwenga gave a grunt and his cock pulsated, sending a gush of semen into Lisa's mouth. He came quickly, his spunk squirting from him in short, sharp spurts that she gulped down, barely able to swallow, so full was her mouth. When he had shot his load he withdrew at once, leaving Lisa writhing frustrated on the bed, her hips thrusting up at him. She was of no interest to him any more though, and she saw that his member was already detumescing as he wrapped the gown about him once more.

She gave another faint, plaintive moan, but already he was heading for the door, and it was an intensely frustrated Lisa who watched it close behind him and heard the key turn in the lock, leaving her alone with her fantasies.

It took Lisa some time before she finally managed to drop off again, her head filled with erotic images, but eventually she drifted into a troubled sleep.

It was still dark when she was woken by the sound of the door opening and one of Okama's men coming in. He undid her bonds without a word and pulled her to her feet. She was barely allowed time to stretch her delicious young body and massage the feeling back into her limbs before he had hold of her arm and was leading her back down to the bar again.

When she entered the room Okama was seated at one of the tables with his men about him. Lisa was shown to a chair, then Ndwenga emerged from a door at the back with a bowl of steaming gruel in his hands which he put down in front of her. He did not catch her eye, and she glanced across at Okama, who was talking earnestly with the man beside him. She wondered again if he knew of Ndwenga's nocturnal visit. She decided he probably didn't because of the way the man had chosen to fuck her mouth. Had he come in her vagina, the evidence would have been there for all to see.

She turned her attention to the gruel. There was no cutlery and she was forced to drink it straight from the bowl. It was thin and watery, with a salty taste, but it was warm and she drank it down hungrily, chewing and swallowing the small pieces of meat and vegetable she found at the bottom.

"Your fun last night made you hungry, Slut," said Okama with amusement.

She did not reply, staring down at her bowl and wishing there was some way to cover her breasts, which jutted over the table top in what seemed to her a very conspicuous way.

137

The men talked on for about another ten minutes, then Okama rose to his feet. This was a signal for the others to follow suit, and Lisa did the same. The man beside her grasped her arms and pressed her forward over the table. For a moment she thought she was about to be fucked, and spread her legs apart in anticipation. Then she felt the familiar sensation of the rope being wrapped about her wrists, and her face reddened as she caught Okama's eye, knowing he had read her thoughts.

"No more now, Slut," he said. "Later, if you are good, you will feel a cock inside you, as I see you desire. Now we must be moving."

Once her wrists were secure, a second length of rope was used to bind her elbows together, thrusting her breasts forward in a way that made her blush. Then Okama reached into a bag and pulled something out.

"There is much walking to do today," he said. "Take these."

He threw the objects down at Lisa's feet and she stared at them. It was a pair of open leather sandals. She slipped them on, gratefully. The previous day's trek had been hard on her feet, and that had mainly been over soft sand. She knew she would have been in trouble had they encountered a harder surface for any distance. She wished he would offer her something more, though. The simplest of loincloths would have been preferable to being forced to walk about with her breasts, sex and behind in full view of anyone she encountered.

Okama went to the door and pushed it open. The first rays of the dawn were beginning to filter through the trees outside, and the air felt chill against Lisa's naked skin. She shivered slightly as she stepped through the door.

Outside the place was deserted. Okama led the way down the path away from the bar, past the pile of beer crates on which Lisa had been so publicly rogered the evening before, and on into the bush.

By the time it was fully light they were some distance from the village, following a dusty track through the trees. They walked at a fast pace, for which Lisa was grateful since it soon began to warm her up. Once clear of the trees they headed in single file out across a broad plain towards a low range of hills in the distance.

For the next two hours they progressed in silence as the sun climbed slowly into the sky. They encountered nobody, for which Lisa was grateful. She maintained a good pace, all thoughts of escape or rebellion having faded from her mind for the time being. She followed her captors obediently, rendering the whips unnecessary, much to her relief.

By midday the group was nearly at the foot of the hills which rose up steeply before them. They were very high, mountains almost, with rocky outcrops. It was from one of these that Lisa's eye was suddenly caught by something glinting in the sunlight.

She squinted upwards. There was somebody up there. A figure standing, partially concealed by the rocks. She glanced across at Okama, but he seemed unworried, leading them forward to a gap between two particularly high pinnacles.

It wasn't until they were almost on top of the rebel camp that Lisa saw it. It consisted of a motley set of low, mud structures surrounding a wide open area. The rebels themselves were seated at the entrances to the huts, or deployed about the area with large rifles slung over their shoulders. At the sight of Okama's band a shout went up and they moved forward, crowding around the small group.

The sight of Lisa brought many of them up short in amazement. They gathered around the naked girl, chattering and pointing, their faces split by broad grins. Lisa stood still, her eyes cast down, wishing she had at least the use of her hands to cover herself from the many eyes that now stared at her body.

They made their way to the edge of the open area where

some logs had been set in a square. There Okama and his men sat down with some of the other rebels, whilst Lisa was made to stand behind her master, still very much the centre of attention from the rest of the men. She wondered if they had ever seen a white woman naked before. Certainly they were fascinated by the sight, pointing at her breasts and crouching for a better view of her sex,

A lively discussion began, the group on the logs talking earnestly together. Someone appeared from one of the huts with a crate of beer. He went around the group, handing a bottle to each. When he reached Okama, Lisa saw him pause and speak a few words, all the time looking in her direction. Okama listened, then shrugged and nodded his head. Then he turned to Lisa.

"Why did you surrender yourself to Ndwenga so easily last night?" he asked.

"I-I thought you had sent him, Master," she stammered, completely caught off guard by the question.

"I had not. Yet you took him into your mouth like a common whore, sucking his seed from him. Then this morning you were ready to give yourself again."

"This morning Master?"

"When that man pushed you over the table. You offered him your cunt like some monkey on heat."

Lisa hung her head, unable to find an answer.

"I am your Master now," he went on. "You will only give yourself when I order it. Do you understand, Slut?"

"Yes Master."

"The men wish to witness a punishment, and because of your behaviour I have agreed. Do you understand?"

Lisa's heart sank. "Yes Master."

Suddenly she felt hands grasping her arms and pressing her forward. She resisted for a second, then allowed herself to be led across to where a lone tree stood at the edge of the open area. It was typical of the trees she had seen from the

140

Rover the day before, with wide branches and a strangely flat top, as if it had been cut short halfway up. As she came closer she noted something else unusual about the tree. All about its trunk were dangerous looking thorns, some as much as six inches long, tapering to a needle sharp tip. The thorns covered the trunk completely, making it impossible to place anything thicker than a single finger between them.

As they reached the tree, Lisa was brought to a halt by the men and she felt hands fumbling with the ropes at her wrists and elbows. Once these were freed she was made to stand with her back to the tree, the thorns almost touching her bare flesh. They used the rope to secure her wrists at her front. Then they dragged her arms up and she noticed for the first time a metal ring set into the tree about a foot above her head. It was to this that they tied her arms, forcing them up over her head and obliging her to arch her back to avoid the sharp prongs of the thorns which brushed against her bare skin.

More ropes were brought and tied around her ankles. These were then attached to stakes driven into the ground on either side of the tree. It was only once these were in place that the men stood back to admire their captive.

Lisa was in a most extraordinary position. The way in which her hands and feet were positioned meant that she was forced to thrust her chest and pubis forward in order to avoid the cruel spikes at her back. Standing thus, with her legs spread apart, she gave the impression of one offering herself to the men, pressing herself to them and inviting them to touch her.

And touch her they did, crowding about and mauling her breasts and sex. They slid their hands down her pubic hair and pressed their fingers into her vagina.

Lisa's automatic reaction was to draw back from their groping hands, but the moment she tried to do so she felt the sharp spikes touch her naked flesh and was forced to press herself forward again.

Her ordeal continued for more than an hour, by the end of which her pale skin was streaked with dirt and mud where their probing hands had been, and a silvery trail of moisture ran down both her thighs as evidence of the effect the caresses were having on her. Lisa's body ached terribly with the continuing strain of keeping herself from impaling her body on the spikes. At the same time her sex was burning with desire, the muscles making the lips contract regularly as her body responded to the treatment she was receiving. On at least three occasions she had come close to orgasm, moaning with passion as the men took it in turns to frig her. But they would sense the onset of her climax and cease for a few minutes, watching as she gasped for breath, fighting with all her might to keep her hips still.

At last, though, they seemed to tire of their sport, and a heated discussion commenced amongst the rebels. It went on for some five minutes, with much nodding and grinning. Then a man was despatched to where Okama sat, and Lisa watched with trepidation as further talk ensued. When Okama nodded, a roar of approval went up from the crowd.

The man ran into one of the huts, emerging a short time later with something in his hand. He gave this to Okama, who rose to his feet and strolled over to where the girl was on display. As he came closer Lisa recognised the object he was holding.

It was a horse whip.

He moved close to her, eyeing her up and down.

"The men are amused by my little toy," he said. "You are the first white woman they have ever touched, and they seem to enjoy it. I think this is true of you as well."

Lisa hung her head, saying nothing.

"Still," he went on. "They also desire to see you punished to atone for your behaviour. So they will have their wish."

Lisa stared apprehensively at the whip. It was made of

142

leather, and was extremely thin, tapering from the thickness of a pencil to no more than that of a length of string. As she watched, Okama swished it through the air a couple of times, making it bend as he did so.

"The men find your breasts very good," he went on. "Very soft. They think that you push them forward like that because you want them touched. They think they should be whipped."

Lisa's eyes widened. "My breasts..?"

"Silence! I have not given permission for you to speak!"

Okama's voice was filled with anger and Lisa was reminded once more that, despite his calm words, he nursed a deep hatred for her. She pursed her lips, hoping her outburst would not make the punishment worse.

Okama waved the whip in the air and shouted something. At once a sea of hands went up, the men all shouting at once. He hesitated for a second, then pointed at a small, wiry man who stood near the back. The man pushed his way through, a broad grin on his face.

Okama said a few words to him, then handed him the whip. He turned to face Lisa, whose instincts made her wish to shrink back from him, something she was quite unable to do.

Lisa couldn't believe what was happening to her. To be tied and violated in this way was bad enough. But to have her breasts whipped! Even in her wildest thoughts she had never dreamed they would do that to her! She dropped her eyes to her swelling orbs. There could be no doubt that they were in a perfect position for the punishment; pressed forward, the long brown nipples still slightly hard from the recent attentions. She raised her eyes again and watched as the man took a position beside her.

"Six strokes I think," said Okama. Then he nodded to the man.

Lisa stared fearfully as he tapped the whip on her firm,

creamy swellings. Then he drew back his arm.

Whack!

The cruel weapon came down with considerable force across Lisa's breasts, laying a stripe across them that rapidly darkened to an angry red. The pain was excruciating. The mark stung dreadfully and immediately brought tears to her eyes.

The blow had another effect though. The moment the whip descended, the young captive's nipples began to pucker into hard brown knobs that stood out prominently from her breasts. Her punisher spotted the effect at once, holding out the whip and teasing the dark flesh, eliciting a faint moan of pleasure from the girl.

He raised the whip again.

Whack!

Lisa gasped as a second stripe was laid across her succulent mammaries, making a scarlet X over their surface, the thin end of the whip curling round and catching her a stinging blow beneath her left breast. She bit her lip as the pain coursed through her. Once again her instinct was to draw back as he lifted his arm for the third time, but the pricking of the thorns in her back reminded her that she did not have the option.

Whack!

This time he brought the whip up from underneath, catching the underside of both breasts and making them bounce upwards, much to the delight of those watching. And still her nipples remained stiff, projecting invitingly for all to see.

Whack!

The forth stripe was directed horizontally and caught her just below her teats, momentarily flattening her swellings and leaving a thin line just beneath the edges of both aureole. By now the pain was almost unbearable, and it was all Lisa could do not to scream aloud as the whip fell yet again.

Whack!

This was the twin of the previous stroke, only this time above her nipples, the blow falling with deadly accuracy so that only the white skin was marked. Lisa clenched her fists and closed her eyes as she prepared for the final cut.

Whack!

This, like the first two, fell across the top of her stinging breasts, making yet another thin red line across her otherwise faultless skin.

Then the man stood back to admire his handiwork.

Lisa's breasts were on fire, the pain from the beating almost unbearable. Yet, as she looked down at her jutting breasts, now criss-crossed with the evidence of her punishment, she felt a great surge of arousal. Her mind was suddenly obsessed with what a sight she must make. She gazed down at her body, knowing that the marks of her beating drew attention to the fact of her nudity. She moaned softly, but not with pain.

Okama approached. He reached out a hand and traced the stripes with his finger, making his captive wince as he did so. Then he took her nipple between finger and thumb, smiling as she moaned once more.

"Good," he said. "I think you will be a good source of amusement for my men."

Chapter 18

They left Lisa tied to the tree, her punished breasts red and throbbing, while the men gathered by the fallen trees for a meeting. The day went on, and the heat of the African afternoon became more and more intense. Thankfully the tree's branches protected her from the full force of the sun's rays, but the hot dustbowl in which the tree stood seemed to concentrate the heat and she found herself sweating. The perspiration ran from her face and trickled between her breasts, forming a white streak that ran all the way down her dirt-spattered body to her pubic hair.

Lisa was extremely uncomfortable. Though the pain in her breasts had subsided to a dull ache, the pain in her limbs seemed to be getting worse. her legs and arms screamed out for relief from the strain of keeping her body taut and clear of the thorns. Then there was the thirst. Lisa had not been allowed a drink since entering the camp, and her throat was now parched. She watched with envy as the men swigged from their beer bottles and chatted animatedly. She would have given anything for a bottle herself.

She reflected on the irony of the expression. After all, what had she to give? She had been stripped of everything, even the modesty of clothes. All she had to give was her body, and she knew they would take that without asking, if they wanted it. She had become no more than a chattel. Something to be stared at, touched, whipped or fucked by them at will. She was truly their slave, and her body was theirs for the taking.

It was already late afternoon before the meeting broke up. When it did so the men wandered back across to their captive. Okama stood in front of her, eyeing her up and down.

"The men have been discussing what to do with you," he said. "Some wanted to kill you, but I don't think that is wise. For now you will stay with us then and earn your keep as you can."

He barked an order and two men stepped forward and began undoing her bonds. Once her hands were free she collapsed forward onto the ground, gasping with relief at being freed from the dreadful tension of the bondage. When at last her ankles were untied she curled herself up, flexing and unflexing her limbs as the feeling agonisingly began to return.

They left her on the ground for fully five minutes, then she felt the hard metal of a gun barrel poking her in the ribs.

"Get up," said Okama.

She rose unsteadily to her feet and stood facing him, her arms by her sides.

"You are thirsty, I think, Slut?"

She nodded. "Yes Master."

"You would like a beer?"

"Yes please Master."

"You would be prepared to earn it?"

She looked at him quizzically.

"It is the idea of the men. They note that, once the beer has been finished, a woman can make another use of the bottle."

Lisa stared at him uncomprehendingly for a moment. Then his eyes dropped to her crotch and her mouth fell open as she realised what he was suggesting.

Okama laughed heartily.

"I see you understand," he said. "But why are you so surprised? Surely such an act will give you pleasure?"

Lisa did not reply.

Okama barked an order to the men, and two of them closed in behind Lisa, taking her by the arms. Before she knew what was happening the hapless girl found herself being marched to the logs where the men had held their meeting, whilst the rest followed on behind.

When they reached the logs, the men took her to the largest, which was about six feet in diameter, and lifted her bodily onto it. For a second she had to crouch down until she found her balance. Then she straightened to a standing position and gazed down at the crowd that had gathered about her.

She wondered at the sight she must make, her breasts covered with stripes, her hair tangled, her fair skin streaked with dirt, white trails showing where the sweat had run down her body, as well as the trails made by the moisture from her sex. Yet the men pushed and jostled one another for a sight of her, and standing above them as she was, she knew that they had a perfect view of her sex.

There was a commotion, and somebody pressed through the throng. It was a young man, carrying a large bottle of beer. Lisa shuddered when she saw it, but an odd warmth seemed to fill her crotch as he held it out to her.

She reached down and took the bottle. It felt surprisingly cool, and she guessed that there must be some kind of stream running down from the hills in which it had been standing. She looked about, then raised the bottle to her lips.

The lager tasted delicious, and she gulped it down, suddenly aware of just how thirsty she had been. The liquid felt wonderful as it flowed down her dry throat. She tipped the bottle higher, and a dribble escaped from the corner of her mouth, running down her chin and onto her breasts.

She lowered the beer, taking a deep breath. The liquid was more than half gone now, and the crowd gave a murmur of approval.

"Finish it." The words came from Okama, who stood at the front of the throng.

Lisa lifted the bottle to her lips and tipped it, taking a long swig, once more relishing the taste of the beverage. In a few gulps the bottle was empty and she lowered it to her side, running the back of her arm over her mouth to remove any vestiges that remained. Again the men nodded to one another.

"Was that good?" asked Okama.

"Yes Master."

"Then put the bottle to further use."

Lisa's heart was thumping in her chest as she lifted the bottle and examined it. It was made of brown glass, the neck tapering evenly down half its length, then running parallel along the rest, a little over two inches in diameter. She ran her fingers along it, feeling the hardness and thickness of it, then looked up at the men, all of whom were watching her earnestly. She swallowed hard, unable for the moment to move as she contemplated the outrageous act that was being demanded of her.

"Do it!" said Okama in a low voice.

Lisa let the fingers of her right hand slip from the bottle onto her breast. She moved her fingers over it, wincing at the pain as she touched the red stripes from her beating. She took her nipple between finger and thumb and rolled it back and forth, the sensation sending a delicious tingle through her body.

She glanced at the men once more. They were silent now, every eye fixed upon her. She dropped her eyes, watching almost detachedly as her hand left her breast and slid down her rib cage, over her trim stomach and on toward her dark pubic triangle.

"Mmmm." She groaned quietly as she found her clitoris. It was hard and wet, as she had known it would be. This was the first opportunity she had had to masturbate since her capture and it felt good to be touching herself so intimately once more, though she would have preferred some privacy to perform so intimate an act. There was, however, something undeniably exciting in being watched, and as she ran her finger back and forth over the hard bud of flesh, her body shuddered with desire and she began to rekindle the fire of lust that seemed to be forever smouldering inside her.

Her eye caught that of one of the men in the crowd, and for a second held his stare. At that moment the full enormity of what she was doing struck her. Here she was, Lisa Carling, the modest little computer programmer who kept herself to herself and never normally wore so much as a low-cut dress. And now she was standing naked and brazen before this group of strange black men, her breasts and behind striped with the marks of the whip, her nipples erect and hard, masturbating herself openly.

"Ahhh!" The image was almost too much for her and for a second she thought she might come then and there. She tore her eyes away from the man's and glanced down at her body once more.

"The bottle," said Okama quietly.

Lisa knew she could delay no longer. Slowly she raised the neck to her lips. She opened her mouth and took it inside, not tipping it this time, but sucking it, like she would a man's cock. As she did so she raised her eyes, gazing out provocatively at the watching men.

She slid the bottle out from between her lips and began to move it down her body, keeping the neck in contact with her skin, leaving a silvery trail of saliva down over her breast and across her stomach. She slid it lower still, over the short, coarse hairs of her nether thatch until she felt the cool, moist glass come into contact with her love bud, sending a ripple of pleasure deep into her burning sex.

For a moment her legs seemed frozen to the spot. She knew she had to widen her thighs in order to contain the thickness of the bottle, yet to do so, standing as she was above the sea of faces, seemed such a totally wanton act as to be unthinkable. Then she saw Okama's face watching her and she thought of the breast lashing she had received that afternoon and knew that she had no choice. She was his slave, and she had to obey.

Slowly she shuffled her feet apart, until her thighs were stretched wide and her sex was open for all to see, it's pinkness glistening with love juices. Then, her face scarlet, she manoeuvred the neck of the bottle to the portal of her love hole and began to press.

She pushed gently, twisting the bottle. At first the flesh resisted. Then, with a gasp, she felt it penetrate her. She pressed harder, bending her legs as she did so, and the bottle slid inside, the hard, cool glass feeling delicious as it forced apart the walls of her sex and slid ever deeper into her.

All of the neck was inside now, yet still she pressed, her vagina feeling stretched almost to breaking point as she forced the rest of the improvised dildo inside her until only the base was visible, distending her love hole in an almost grotesque way.

Lisa paused, allowing the muscles in her sex to contract about the object. She was extremely aroused now, every fibre of her being alive with the sensation of her penetration. She cast her eyes over her rapt audience. Then, taking the base of the bottle between her fingers she began to work it back and forth.

"Ahhh!"

The moan of pleasure echoed about the clearing as the thick bottle moved in and out of her. It was the most extraordinarily stimulating sensation, made the more so by the fact that she was being watched whilst she pleasured herself. It was almost as if the men's eyes were touching her physically, caressing her naked flesh, urging her on in her masturbation. All of a sudden she felt more aroused than she had imagined possible, and a new urgency crept in, making her work the bottle back and forth with increased vigour.

She widened her legs still further, bending her knees and thrusting her sex forward, wanting the men to get the best possible view of what she was doing, no longer caring about the shamefulness of her behaviour, simply lost in the pleasure that her actions were giving her.

Suddenly, on an impulse, she changed her motions, holding the base of the bottle with both hands and thrusting her hips forward against it, working her backside back and forth in a lewd dance. She was groaning aloud now, her head thrown back, her breasts pressed forward, wanting to be watched. Wanting the men to feast their eyes on her nakedness and to see the desire in her as she gave herself up to her lust, her supple young body gyrating sensuously.

All of a sudden the urgency came upon her once more, and she knew her climax was close. She began to move faster and faster, ramming her hips forward onto the cold, hard bottle, her breasts bouncing up and down as she did so. She was lost in herself now. Oblivious to everything except her desires, the juices from her sex dripping from her fingers and forming a damp, dark circle on the wood between her legs.

"Ah! Ah! Ah!"

She came suddenly and noisily, a shout escaping from her lips as her body shook with spasm after spasm of pleasure. She stood, her backside jabbing forward against the bottle, her eyes tight closed, her head shaking back and forth. The orgasm seemed endless, the bottle stabbing in and out of her, her body jerking like a puppet on a string as she let herself go.

Then, just when she thought she would die with the joy of it, her passion began to ebb, her motions slowing as she started down the long slide back to normality. As she came down she sank to her knees, still moving the bottle back and forth, but more gently now, her cries turning to moans, then to gasps as she began to regain her breath.

When, at last, her body was still, she realised her head to stare out at the faces of the men, whose eyes were fixed on the bottle that still projected from her sex. For a moment there was silence, then a slow round of applause rose from the watchers.

Chapter 19

"What is it?"

The words were half spoken, half mumbled by the sleepy

152

girl as she felt a hand shaking her shoulder. Who could be waking her at this time, when all she wanted was to sleep? She reached down for her bedclothes, but found none, fumbling about her on the hard, dry earth. Her hand went to her body, finding only naked flesh, and she winced as she touched her punished, tender breasts.

Then she opened her eyes and remembered, and her heart sank.

Following her display, Lisa had been taken to a stream, where she was allowed to wash the grime of the day from her whilst her guards watched. The water had been extremely cold, but she hadn't minded, being glad to immerse her body. Her breasts, in particular, were extremely tender after the lashing they had received and the water soothed the pain.

Afterwards they had taken her to one of the huts where, her collar lashed to a stout pole, she was allowed to lie down on the floor and rest. She had fallen at once into a deep sleep in which she dreamt of freedom. In her dream she saw herself back in London at a sumptuous party where she wore a long and elegant gown and was being chatted up by a handsome young man. She was about to take his hand and accompany him to the dance floor when she felt the hand on her shoulder.

It was one of her guards, and he was shaking her awake. Lisa gave a little cry of dismay as the elegance of the party, and of her clothes, dissolved about her and she found herself naked in the dingy hut, staring into the face of one of her captors. He said nothing, simply taking her by the collar and pulling her to her feet.

He detached the other end of her lead and took her out into the warm night air. In the sky above were a million stars and there was barely any wind at all. On any other occasion, Lisa would have paused to savour the beauty of the evening, but in the circumstances that prevailed she had no time for that.

The men were gathered around a fire, on which they were roasting a slab of meat. Lisa saw the light from the fire and heard the laughter of the men, and for a second she hung back, fearful of what awaited her amongst the crowd of lusty rebels. But her guard would have none of it, dragging her along as he made his way down towards the noise and laughter below.

A small cheer went up as Lisa was led into the centre of the camp. She lowered her eyes, mindful of her shameless behaviour that afternoon and unwilling to look any of them in the face as she was paraded once more in front of them. At one side, sitting facing the fire, was a group apart, in the centre of which sat Okama, and it was to these that she was led. The man brought her to a halt before them and she stood silently, her hands hanging at her side, awaiting what orders he might have for her.

For a few minutes he ignored her, continuing his conversation with his companions. For some strange reason this annoyed Lisa slightly. It wasn't as if she wanted to be placed on show, her breasts and cunt bared to the men, but to be ignored seemed somehow insulting. There was something else that Lisa didn't like about having to stand and wait, though. It gave her the opportunity to reflect on what was in store for her that evening. Being the lone female, and a naked slave to boot, she had few illusions as to what the men might have in mind for her, and she stared about at them, wondering what was to follow.

And the contemplation was beginning to make her horny once more. She wondered at the perversity of her nature. Here she was, enslaved by a group of savage strangers, some of whom would be happy to see her dead, and had revelled in watching her being whipped and humiliated that very afternoon. Yet when she thought of their thick, black cocks plunging into her vagina, the wetness came back at once, and her nipples hardened without even a single caress.

At last Okama raised his head to look at her.

"Well, Slut," he said. "Are you hungry?"

Suddenly Lisa realised that she was ravenous. It seemed ages since she had last eaten and the sight of the platter of meat in front of the men made her mouth water. Okama picked up a bone from the plate and tossed it to her. She caught it. The meat was tough and greasy, and of an indeterminate source, but she didn't care. She bit greedily into it, the grease coating her fingers and lips as she devoured it.

She gnawed all the flesh from the bone, throwing the remains into the fire. Then Okama made a sign and a bottle of beer was brought to her. When he saw the embarrassed expression on her face the rebel leader smiled.

"Do not worry, Slut," he said. "Tonight it is merely for drinking."

Lisa swigged down the beer, and as she did so she was struck by the contrast with the dream she had been enjoying just before. There she had been elegantly dressed, sipping cocktails from a glass and nibbling at canapes in the company of a handsome young man. Here she was totally nude, swigging beer from a bottle whilst surrounded by a band of hostile rebels, all of whom lusted after her body. And yet she made no protest, simply accepting her fate.

She finished the beer and placed the bottle on the ground. Then she stood and waited to see what would happen next. She didn't have to wait long.

Okama rose to his feet, and the crowd went suddenly quiet. He began to speak, his words drawing laughter from the men. Suddenly a cheer went up, and the men began fiddling with the guns that they seemed to carry at all times. Lisa watched, mystified as the men each extracted a bullet from his magazine and began to scratch something into the lead. Then Okama beckoned her forward.

"Take this bag," he said, holding out a tatty cloth sack. "Collect a bullet from each man, then return to me."

Lisa gave him a puzzled look, but knew better than to ask why. She took the bag from him and, turning to his companions, began to collect the bullets. Then she headed out into the main crowd.

It wasn't easy going. Wherever she turned she seemed to encounter hands reaching out for her. Her breasts were caressed, her nipples grabbed and pinched, and hands slid up her thighs, coarse fingers worming their way into her sex and making her gasp with the sensation as her body began to respond to their touches. For every hand that dropped a bullet into her bag, there seemed to be three more taking liberties with her lovely young form, and she found herself twisting and turning in a vain attempt to avoid them.

At last, though, she had collected a round from every man, the bag now feeling considerably heavier. She pushed her way back between them, finally breaking out in front of Okama, red-faced and panting, her body tingling with arousal.

Okama allowed his eyes to travel down her body, and she knew he was taking in the hard knobs of her nipples, the wet sheen on her sex lips, and her clitoris peeping from between the pink folds. He smiled and took the bag from her.

Lisa watched in silence as he checked the bag's contents, then screwed the neck shut in his fist and began to shake it. Then he opened it again and held it out to her. The crowd went silent.

"Take two bullets," he said.

Lisa hesitated, staring at him.

He shook the bag impatiently. "Come on."

Gingerly Lisa reached into the bag. She picked two of the bullets, then withdrew her hand. She stared down at them. They were heavy and evil-looking, and each one had something lightly scratched onto its surface. Close inspection revealed it to be a pair of initials.

"Give them to me." Okama reached out his hand.

He studied the two bullets, then read out the two inscriptions. From the crowd came a whoop and, after a certain degree of jostling two men pushed their way to the front. Okama called them forward, then handed each one of the bullets. The two men turned to her, their faces split by wide grins.

All at once Lisa realised what had been happening. It was a raffle. Each man had marked a bullet with his own initials, and had dropped it into the bag. Then she had chosen two, and in doing so, had chosen her partners for the evening. She gazed at the two men in amazement, suddenly realising she was about to be fucked.

They were a motley pair, one short and paunchy with a balding head, the other much slimmer. Each wore a dirty white shirt and torn jeans, and each had a rifle slung over his shoulder.

They closed in on the girl, grasping her arms. She tried to twist out of their grip, but it was hopeless. They reached for her breasts, making her wince as they squeezed them hard, reminding her of the painful stripes that covered them.

They began to march her away, the men behind cheering as they did so. Lisa tried to protest, but they simply dug their fingers into her arms as they dragged her away. She threw a glance over her shoulder at Okama, who sat expressionless, as he watched her being taken off to be ravished. Then they were out of the firelight and heading up towards the huts.

They walked without speaking, each holding firmly to an arm as she stumbled along between them, her pale, slim body making a stark contrast to their own dark skins. They took her to one of the huts closest to the campfire, then shoved her inside.

It was gloomy and rather smelly in the rude hut, but Lisa was given no time to contemplate her surroundings. The paunchy man threw himself on the floor, sitting with his legs spread apart, then indicated his fly and nodded to her.

Slowly Lisa dropped to her knees, her eyes fixed on the man's jeans. All her instincts told her to refuse, to try to escape from this ugly, overweight stranger, but she knew she dare not. The pain in her breasts told her that these men were not to be refused. She reached out a shaking hand and began fumbling with his waistband, undoing the button and then sliding down the zip.

She reached inside. His cock, like the man himself, was short and fat, a great brown sausage that was as yet only semi-erect. She pulled it clear of his pants, feeling it harden under her fingers as she did so. His balls were large and heavy, and she cupped them in one hand, squeezing them gently whilst her other worked his foreskin slowly back and forth, his weapon becoming harder with every stroke.

He took hold of the back of her head, forcing it down towards his ever stiffening member. Lisa could smell him now, and the scent of his arousal sent a wave of excitement through her as she closed her lips about his cock. She sucked at him, feeling him swell still more as she did so, and all at once she was hungry for him. The sensation of his thick pole in her mouth brought her own desires to the fore. She grasped hold of his shaft, working her hand back and forth as her head bobbed up and down, sucking greedily at his hard, black manhood.

Suddenly she felt a hand on her behind, and she was reminded of his companion. The man was rubbing his hand over the soft flesh of her backside, grasping hold of her cheeks and pulling them apart. Then something else touched her. Something hard and hot that probed down into the crack of her bottom, making her gasp with the pleasure of its touch. She pressed her behind back, spreading her legs and presenting him with what she knew to be a perfect view of her open sex.

Suddenly Lisa knew she wanted to be fucked. The fact

that the man behind her was a stranger who spoke in a tongue that was incomprehensible to her was somehow irrelevant, as was her wanton behaviour with the man in whose lap her head was buried. The sensation of double penetration was one that she craved, and she shuddered as she felt the man behind her move closer.

But she wasn't prepared for what happened next, and she gave a cry of surprise as, instead of sliding his cock into her pulsating sex, he began pressing it against the tight little hole of her anus.

Lisa couldn't believe what he intended. She had resigned herself to being fucked, but to have him in her rear seemed unthinkable. Surely she couldn't accommodate his thick member there? And yet he continued to press against her, twisting his cock in his hand to try to worm his way inside.

"Mmmf!"

Her cry of surprise and pain was muffled by the fat cock that filled her mouth as she felt him penetrate her. Instinctively the muscles of her sphincter tightened about him as he continued to press into her. She tried desperately to relax her backside and allow him the access he was demanding, though the pain was dreadful. At the same time she was forced to concentrate on the man in front of her, whose grunts indicated that the work of her hands and mouth were having the desired effect.

With a sudden heave, the man behind her thrust his cock all the way in, penetrating her to the hilt. For Lisa the sensation was extraordinary, her rectum filled with his rigid flesh whilst the lips of her sex tightened about empty air.

He began to move, ramming his hips against her soft behind, gasps of pleasure escaping his lips as the tightness of her anus stimulated him. His cock seemed to swell even larger as he did so, bringing more faint cries from the young slave girl. For her part, Lisa was totally frustrated, her body penetrated by two men simultaneously, yet her rigid little clitoris receiving no attention whatsoever as the juices leaked from her sex and trickled down her thighs. But still she persevered with fellating the man in front of whom she was prostrated, knowing that her duty was to bring the men pleasure and that any she should gain herself from the encounter was of no consequence to her ravishers.

The first man was becoming more animated now, his hips thrusting hard against her face, and she sensed that he was approaching his peak. She sucked harder at him, her hand flying up and down his shaft, bracing herself to receive his semen down her throat.

Two more violent thrusts, then a hoarse cry and he was coming, his spunk squirting into her mouth and splattering against the back of her throat. For a second Lisa almost choked. Then she was gulping down his seed, relishing the strong male taste of his semen and determined not to lose a drop, despite the way her body was being shaken back and forth by the urgent movements of the man buggering her.

Even while she was still receiving great mouthfuls of the man's seed, she felt her other violator let himself go, and was rewarded by the sensation of a dollop of hot spunk spurting into her rectum, followed by another and another. Lisa's frustration was now complete; two men coming inside her, two shattering climaxes filling her with sperm, yet her own desires completely unsatisfied. Even a simple finger ramming its way into the dripping cavern of her cunt would have brought her off just then, but it was not to be. Instead she was merely the instrument of these two panting strangers' desires, like a sex toy that can be used and then discarded.

The two men withdrew from her simultaneously, shoving her over so that she sprawled on her back, gazing up at their dark faces. One of them picked up his jeans from the floor of the hut and took out a packet of cigarettes, offering one to his companion. He lit them with a match, the sudden flare of light illuminating the two mens' faces. Then they settled themselves against the wall, drawing hard on their cigarettes and contemplating the pale naked figure before them. Neither made any attempt to put his trousers back on. They simply chatted quietly.

Lisa lay on her back, aware of the sperm that was beginning to ooze from her anus, and aware too that they had not yet finished with her. She only hoped that one of them at least would fuck her vagina before the night as out and ease the burning frustration within her.

And with that hope came the final realisation that she, Lisa Carling, had completed the journey she had begun in Conrad Lang's office such a short time before. A journey that had transported her from chaste young girl to wanton, lascivious whore.

Chapter 20

Time passed, and Lisa's life began to develop something of a routine, though it was like no routine she had ever encountered before, or even imagined she would ever encounter. By day she was largely left to herself, tethered by a lead to a tree in the compound and performing minor duties such as repairing the men's clothing or washing. Sometimes Okama would order her tied to the thorn tree, where she would become once more the object of the men's attention, their hands groping her lovely young body as she hung helpless before them. Sometimes it would be too much for her and an orgasm would shake her frame, the cries that escaped her lips echoing back from the hillside as if to taunt her and remind her of her lasciviousness.

In the evenings she would be paraded before the men, as she had been on that first night, and would be forced to draw lots for those who would have her that night. Then she would be led away to some corner of the camp where she would give them what they demanded, bringing them off with her hands, mouth, backside and vagina, and sometimes even between her breasts, before finally being allowed to curl up in one of the huts for the night.

Okama maintained strict control of her whoring, ensuring that the nightly ballot was a fair one and that only the winners were allowed access to her, though the men took every opportunity to feel her up whenever they encountered her during the day, sometimes triggering unexpected orgasms in the wanton young girl as they slid their hard, thick fingers between her thighs.

Once a day Lisa was taken by one of her captors to the nearby water hole in order to be allowed to bathe. It was a part of the day she looked forward to; the opportunity to cleanse the sperm, sweat and grime of the hot day from her body being a welcome one. It was on one of these visits, however, that the trouble started.

The walk to the water hole took about ten minutes, down a winding path through trees which grew thicker as they approached the water. Generally she was accompanied by a single guard, a rifle slung over his shoulder, the lead to her collar gripped in his hand. One evening, about two months after her arrival at the camp, they were progressing as normal, Lisa walking ahead of him, when she was surprised by a sudden movement in the bushes to the side of the track.

At first she thought it must be some kind of animal, and she shrank back, causing her guard to bump into her. Then two men emerged from the bushes. Lisa recognised them both as members of the rebel gang. In fact one of them had fucked her only two nights earlier and had impressed her with his prowess, managing to come twice in her mouth and twice in her vagina before finally releasing her in the small hours.

The pair addressed Lisa's guard, and a short argument ensued. They were both much bigger than him and, Lisa suspected, superior to him in rank. The discussion lasted no more than two minutes, after which the guard gave a shrug and a nod. The pair then moved quickly, grabbing Lisa and pulling her into the bushes.

They laid her out on a small patch of grass and took it in turns to fuck her, one holding her down, a hand across her mouth to silence her cries whilst the other thrust his cock into her. It took no more than five minutes before Lisa, still slightly dazed and with her thighs spattered with semen was returned to her guard who then led her down to the water without a word.

Two days later they struck again, dragging her from her escort and taking their pleasure quickly and silently. The following day three other men were on the track and Lisa was forced to submit once more.

Over the next two weeks it became a regular feature of her bath that she would be ravaged beforehand, and she found herself heading off down the track each day dreading the attack and violation she knew was inevitable.

What was inevitable too, though, was that Okama would find out. With so many men now taking this extra helping of her body he was bound to know sooner or later, and she awaited with trepidation the time that it would happen.

When the incidents finally came to his attention she was never certain whether it was by chance, or whether he had been acting on a tip-off from one of the guards. All she knew was that, when he burst upon the scene that afternoon, there was no more compromising a position she could have been in.

Lisa was stretched across a large fallen tree, the trunk of which was more than three feet in diameter, her back arched, her breasts thrust upwards, her thighs spread wide. Between her legs stood one of the rebels, his jeans about his ankles, his long black cock ramming into her open vagina. The girl's head hung back over the back of the tree, her hair trailing on the ground, her mouth filled by another rebel's erection, which she was sucking hard. As the two men came, she came too, her cries of pleasure muffled by the thick weapon that filled her mouth. It was only when the two withdrew and she was allowed to sit up that she saw Okama.

The sight of him sent a shiver of fear through her. His brow was creased with anger, and he stood, his hands folded, glaring at the trio. By this time the men had seen him too and were pulling up their trousers, sheepish looks on their faces as their cocks shrivelled back to normal size.

Lisa couldn't understand a word he said to them, but she understood his mood well enough and watched in silence as he berated the two men before calling two guards who escorted them away. Then he barked an order to Lisa's escort, who quickly grabbed her lead and began dragging her off up the path toward the camp.

Lisa knew where she would be taken. As soon as they reached the camp they made straight for the thorn tree, and Lisa was made to stand silently before it whilst the man bound her wrists. This time she was secured facing the tree, her hands held high above her head, her ankles pulled apart and fixed in position. She stood, straining to hold her pale young body clear of the cruel spikes that hovered less than a quarter of an inch from her jutting breasts, threatening to puncture her flesh at any moment.

Okama did not stand on ceremony. He simply barked: "Twenty strokes," then stood back as more of the men gathered about the tethered girl.

A few weeks before Lisa would have been appalled at this injustice. After all, it wasn't as if she had encouraged the men to ravish her as they had. But by now she knew better than to protest. For her, life was cruel, and her simple compliance with the mens' desires, as well as the obvious pleasure she had taken for herself, were enough to single her out for punishment.

The beating was administered with a long, thin bamboo cane, the strokes falling across her backside. After the first ten her skin was glowing bright red and the tears were coursing down her cheeks. Every time the stick landed on her flesh it had the effect of rocking her body forward, bringing her dangerously close to the dreadful spikes, and on more than one occasion her breasts and belly were grazed by their savage points.

The man paused, then began the second ten strokes.

Swish! Whack!

Swish! Whack!

Swish! Whack!

The blows fell with a steady regularity, each one bringing a new spasm of pain to the girl, and each one increasing the perverse arousal that always now accompanied the pain. Her body was coated in a sheen of sweat, the cane raising a small spray every time it landed.

Swish! Whack!

Swish! Whack!

Swish! Whack!

With two more strokes to go, the man paused, panting with the exertion. Then he raised the cane again.

Swish! Whack!

Swish! Whack!

And then it was over. The man dropped the cane to his side as the crowd looked on at the panting girl, her backside a mass of criss-crossed stripes, her breasts rising and falling quickly as she fought to regain her composure.

Her ordeal was not over yet though, as, to a gasp from the crowd, the man suddenly dropped his jeans, revealing a penis as stiff as a ramrod standing out from his groin.

Lisa braced herself as he moved close, closing her eyes as she awaited the sensation of his thick tool entering her vagina, which she was forced to press back so temptingly. But it was worse than she imagined, for it wasn't her vagina he wanted.

The man wasted no time on ceremony. He simply grabbed the cheeks of Lisa's behind and rammed his cock into her anus, oblivious to her cries of pain. At once he began fucking her hard whilst she struggled desperately to keep her body clear of the cruel thorns.

For Lisa this was the ultimate humiliation; having to undergo the shame of a flogging, followed at once by a public buggering. She kept her eyes tight shut, trying not to think of the sight she must make, naked and helpless, the man's thighs thrusting forward against her as he slid his weapon back and forth inside her rectum.

Mercifully for Lisa he came quickly, spurting the contents of his balls into her backside with a triumphant shout that brought a cheer from the onlookers. He stayed inside her until every drop of his spunk had been deposited inside her rectum. Then he simply pulled himself out and yanked up his jeans once more.

The crowd was strangely subdued as it dispersed, leaving Lisa still bound to the tree, her backside on fire, her sex pulsating with the frustration of desires aroused but unfulfilled. It was more than two hours before she was finally released, by which time she was exhausted, the constant strain of holding her body clear of the thorns having taken it all out of her. Indeed, when she looked down at herself, her breasts and belly were covered in tiny scratches where she had come into contact with the tree. Here and there tiny beads of blood revealed where her skin had been punctured.

They took her to the circle of logs where Okama held his parliament. He was alone now though, seated on one of the logs. He watched as the exhausted girl was led across to him.

"So, Slut," he said, eyeing her. "Did you think the punishment unfair?"

Lisa said nothing, her eyes downcast.

"You understand that it was necessary then, for the men's discipline. Those you were giving pleasure to will also be punished. The loss of wages will hurt them just as much as the flogging did you."

Again Lisa did not answer.

"But this incident has told me something," Okama went on. "Having a woman in the camp is not good for discipline, especially a naked young white woman with such a hunger for sex. Therefore you must go."

Lisa looked up at him. Go? Did this mean he was releasing her? She could scarcely believe it could be true. But his next words dashed any hopes she might have had.

"I am selling you," he said. "There is a wealthy tribe near here who can supply me with guns and ammunition. I will trade you there. You will fetch a good price."

Lisa stared at him in dismay. She was to be sold! But to whom? What sort of fate awaited her at the hands of yet another master? She had no wish to remain where she was, satisfying the desires of Okama's men, but the prospect of moving on to a new owner was no more attractive to her. She looked questioningly at the man who had held power over her for so long.

"You are to leave tomorrow," he said. "At dawn. Meanwhile you must sleep. It is a long journey."

And with that he dismissed her, and she was led away to one of the huts.

Chapter 21

There was barely a glow in the eastern sky when Lisa was woken from her slumbers the following morning. A fire was burning outside and she was made to squat down beside it, a bowl of gruel placed in her hand. She ate the food hungrily, aware that it might be some time before she was given any more. She had hoped that they might clothe her for the journey. It had been bad enough being naked about the camp. The thought of having to walk back into the world outside with her breasts and sex uncovered was one that filled her with trepidation. But all they brought her was a pair of sandals, which she slipped onto her feet and then stood quietly whilst her wrists and elbows were bound. Once this was done a rope was attached to her collar and they were off. She looked about for Okama as she was led from the camp, but he was nowhere to be seen. In fact there was nobody about but her and her three escorts.

By the time it was fully light, the hill that towered over the rebels' camp was far behind them. They trekked on at a steady pace, one man ahead of Lisa, two more behind. She was thankful that they met nobody as they made their way across the plain.

The sun rose higher and the day became hot. The ground shimmered with mirages and Lisa began to feel thirsty. She was grateful when they found a waterhole in the late morning and settled down beside it.

Lisa was given a drink, though her hands were not released. Then they laid her out on the grass and fucked her, each man taking it in turns to ram his cock into her. All three made her come, crying out with passion as she felt herself filled by their semen. Then, once they had had their pleasure, they dragged her to her feet and moved on.

As she walked, Lisa could feel their semen leaking from her sex and dribbling down her legs. She looked round at her three captors, who were obviously highly delighted at having her to themselves. It was clear to her that Okama would not have permitted them to use her so freely to satisfy their carnal desires, but it was equally clear that they felt safe being so far from the rebel camp, and that it was their intention to use her in any way they pleased during the journey.

Towards the end of the afternoon Lisa spied a village ahead. The track they were taking became more worn the further they walked, and shortly they encountered the first humans they had seen since leaving the camp. They were two men, both in their thirties and scruffily dressed in torn vests and shorts. Lisa averted her eyes as they came closer and the men whistled in appreciation at the sight of the naked white girl, her thighs striped with dried semen.

Lisa's captors stopped and a good deal of chatter went on whilst she stood, her eyes cast down, waiting to move on, her cheeks glowing as the men studied her lovely breasts, which were thrust forward by the bonds at her elbows. The rebels were clearly questioning the pair, and there was much talking and pointing. Eventually they seemed to be content with what they had heard, and they made as if to depart. As they did so, however, one of the men blocked their way. He pointed at Lisa and asked a question.

Lisa watched in silence as a further discussion commenced. It went on for about two minutes, then the rebels nodded in agreement. One of the men reached into his pocket and pulled out a handful of copper coins, counting them out into the open palm of one of Lisa's escorts. The rebel counted them again for himself, then nodded his head and slipped them into his pocket. The man turned to Lisa and grabbed her by the arm, indicating a patch of bushes nearby.

It was then that Lisa realised what was happening. Her body was being sold to this scruffy stranger for what looked like no more than a few pence. She made to protest, but one of her captors caught her eye and she thought the better of it. Instead she allowed herself to be led off by the man towards the bushes.

No sooner had they reached the meagre shelter that the

bushes offered from the eyes of the others than the man took her by the shoulders. He turned her round and pressed her down onto the rough earth. Lisa lay back on the hard ground, watching him as he unbuttoned his shorts. The way her arms were tethered behind her made lying down awkward, and she found herself thrusting her breasts and backside up at him as she tried to find comfort. The man dropped his shorts. He wore no underpants, and was already hard, his long black cock curving upwards from above his tight scrotum. Its length twitched as he contemplated her lovely young body.

There was no foreplay, no ceremony. The man simply wanted relief and the chance to use the young girl's body. He dropped to his knee, then flopped forward onto her and Lisa gave a gasp of passion as she felt him slide his length into her. Then he was screwing her, his backside working back and forth with a sense of urgency that at once unleashed a surge of passion in the wanton girl. Even here, stretched out on a hot dusty track, being fucked by this scruffy stranger, she still had no control over her desires. As he came in her she cried aloud with the onset of her own orgasm.

It was only when he withdrew that she saw his friend standing behind him already stripped for action, and in no time yet another thick manhood was filling her cunt with sperm whilst she gasped and writhed beneath him.

In less than ten minutes from when they had first stopped, they were on the move once more, leaving Lisa's two satisfied customers staring after them as they headed off down the track. As Lisa felt new rivulets of spunk leaking onto her thighs she realised that yet another step into the depths of her depravity had been taken. She had allowed herself to be sold for mere cash. Her escorts had become her pimps, and she their whore.

The town was a small one, not unlike the one in which she had spent her first night on the Dark Continent, though this time the men had the confidence to parade her along the main street, clearly unworried about being detected by her original captors. This village was much deeper in the bush, and there was little sign of any vehicles having visited it for some time.

As Lisa was led down the track that ran through the middle of the squat houses, the people began to emerge, staring in wonder at the naked girl, her skin so pale in contrast to their own, her long, flowing locks so unlike the tight black curls that adorned their own heads. They looked too at her swelling breasts and her bare crotch, the evidence of her recent behaviour clear for all to see. There was much chatter from the crowd, the men grinning and pointing whilst the women frowned their disapproval of the naked newcomer, some shouting abuse or spitting in Lisa's direction.

Lisa hoped they would pass through the village quickly and continue their journey, but to her dismay the men halted beside a two-storey building and one of them knocked on the door.

They waited a short time, then the door swung open. A woman stood in the entrance. She was a large woman, in her forties Lisa estimated, and she cast a look of disdain over the small party, a look that turned to disgust as she eyed Lisa.

A conversation followed, with much argumentation. The crowd gathered round to listen as the men talked animatedly with the woman, constantly gesticulating towards Lisa. At one point one of the rebels grabbed hold of her, turning her to face the crowd. He cupped her breasts, holding them up for the people to see and demonstrating the hardness of her nipples. Then he forced her to open her legs and ran his finger over her slit. He held his finger up to show her wetness mingled with the sperm of the men who had had her earlier. He placed his glistening fingers to her lips, and a murmur of approval came from the onlookers as Lisa licked them clean.

Lisa felt like an animal at a cattle auction, her body on show for all to see, forced to display her charms to this scruffy crowd with no concession whatsoever for her modesty. Here she was, stark naked, in the middle of a crowded street, her hands bound behind her whilst her breasts, backside and cunt were caressed and probed in the most overtly sexual manner for the benefit of the onlookers, and there was nothing she could do about it.

At last, though, the rebels turned back to the woman at the door, who appeared to be wavering. She argued for a little longer, then she nodded her head and stood back from the entrance.

The first of the rebels entered, followed by the other two, but when Lisa made to do so the woman barred her way, shouting something to her captors. There followed another brief conversation, and then the sound of laughter. One of the three men stepped back outside and Lisa watched as he picked up a hose pipe that lay on the ground beside the building. He indicated for her to stand in front of a tree, then moved behind her and undid her bonds. Once her arms were free he went to the tap to which the hose was attached and turned it on.

Lisa braced herself as he aimed the jet of water in her direction. Even despite the warmth of the day the water was freezing cold and it took her breath away as it caught her body, splashing onto her breasts and causing the nipples to harden at once.

Despite the fact that she was being forced to make her toilet in front of half the village, Lisa was glad of the opportunity to wash herself, rubbing her arms and upper body with her hands to dislodge the dirt. Once this was done he aimed the hose at her crotch and she was forced to wash out the sperm that was still within her and which was streaked down her legs. Her face glowed red as she spread her thighs

172

and delved deep inside her vagina in an effort to remove all vestiges of the men's seed.

When at last she was clean, the rebel switched off the water and called into the house. The woman emerged shortly and walked round Lisa, sniffing disdainfully as she inspected her. Only once she was completely satisfied did she nod her head and Lisa entered the house, relieved to be away from the gaze of the townspeople..

Inside, the place was no more prepossessing than it had appeared from outside. It had a musty smell about it and what little furniture there was was worn and stained. The curtains at the windows were no more than rags, and the stone floors were bare.

Lisa was led down a corridor and into a large room. There were tables set about with an odd assortment of unmatching chairs drawn up to them. The atmosphere was heavy with sweet-smelling smoke and the men seated at the tables were quiet, eyeing her with no more than a drowsy interest. Her escort took her to the centre of the room and made her stand, staring about at the occupants.

The room reminded Lisa somewhat of the bar that Okama had taken her to on that first night, though it was more dimly lit and the occupants seemed considerably more subdued. The two rebels who had gone into the house before her were lounging at a table with beer bottles in front of them, and their companion joined them. Lisa stood beside the table, eyeing the beer enviously.

One of the rebels reached out to her, stroking her inner thigh. A shiver ran through her body as he did so and he grinned to his companions. He had an odd-shaped cigarette hanging from the corner of his mouth and he took it out and offered it to her. Lisa shook her head, but he made an insistent noise and offered it to her again. This time she recognised it as an order and took it from him.

She placed it in her mouth and drew upon it, then breathed

in the smoke. For a second she almost choked as it burned the back of her throat and the men laughed as they saw the tears come into her eyes. She blew out the smoke and held the cigarette out to the man, but he shook his head, indicating that she should smoke some more.

By the time Lisa had taken two more drags from the rollup she knew that it was not tobacco that she was smoking. A strange euphoria seemed to be overtaking her and the smoke ceased to burn her throat. She drew on it twice more, then realised that the man at the table was speaking to her, holding out his hand. She passed the cigarette back to him.

All of a sudden Lisa realised that the man still had his hand on her inner thigh, stroking it gently, his fingers brushing against her sex as he did so. She watched him, fascinated by the movement of his hand, momentarily forgetting the eyes that were upon her as she felt her body respond to his touch.

"Mmmm."

She closed her eyes, pressing her pubis forward and opening her legs, encouraging him to become more bold as the drug began to dull her senses. His caresses felt wonderful. Her body was suddenly responsive to him. She gazed dreamily across the table to where coins were changing hands between one of the rebels and a man who had just entered the room. She knew the transaction had some relevance to herself, but momentarily she could not think what, and when the man took her arm and led her toward an alcove at the side of the room she went willingly.

The alcove was screened from the room by an old blanket, and the man pushed it aside, beckoning Lisa to go through. Inside there was a mattress on the floor and little room for anything else. The man motioned Lisa to lay on it, and she did so, stretching out on her back and spreading her legs. She watched as he lowered his trousers.

The man knelt between her legs, his rampant cock rising

from his groin. She felt as if she was in a dream, and a mere spectator to what was about to take place, though when she felt the thick end of his erection pressing against her sex the sensation was real enough. She groaned as he penetrated her. She was suddenly extremely aroused, the drug they had given her taking on an aphrodisiac effect as she felt all her senses heightened.

He fucked her quickly and without passion, his hips pounding against hers, shaking her body back and forth and bringing small cries of pleasure from her lips that she knew must be audible to those in the room.

He came, jets of semen spurting into her and triggering an instant orgasm, her cries even louder as the waves of pleasure rolled over her. She felt completely detached from what was happening to her now, and scarcely noticed when the man withdrew and was at once replaced by another, who dragged her up onto all fours and immediately penetrated her from behind, his rough hands kneading her dangling breasts and kindling her passions anew.

And outside the jingling of coins continued.

Chapter 22

Lisa woke next morning with a dull headache, blinking wearily at the shaft of light that penetrated the dirty windows of the house and fell directly on her face. She sat up, wincing slightly at the way her body ached.

She gazed about her surroundings. She was still on the mattress in the alcove, though the blanket that had afforded her some privacy had long since been torn down. She looked at her body. Her breasts and belly were spattered with semen, which was matted in her pubic hair and coated her thighs. She tried to remember how many men had slipped into the alcove the night before and taken her, but she couldn't. The whole evening seemed merged into a mad, unceasing bout of copulation in which every orifice of her body had been filled by an unending queue of partners.

She rose unsteadily to her feet. As she did so the door opened and the woman entered. She eyed Lisa with the same distaste as she had the previous day, then beckoned to her. Lisa padded down the corridor behind the woman, who unlocked the front door and motioned for her to go outside. It was cool in the morning air, the sky turned red by the light of the dawn, but the air was fresh after the musty smell of the house and the stuffiness of the alcove, and Lisa breathed it in gratefully.

The woman nodded at the hose, and Lisa picked it up, turning on the tap and spraying the water onto her bare skin. It was cold, but intensely refreshing, and she was anxious to cleanse her body of the evidence of the previous night. The woman offered her a bar of soap and she accepted it gratefully, glad for the opportunity of a proper wash.

The woman watched her throughout her ablutions and, when Lisa was finally clean, allowed her back inside. She took the girl to a small kitchen, where a pot was boiling on the stove. She spooned something into a bowl and offered it to her.

It was a kind of porridge, with a slightly salty taste, but it was food, and that was what Lisa wanted. She devoured it hungrily, accepting a second bowl and washing it down with a glass of milky tea.

By the time she had finished there were sounds of stirring in the rest of the house, and soon her three escorts emerged, grinning sheepishly at one another when they saw their naked captive once more. Lisa wondered if the three of them had had her the night before, and suspected that they probably had.

One of the three pulled a handful of coins from his pocket

and began to divide them between his colleagues and their hostess, each taking a large pile. Lisa watched as they pocketed the cash she had earned for them. She wondered if Okama would have approved of what they had made her do. She suspected not. Perhaps one day he would find out and the men would be punished. After all, it couldn't be that often that the village was visited by a naked white woman who prostituted herself for so little cash. It was bound to be talked about for some time to come.

The men bound her wrists and elbows once more, and she was led from the house. Half an hour later the village was no more than a speck on the horizon as they trekked on through the bush.

They walked for most of the day, stopping only briefly for lunch, which consisted of a loaf of bread and some water from a nearby stream. Then, in the late afternoon, they stopped again by a small oasis. Lisa fully expected that the three would ravage her once more, but instead they made her bathe in the stream, then stood her by the side whilst they combed her hair and checked that she was presentable. Only then did they bind her arms once more and continue their trek.

It was less than twenty minutes later that Lisa smelt the woodsmoke. Soon afterwards she saw it, a plume of blue rising up into the evening sky from a copse of trees ahead of them. Five minutes later they encountered a lone figure, who silently emerged from the bushes.

The man was dressed completely unlike her captors. He wore a brightly coloured cloth about his waist and his chest was bare. Around his neck were beads that seemed to be made of animal teeth and on his head he wore a headdress fabricated from some kind of hide. In his hand he carried a long, dangerous looking spear. This he pointed at Lisa's party as he barked out some kind of challenge.

One of the rebels stepped forward, his arms outstretched,

and said a few words. The man turned his eyes on Lisa, his gaze travelling up and down her body. Then he nodded and turned, leading them along the path.

As they came closer to the place from where the smoke was issuing, more and more people emerged. The men were all dressed in a similar manner to the one they had first encountered, whilst the women wore smocks apparently made from the same material as the mens' cloths. All stared at Lisa as she was led past them, many of the women giggling at the sight she made.

They followed the path round a bend, and suddenly the village was in front of them. It was like nothing Lisa had ever seen before. The dwellings were circular huts made of mud, with thatched roofs. There was no sign of any brick building, nor of any vehicular roads. As they made their way past the huts the path opened out into a circular arena, in the centre of which was a platform with a sort of totem rising from it. On the far side of this was an area surrounded by a stout fence made of vertical staves. Through the gaps in these Lisa could make out a much larger house than the others, though of a similar construction. Even as they stepped into the open area, people were emerging from all sides, stopping at the edge to watch the small band as it made its way to the centre.

The men stopped beside the stage, one in front and one on either side of their naked captive. Lisa looked about her at the many faces that now surrounded them. The crowd jabbered and pointed at the lovely young white girl.

They waited about five minutes, during which time nothing seemed to be happening. Then, all of a sudden, a hush fell upon the crowd and Lisa looked up to see the people parting in front of her. As they stood aside, a broad gate opened in the fence and a man stepped through.

He was about fifty years old, broad chested and big bellied. He wore a lion skin about his shoulders and on his head was an elaborate crown made of birds' feathers. Like the warrior who had led them into the village he too carried a spear, but his was made of a metal that gleamed brightly in the sunlight. The jewels about his neck were equally glittering and his hands were bedecked with rings. Behind him came an entourage of five women, all similarly grandly adorned. Clearly this was the village Chief.

The man made his way at a stately pace across to where the rebels and Lisa were standing. As he approached them the three men dropped to their knees and Lisa followed suit. The Chief nodded and they rose to their feet again, Lisa somewhat unsteadily due to the ropes that tied her hands.

The leader of her escort began to speak. He and the Chief exchanged a few words, then he beckoned to Lisa. The girl stepped forward nervously, her eyes lowered. The man took her by the shoulders and shoved her forward until she stood just in front of the Chief. For the first time she realised how tall he was, her eyes reaching only the level of his chest.

The rebel began to speak again, apparently outlining her charms to the large man. He cupped her breasts, bouncing them in his palms and demonstrating how sensitive Lisa's nipples were, making them pucker to hard points as he toyed with them. He slapped her belly to show its firmness and ran his fingers through her pubic hair. Then he made her turn, pressing on her shoulders and bending her forward. At the same time he kicked apart her ankles and took hold of the cheeks of her behind, stretching them open and running a finger over her anus, making the muscles contract as he did so.

When his fingers found her sex Lisa gave a little gasp, her body shuddering as he teased her clitoris out from between her nether lips and prised the portals open to reveal the pink, wet interior. Then he pulled her body straight again, turned her around and forced her down onto her knees in front of the Chief.

The conversation between the two men continued for some time, and Lisa could tell they were haggling. Men were despatched into the compound behind the fence and returned with armfuls of weapons which the rebels inspected. The light grew dimmer as the sun slowly sank to the horizon, yet still they talked whilst the crowd looked silently on.

It was almost dark when the deal was finally struck, by which time fires had been lit about the compound, their flickering orange flames illuminating the mens' faces as they talked. An exclamation rose from the crowd as the Chief held out his hand and the rebel slapped it with his own. Then a solemn clapping rang round the square, like that which might be heard following a political speech or a lecture.

The Chief turned to the entourage of women, who had stood behind him throughout the proceedings, saying nothing, but occasionally giggling and nudging one another during the intimate inspection of Lisa's body. He spoke to the leading woman, and once again the group collapsed into laughter. Then she stepped forward and took hold of the lead that dangled from Lisa's collar.

The woman gave it a tug, yanking the hapless girl to her feet. She eyed the youngster's body up and down, then set off for the fenced compound, dragging Lisa behind her and followed by the rest of the women.

As they approached the gate a man opened it for them and they passed through. They took Lisa straight to the large building she had seen on arrival in the village, and shoved her through the door.

Inside was a large, dark room that smelled of wood smoke. All about the walls were flaming torches that flooded the room with an eerie flickering light that made their shadows dance on the walls and ceiling. Once inside they gathered round Lisa, poking and pinching her skin. They felt her breasts and backside and tugged at her pubic hair, as if they

180

had never seen a naked European girl before, which was probably the case.

One of the women was taller than the others, aged about thirty - Lisa estimated - and rather more smartly dressed. This was the one who had led Lisa into the compound and it was she who now took charge, barking orders at her giggling companions. At once they dragged Lisa across to the centre of the room, where a log lay on the floor about a foot in diameter. They turned the girl round and began to undo her bonds, releasing first her wrists, then her elbows. It was a relief to Lisa to be able to relax her arms once more, but a relief that was short lived as they forced her down onto her back, making her lie at right angles across the log whilst they tied her wrists to rings set wide apart in the floor. Other hands grasped her ankles, pulling her body taut and securing them to more points on the floor, leaving her thighs open wide.

Lisa was in an extraordinarily vulnerable position, her body stretched wide, the log positioned under her backside so that her pubis was thrust upwards in the most provocative manner, and her sex wide open to their gaze. But the women had not finished yet. One of them produced a bag, and dipping into it, pulled out three shiny metal clips to which were attached long, fine chains. They held the clips under Lisa's nose so that she could investigate them. They were wide, like the jaws of a shark in miniature, and each had a row of needle-sharp teeth that locked together as the springs forced them closed. Lisa couldn't think what they could possibly be for, but when the women began to toy with her breasts she began to get an idea.

Two of the women positioned themselves on either side of her and started to caress her creamy mammaries, kneading them in their palms and laughing as Lisa's face reddened, small gasps of pleasure escaping from her lips. In no time her teats were hard and protruding upwards toward the ceiling like long brown points. Only then did the women bring the clamps forward, squeezing the jaws open, then closing them over their captive's nipples. Lisa gave a cry of surprise and pain as the teeth bit into her tender flesh, bringing delighted smiles from her tormentors.

The two women who had placed the clamps on her then took hold of the chains that hung from them, pulling them upwards. It was then that Lisa realised that their companions had not been idle whilst they had been preparing her for this torture. Two narrow cords had been slung over a rafter above her head and, as she watched, the chains were attached to these. Then the cords were pulled tight, bringing tears to the girl's eyes as her flesh was stretched by the tension until she felt sure that it must tear. They fastened the cords about the rafter, laughing and clapping as they saw the obvious discomfort this caused their prisoner.

But the worst was to come, and Lisa reacted with shock as the senior woman knelt between her legs and reached for her clitoris.

"Ahhh!"

The exclamation escaped Lisa's lips as the woman began to toy with her love bud, teasing it with her fingers and watching as it hardened. Only once it was erect, its tip peeping out between her sex lips, did she produce the clamp.

"Oh!"

This time the cry was one of pain as the teeth of the clamp closed over Lisa's most sensitive place, sending pangs of agony through her body as this too was attached to the roof above and pulled taut. Only once this third chain was secure did the women stand back and look down at their captive.

Lisa knew she must make an extraordinarily erotic sight, her naked body open, her pink slit thrust upwards as if inviting penetration. The silver coloured clamp stretched her clitoris to twice its normal length, the pink flesh turning deep red as the teeth bit deeper. Her breasts, the nipples squeezed tight by the clamps, were pulled almost conical, the pale skin tight.

At that moment another, larger shadow fell across Lisa's face. She looked up to see that the Chief had entered and was staring down at her with obvious approval. The women had moved back, whispering and nudging one another as they watched the Chief. He walked all the way around Lisa, testing her bonds and feeling the tightness of the chains that were torturing her breasts and sex, bringing cries of pain from her as he pulled them still tighter. Then he gave an order and the leader of the women ran to the corner of the room and retrieved a long canvas bag. She undid the cord that tied the neck, then offered it up to the Chief.

He reached inside and withdrew something long and thin. Lisa stared at the object with some trepidation. It was a cane, about two and a half feet long and extremely thin. The Chief was able to bend it almost completely double as he tested it in his hands. He flexed it once or twice, then nodded his approval and handed it back to the woman. She smiled and passed the bag to one of her companions. Then she took up a position between Lisa's legs, staring down at her naked body.

Lisa watched fearfully as the woman swished the vicious little cane through the air. There was little doubt that it was to be used upon her, but how? There was no way it could be her backside, pinned down on her back as she was. She shivered as she gazed into the woman's eyes.

But it wasn't just fear that made her body shake. Along with the sense of foreboding that she felt, her vulnerable position and the searing pain in her nipples and clitoris suddenly induced an intense sensation of sexual arousal that flooded through her body, bringing a gush of wetness to her sex that she knew must soon be visible to those watching.

The woman tapped the cane against Lisa's inner thigh, about two inches from her sex. Lisa's body reacted automatically, the muscles of her vagina giving a sudden spasm that forced a drop of moisture out onto her thick pink lips. The woman shook her head on seeing this, moving the cane up and collecting the drop on the tip, then holding it up for all to see. Then she wiped it in Lisa's pubic hair and tapped her thigh once more.

Swish! Crack!

Lisa gave a yelp of pain and surprise as the cane came down hard on the tender flesh of her inner thigh, leaving a thin white line across her skin that immediately began to darken to red. The woman with the cane grinned at her reaction and pulled back her arm again.

Swish! Crack!

The second blow fell in the mirror position to the first, the dreadful stinging pain making Lisa writhe in her bonds, the movements simply serving to tighten the tension in the chains and stretching her breasts and love bud still further.

Swish! Crack!

Swish! Crack!

Two more stripes were laid across her smooth flesh by the woman, the whippy cane wrapping itself about her leg so that the weals ran all the way around to the back.

Swish! Crack!

This time the end of the cane caught the top of Lisa's sex lips, making contact just below the clamp that held her clitoris, much to the delight of those watching.

Swish! Crack!

Swish! Crack!

So close to Lisa's sex did the next strokes fall that they dislodged a drop of moisture from inside and she felt a cold sensation as the wetness trickled down over the marks already made by the cane.

Swish! Crack!

Swish! Crack!

Swish! Crack!

Each blow found its target perfectly, leaving the flesh at the top of the hapless girl's legs criss-crossed with thin, angry marks, the pain from which was almost unbearable.

Swish! Crack!

Swish! Crack!

Swish! Crack!

And yet still the heat in the naked girl's sex increased as each stroke was laid across her pale skin. Her muscles were working uncontrollably now, the lips of her sex twitching violently and forcing yet more of her shining love juice into the open so that it ran down to her backside and dripped onto the earth below.

Swish! Crack!

Swish! Crack!

Swish! Crack!

The woman paused, the sweat running from her face as she gazed down at the writhing girl. Then she drew back her arm once more.

Swish! Crack!

The final blow fell with deadly accuracy along the length of Lisa's gaping slit, the tip cracking down on her love bud and splashing moisture out on both sides, making Lisa cry aloud with a mixture of pain and passion.

The woman lowered the cane and the others gathered round, standing over the panting white girl whose hips pumped back and forth, her sex thrusting up at them in an almost uncontrollable display of lust, each movement causing her clitoris to stretch and contract. Lisa's arousal was almost total now, the pain from her thighs and from the dreadful clamps suddenly as nothing to the sheer desire that gripped her as she lay before them, her sex positively on fire.

The Chief moved forward and said something to the woman with the whip, who cackled with laughter. She stretched out her arm and teased the fleshy lips of Lisa's sex with the end of the whip. The effect on the girl was electric. A moan escaped her lips as she pressed her thighs upward against the wood.

The woman withdrew the weapon, evincing a groan of disappointment from the writhing beauty. She turned to the Chief and raised an eyebrow. He nodded.

She brought the cane down between Lisa's legs again, this time rubbing it back and forth with a sawing motion. The roughness of the bamboo scraped over that part of Lisa's tender love bud that was not concealed by the clamp. It was a crude gesture, but to the horny youngster it was enough, and she almost cried with relief as she felt her orgasm building.

Ah! Ah! Ah!

The screams of passionate joy rang about the room as Lisa's climax overwhelmed her. Unable to control herself she began undulating her whole body as she pressed up against the object that had transformed so rapidly from tormentor to relief bringer. The chains flexed and pulled at her punished nipples and clitoris, the teeth biting ever deeper into her, but she didn't care. All that mattered was the glorious orgasm that shook her body with spasm after spasm whilst she continued to shout aloud with the pleasure of her relief.

Chapter 23

Lisa woke the next morning to find herself hanging by her wrists from a stout tree. Her limbs ached dreadfully, and she couldn't believe that she had actually slept in such an awkward position. Her arms were roped together and tied above her head. She gazed bleary-eyed about her. She was outside the large building in which the Chief lived, though still within the boundary of the fence. She was in a cage made entirely from bamboo poles set at right angles to one another, leaving squares about six inches by six inches through which to gaze out at the world. The cage was built around the tree, the bars above her embedded deep into holes in the trunk. It was about ten feet square, no more than a tiny cell, with a door secured by a stout chain and lock. The ceiling was about two feet above her head, so that her arms were actually reaching through the bars above her.

She gazed down at herself. Her nipples were red and swollen, the tiny marks of the teeth forming regular patterns above and below each. Her thighs were covered in the thin stripes that the cane had made on the soft flesh, and she still felt extremely sore down there, especially where the clamp had bitten into the tender flesh of her clitoris. She wondered at this introduction to her new life. Clearly these people, like the rebels, had not been treated well by their colonial masters, and saw her as a scapegoat for all their mistreatment. She wondered what was to come for her in this savage place, as a naked and submissive slave to these proud people.

The village began to wake up about her. Her cage was set some way back from the stockade that separated the Chief's house from the rest of the dwellings, but she could see the people clearly enough, and that meant that they could see her, many of them stopping to gaze through at the Chief's new acquisition.

It was about an hour before she saw any movement in the compound, however. It was a lone man, carrying a tray with a bowl and a jug on it, and he was approaching the cage.

At his belt was a bunch of keys and he used one of these to unlock the door, swinging it open. He placed the tray on the floor of the cage, then turned to the suspended girl, his eyes travelling down her body and taking in her luscious charms that were so openly on display.

He moved to her and, taking her by the shoulders, turned

187

her round so that she faced the tree. Lisa expected her hands to be released, but when she turned to see what the man was doing she gave a small gasp of dismay. He had drawn a long cane from his belt and was flexing it in his hands. Then he drew back his arm.

Swish! Whack!
Swish! Whack!
Swish! Whack!
Swish! Whack!
Swish! Whack!
Swish! Whack!

Six strokes, delivered dispassionately and accurately across Lisa's behind. As they fell she danced about like a puppet on a string, trying desperately to avoid the blows but simply succeeding in offering the man new, virgin flesh on which to lay another stripe. The beating was swift and hard, and at the end Lisa's backside was on fire as tears coursed down her cheeks.

The man, still stony-faced, took her by the shoulders once more and turned her round to face him. He reached for her breast, pinching the already sore nipple between finger and thumb and watching the expression of pain that passed across Lisa's face. Then he felt for her crotch, sliding a finger into her vagina as Lisa groaned quietly with the sensation. He removed his finger and examined the sheen of wetness that now covered it. Then he nodded with satisfaction and wiped it on her pubic hair.

He moved even closer, so that Lisa could smell his body, his closeness bringing a tingle of anticipation to the lustful youngster. But he simply reached above her head, releasing her hands from the rope above, though leaving them still tied together. He indicated the tray he had carried in.

Lisa dropped to her knees and picked up the bowl. It was filled with a white maize meal with the consistency of mashed potato, and she scooped a handful into her mouth.

It was tasteless, but filling and she consumed it all, washing it down with the water in the jug. Once she was done he took the tray and left her, locking the door of her cage behind him.

For the next three days Lisa's life was relatively uneventful. She was not allowed out of the cage at all. To satisfy her bodily needs they supplied her with two buckets, one of which was full of water, in order to allow her to keep clean. Three times a day she would be fed, the meal often accompanied by a brief but painful beating. She would be suspended by her wrists for this, and a different part of her anatomy would be chosen each time. Sometimes it would be her breasts. Sometimes her belly. Sometimes her thighs, her back, her legs or her backside. Soon her body bore stripes in almost every area, and it became difficult to find a part on which she could lie at night without discomfort.

She worked out that the area in which she was being kept was a kind of royal compound, entered only by the Chief and his entourage. The women appeared to be his wives, and at night Lisa could hear much shrieking and merriment coming from inside the large hut. Sometimes they would visit her, usually to beat her, their punishments harder and more painful than those administered by the guards. Afterwards they would inevitably check the state of her arousal, laughing aloud when they saw how wet she had become, though she was not permitted an orgasm as she had been on her first night.

Apart from the Chief's wives and their guards, the only other living creatures in the compound was a small flock of goats. These wandered freely about, nibbling at the grass and bushes. Each animal was kept beautifully groomed, and each bore a small brass ring, about an inch in diameter, through its nose. On their rumps was a brand depicting a leaping lion, just over an inch long. There were other goats outside the compound, but none was so well-kept and none was marked in this distinctive manner.

It was on the third day that Lisa saw her first hunting party. There were about twenty of them, all men, and all dressed like the one she and the rebels had encountered on entering the village, though, in addition to their loincloths, these men had their bodies painted in bright colours.

They paraded in the open area in front of the Chief, banging their spears against their shields and chanting whilst he looked on. Lisa watched too, her face pressed against the bars of her cage as they performed their antics.

Suddenly another figure appeared, It was the woman who had beaten Lisa on that first night, and who appeared to be the Chief's senior wife. She was leading one of the goats on a piece of chain that was attached to the ring in its nose. The goat clearly had some significance, as a murmur of approval arose from the men on seeing it.

The animal was paraded in front of the men, then the lead was detached. At first the animal simply stood, gazing about itself in a bemused manner. Then the woman clapped her hands and shouted at it, making it run from her. At this a group of the villagers took up the initiative, chasing the animal down the track and out of the village, shouting and hurling stones after the frightened beast until it was well out of sight.

The parading went on for a further half hour. Then one of the men shouted an order and they were off, yelling and screaming as they disappeared down the track.

It was nearly dusk when they returned, and the village gathered in the square as they marched up the track, chanting rhythmically. As they came into the centre, Lisa could see that they had the goat on a pole, strung up by its legs, and there was much cheering as it was laid down before the Chief.

That evening the smell of roasting meat wafted across to

Lisa's cage, and the celebration went on long into the night.

For the next four days the beatings ceased. Lisa was still kept caged and naked, her wrists tied together, but her meal times passed without punishment and even the wives restricted themselves to taunts through the bars and occasionally spitting on her. For the confused girl, this respite was something of a relief, though the strain of being constantly caged and, worst of all, forcibly naked, still told on her.

Then, on the fifth day, things changed.

She knew something was afoot when she saw the fire being built in the centre of the square beside the platform. All morning wood was dragged in from outside and thrown onto the blaze, which rose high into the sky, crackling noisily. At any moment Lisa expected some kind of ceremony to commence but, apart from those attending to the blaze, the square remained quiet. As the day wore on, the flames died down, and the men tended to the embers, from which a shimmering heat haze began to rise. Then, late in the afternoon, the villagers began to gather about the square.

When the guards came for Lisa, it was completely unexpected. One minute she had been sitting in the corner of her cage gazing out, and the next the door was open and two men were pulling her to her feet.

They each took her by the arm and frogmarched her out of her cell and toward the compound gates, which were swung open as they approached. Lisa was surprised at the size of the crowd that had gathered. She hadn't seen this many people in the square since her arrival, and there was a definite air of expectation as she was led out into the centre.

They took her to the edge of the platform, which was about three feet high, and indicated that she was to sit on it. It was made of stone, like some kind of primitive altar, and it felt hard against her backside as she hoisted herself onto it. They took her arms and pulled them up over her head, securing them to the post that projected from the centre of the slab. Then they grabbed her ankles and dragged her legs apart, tying them to rings set into the side of the platform.

Lisa was trapped and helpless before them. She raised her head and stared down between her breasts at the watching crowd. What could they have in mind? Was she to be publicly fucked? Or flogged? At once her mind was filled with erotic images of what they might do to her, images that sent a spasm through her body making her nipples harden at once.

But there was no sign of a rampant cock about to penetrate her, or of a whip or cane. Instead the crowd parted and a small, wizened old man made his way to the centre. He was decorated in the most extraordinary manner, with a bone necklace and bone earrings, his skin painted bright colours and his head adorned with brightly coloured feathers. At his waist hung a large bag and in his hand he held yet another bone. This looked suspiciously like a human femur, and Lisa watched him warily as he waved it over her prone form.

He began chanting, moving the bone back and forth over her as he did so. For a horrible moment Lisa wondered if this could be some kind of human sacrifice, but she could see no weapons.

The chanting went on for about ten minutes, then the man placed his bone down on the slab beside her and pulled the bag from his waist, opening the top and placing it on the platform.

He reached inside and Lisa squinted to see what he held in his hand. Her heart leapt when she saw. It was a cutthroat razor that gleamed brightly in the sunlight. Once again thoughts of human sacrifice crossed her mind, but when he approached her it wasn't her neck that he reached for. It was her pubis.

He began to run the razor down her mound, each stroke

carrying away a swathe of the short, dark hairs that adorned it. He worked quickly, denuding her mons in no time and then starting on her sex lips, scraping away every wisp of hair until she was as clean as when she had been born.

Lisa watched the whole exercise, her head raised, wincing as the razor was brought so close to the centre of her desires. She wondered what she must look like, her sex so ruthlessly displayed. The lack of hair felt strange to her, the air oddly cool against her flesh, and she felt a heightening of her arousal as she contemplated the sight she must offer.

The man reached into his bag again and withdrew something else. It was a long spike, needle sharp at the tip and widening to a few millimetres diameter at the base. He held it up and examined it, then picked something else from the bag and showed it to the crowd, who gave a murmur of approval. He carried the two objects over to where Lisa lay and showed them to her.

An odd, cold sensation suddenly invaded Lisa's stomach. The second object was a brass ring, of the sort worn by the goats through their noses. It was nearly an inch in diameter, the brass being at least an eighth of an inch thick. The ring was not a complete circle, a gap of about a quarter of an inch having been opened in its circumference.

Lisa drew in her breath. The ring was for her. There could be no doubt about it. But where would they put it? The goats wore theirs through their noses. Surely they wouldn't disfigure her face in the same way? But where else was there? Her ears?

She didn't have to wait long to find out, and when she did she could barely believe it. The man began running his fingers up her newly shaven slit, holding the lips between finger and thumb and sliding up towards her clitoris. He fumbled around for a few seconds, testing the thickness of the flesh, then grasped the skin just beside her love bud and picked up the spike.

"No!"

The word barely escaped Lisa's lips before a hand was clamped over her mouth from behind. She watched wide-eyed as the man brought the sharp point of the spike against her flesh.

It must have been even sharper than she had expected, because it penetrated her flesh quickly and cleanly, giving her no more than a pinprick as he slid it through the fold of pink flesh, wiping away the drop of blood that began to well from it.

He worked quickly and expertly, picking up the ring and forcing it through the hole he had made. Then he pulled a hammer from the bag and, positioning the ring on the stone, gave it a single sharp knock, closing the ring so well that the join was virtually invisible. He reached into his bag once more, withdrawing a small jar. He dipped into it with one finger and smeared a small amount of paste onto the wound. The paste stemmed what little bleeding there was instantly.

It had all taken no more than ten seconds, and there had been hardly any pain at all. Lisa couldn't believe what had been done to her. She shook away the hand that covered her mouth and stared down at herself. The ring gleamed brightly against her bare thighs, an extraordinarily erotic adornment that she knew would draw attention to her crotch and would excite any man that saw it.

But Lisa's ordeal was not over yet. No sooner had the man finished than she felt hands at her wrists and ankles again. They turned her over to lie on her stomach, her breasts pressed flat against the stone. Then they tied her legs to the platform once more so that she was bent forward over the slab, her arms pulled out in front of her, her backside raised for all to see.

It was then that she remembered the other distinguishing mark on the Chief's goats.

The brand! Every one of the animals bore the mark of

the leaping lion on its rump! With a sense of deep foreboding Lisa turned to the fire, just in time to see the old man withdraw the brand from the embers.

Suddenly something was being held close to her face. She blinked at it. It was a thick piece of leather. The hand pressed it against her mouth, then she understood. She opened her mouth and took it between her jaws, biting down hard. Then she clenched her teeth and, taking one last look at the man approaching her with the glowing rod, closed her eyes.

"Mmfff!"

Her cry was muffled by the leather as the searing pain of the brand swept through her body. It had been thrust onto her right buttock, and she could hear the sizzle as it burnt into the soft flesh there. The man held it in place for about three seconds, although to Lisa it seemed forever, the pain of the red-hot metal more dreadful than anything else that had been inflicted on her since her enslavement. She clenched the leather between her teeth, biting so hard she felt as if she would actually take a chunk out of it, the tears running down her face as the agony continued. When, at last, the man removed the brand, she was sobbing uncontrollably and she barely heard the low cheer that went up from the onlooking crowd.

Something was slapped over the burnt flesh. Some kind of ointment that smelt oddly sweet, and almost at once the pain subsided. Lisa turned her head to see the man smoothing a white fluid where he had branded her. She had no idea what the potion was, but it felt deliciously cool after the heat of the iron. At the same time hands were undoing the bonds that held her arms and legs and in no time she was rising somewhat unsteadily to her feet.

The man held out a cup to her, which she took in both hands, her wrists being still fastened. She raised it gingerly to her lips and took a sip. It tasted slightly bitter, but not unpleasant. The man gestured for her to drink more, and she lifted it again, this time draining it. The liquid flowed down to her stomach, where it had an odd, warming effect on her. She handed back the cup, then looked out at the crowd again and was surprised to discover that she could not focus properly. She shook her head, and it felt heavy, as if she was wearing an iron helmet. She opened her mouth, but suddenly none of her muscles seemed to work properly. She tried to take a step, but her legs failed to respond to her brain and she found herself toppling forward into the arms of two guards. Then a sudden blackness enveloped her and she fell into a deep stupor.

Chapter 24

Lisa had no idea how long they kept her in her drugged state. She had vague recollections of food being spooned up to her mouth, and of hands dressing the wounds made to her body on that fateful afternoon, but otherwise the whole thing was a blank. She knew she was kept in a hut, because she could remember the smoky smell and the softness of the blanket on which she lay, and the lingering bitterness in her mouth told her that they had continued to administer the drug that had knocked her out originally. Of the rest of the time, however, she remembered nothing.

She awoke to find herself lying on the floor of her cage in the Chief's compound. She opened her eyes and blinked up into the sunlight that flooded her small cell. She felt no ill effects. It was as if she had simply been asleep. As if the days and possibly weeks that had passed were but a single night.

She looked down at herself. Her wrists were bound behind her, but the rope used previously had been replaced by iron manacles joined by a short chain. These must have been made for her whilst she was drugged. They fitted snugly about her wrists, with no way that she could see of removing them, though the chain between had a catch in its centre. The manacles were attached to the bars of her cage by about six feet of stout chain.

Something else had changed too. Her collar had been removed, and for the first time in a long while she was able to move her head without it chafing.

Then Lisa's eyes fell on her sex and she gave a gasp of surprise. Her mound was still quite devoid of hair. Not even any stubble showed. Clearly some kind of permanent depilation method had been used on her whilst she was unconscious.

But it was the ring that really caught her attention. There it was, large and shining, piercing her in her most intimate place, its presence drawing attention to her sex and accentuating her nakedness and vulnerability. It was the most extraordinary body ornament she had ever seen.

Then she remembered the brand. She rolled over and struggled to her feet. This took more effort than she expected and she was obliged to lean against the side of the cage for a few seconds to regain her breath. She soon felt better though, and twisted her body round, squinting down at her backside.

There it was. The rampant lion. The Chief's mark indelibly printed on her pale flesh. She had expected an ugly disfigurement, but it was more like a birthmark, not more than an inch long, etched into her behind, high on the right cheek. To Lisa there was something oddly erotic about its presence, especially combined with the ring. They were marks of the Chief's ownership of her. Signs that she belonged to another. Signs that would only be seen when she was naked, confirming once and for all that that was how she would remain for as long as she was his. Naked and branded for all to see.

She walked across the few feet the cage allowed to gaze through the bars into the village, and at once another feature of the ring in her sex became clear to her. It had been positioned most artfully, so that, whenever she walked, it would rub against her clitoris. The effect was instant, her sensitive little bud hardening at once, making the friction even more pronounced. Lisa's face reddened as she realised how aroused the sensation was making her, and she stood still, waiting for the feeling to subside.

The guard visited her about an hour later, bringing her food, releasing her wrists and standing silently by whilst she ate. Then he secured her arms once more and was gone, leaving her alone with her thoughts.

For the next three days Lisa was undisturbed, her only visitor being the guard who came with her food and to replace the buckets supplied for her ablutions. She spent much of the time staring out into the village, afraid to move about too much because of the effect that the ring had on her. Then, on the fourth day, she saw the young warriors being paraded and she knew another of their tracking exercises was about to begin.

She watched the young men marching back and forth, shouting their war cries. Then the gate to the compound was opened and she waited to see which of the unfortunate goats was to be the subject of their hunt.

But this time it was different. This time the senior wife headed, not for the small herd of goats, but for Lisa's cage. The young captive watched in puzzlement as the woman unlocked the door and stepped inside. She gestured for Lisa to turn round, releasing the chain that held her to the bars. Then she turned her round again, kicking her ankles so that she was obliged to stand with her legs apart. The woman knelt down before her and, from her belt, produced a shiny chain, like a dog's lead. She reached for Lisa's sex, taking hold of the ring, her fingers sliding surreptitiously into the girl's vagina as she did so, eliciting a small gasp from her.

There was a click, and Lisa realised with a shock that the chain had been fastened to her ring. No wonder they had dispensed with her collar, she thought. Once the woman had made certain that it was secure, she rose to her feet and gave a little tug, pulling Lisa's hips forward in a most provocative way. Then, apparently satisfied, she beckoned to her, turning and walking out into the compound.

Lisa followed, her face glowing as she walked into the arena, the chain attached to her sex gleaming in the sunshine. The warriors were all watching, their eyes fixed on her body. With each step she felt the wetness inside her increase as the ring rubbed against her love bud, so that by the time she was brought to a halt beside the platform she was panting slightly.

A crowd had gathered around the arena, talking excitedly and pointing at her. All of a sudden they went quiet, and Lisa turned to see the Chief emerging from his hut.

He strode out into the centre, stopping to examine his young slave. His wife gave him the lead and he tugged at it, grinning with delight as he saw how it forced Lisa's hips forward. The girl remained silent, her eyes cast downward. The Chief made his way to the platform and stood before it, surveying the group of warriors in front of him. There were about fifteen of them, banging their spears against their shields and stamping their feet.

The Chief held his hand up for silence, and the men ceased their banging at once. Then he beckoned and Lisa was led forward to stand in front of him.

He began to speak, and Lisa could tell from his gestures and the way the men leered at her that she was the subject of his talk. He indicated the ring through her sex, then made her turn and bend over to show off the brand on her behind. There was much laughter and clapping as this went on, and

Lisa kept her eyes on the ground, unable to face those of the crowd.

Suddenly the Chief barked an order, and one of Lisa's guards sprang out from the crowd. He dropped to his knees in front of her and unhitched her lead, pausing to stroke her sex as he did so. Then he produced a long stick from his belt, and the crowd hurriedly cleared on one side of the square.

Only then did Lisa realise what was required of her. The men were going on one of their hunts all right, but this time it wasn't a goat that they were after. It was her. She was to be their quarry. Naked and alone, her hands manacled at her back, she was to be pursued through the wild bush by a group of excited hunters. And what would they do when they caught her? Lisa shuddered at the thought. No man had had her since the night of whoring for Okama's men. Now she was faced by fifteen lusty warriors, all of whom were clearly chafing at the bit to get their hands on her.

Of course she should have guessed the Chief's plan earlier. For hadn't they decorated her in the same way as they did the goats, with a brass ring and a brand on her backside? These were both clearly intended to show her status as no more than a kind of domestic animal to them.

Whack!

The time to contemplate her fate was suddenly past as the guard brought his cane down across her rump with a hefty swipe, stinging her flesh dreadfully. At once she began to run, making for the gap in the crowd, her guard in hot pursuit.

Whack!

She jumped forward as the stick caught her on the behind once more, making her increase her pace. The crowd were cheering now as she raced across the square, her breasts bouncing with every pace, the ring in her sex glinting in the sunlight.

Whack!

She reached the edge of the square and the people surged forward, grabbing at her breasts and sex, pinching her flesh and laughing aloud at her discomfort. And still her pursuer urged her on.

Whack!

Another stinging blow bit into her behind as she broke through the cordon and headed off down the open track, running blindly now, intent only on getting away from the guard and his awful weapon.

Whack!

Yet again the cane fell across her burning buttocks. Then the man was falling behind and Lisa raced on alone for the cover of the bush, trying to put as much distance as possible between herself and the village before the warriors set off on her trail.

She ran on for some time, until her breath was rasping in her throat. Then she slowed to a walking pace, occasionally glancing over her shoulder to assure herself that she was not yet being pursued.

All of a sudden she realised with dismay that her bare feet were leaving a trail of footprints in the dust. She cursed her stupidity. The men following her were experienced bushmen. At this rate they would find her easily. She looked about. Off to her left was an outcrop of rock. Surely not even the Chief's warriors could track her there. She turned from the path and headed for it as fast as she was able.

Lisa climbed up onto the rocks with the agility of a young gazelle, despite her inability to use her hands. Once at the highest point, she paused for a second, glancing about her to ascertain the best route. Then she set off, jumping from rock to rock, content that she was leaving no clue as to where she had gone.

She followed the rocky spur for some distance, until ahead she espied a patch of vegetation amid the parched African landscape. Such greenery meant there must be water nearby, and a new plan to outwit her trackers hatched in her mind. She headed towards the spot, still trying her best to keep her feet out of the dust of the plain. As she came closer, she had to push her way through the bushes, dodging from side to side to avoid scratching her naked flesh on the thorns. At last she found herself on the edge of a river.

It was then that she put her plan into action. She knew that walking through the stream would mean that she would leave no discernible footprints, and she was determined to do her very best to avoid capture. She stepped forward and felt the temperature of the river with her toe. It was surprisingly cool and she shivered as she moved out toward the centre of the stream. The water rose about her legs, coming higher until she felt its cold touch against her bare sex. Then she turned and began to stride upstream, her movements lumbering as she took on the current.

She walked in this way for more than fifteen minutes. She might have gone further, but she met a high waterfall, and found herself quite unable to climb the steep banks beside it.

She turned inland again, making her way up the side of a large hill that rose up from the plain. She skirted its side, trying to conceal herself behind the bushes as she did so, aware of how conspicuous her pale flesh was. Eventually she found a rocky outcrop high on the side of the hill and paused there in the gap between the boulders to rest.

She stared out across the plain. They were out there somewhere, she knew it, that band of randy young warriors intent on finding the naked slave and carrying her back to their camp. She squinted into the sunlight, trying to pick out a figure in the shimmering heat haze, but could see none.

She sat down on the hot stone, resting her back against it and making herself as comfortable as she was able, despite the awkward way her hands were trapped behind her. She gazed down at her body. Lisa had never felt so vulnerable, totally unprotected against anyone who should chance upon her, even her pubic hair removed so that her sex was on view to anyone who saw her. The thought sent a perverse little thrill through her. The chafing of the ring against her love bud had been a constant distraction ever since she had left the village, and she had struggled to keep her mind off the delicious sensation it gave her as she walked along. Now she was at rest the sensation had ceased, but still she could not help feeling horny. It had been weeks since she had had an orgasm. Weeks in which she had been exposed to all manner of humiliation, punishment and titillation without any actual contact with the strong men who were all around her. She thought of her night whoring in the village, and the number of men who had taken her with no consent asked or given, of the way she had capitulated to their every desire, sucking and fucking them with abandon.

Suddenly Lisa was feeling very turned on indeed. The deprivation of the past weeks, combined with her exposed position and the ring that rubbed so tantalisingly against her clitoris making her sexual appetite increase with every moment. All at once she knew she must get relief. But how? Her hands were trapped behind her, unable to reach the centre of her desires, and there was nothing she could see around that could satisfy her.

Then she remembered the tree she had passed a short time before. It had been old and dead, its branches bare and cleaned completely of bark. One of the branches spread out horizontally less than three feet from the ground, and jutting up from it had been the remains of another branch, about eight inches long, projecting vertically from it. Just like a cock, she remembered saying to herself as she had passed. And now she couldn't get that idea out of her mind.

Dare she go back to it? A shudder ran through her frame as she contemplated the idea. It was outrageous and shameful even to think about. And yet the more she did think about it the more aroused she became, the muscles of her sex convulsing and making the brass ring scrape against her love bud once more.

She stared down at herself. Her nipples were like bullets, her breasts shaking slightly as her hips began to gyrate. What was it that gave her these carnal cravings? Why was it that she was so lascivious that even the idea of fucking a tree brought a desire that she found herself barely able to control? Surely other women didn't respond as she did? But she knew she was past the point of resisting the urge to bring herself off. The cravings within her were just too great. She needed to relieve this tension inside her, no matter how immodest her behaviour would have to be in order to do it.

She struggled to her feet and peered over the rock. There was nobody in sight. It was as if she was completely alone in this wilderness, though she was only too aware if the hunting party which even now was seeking her. She stepped out from her hiding place, glancing guiltily about as she did so. Then she began to make her way back down the track.

She continued to check all around her as she walked. Now that she knew what she was going to do, the sensation of her ring seemed even more intense, her love bud protruding between her bare sex-lips, small drops of moisture threatening to escape onto her thighs at any moment.

She rounded a bend in the track, and there was the tree in front of her, just as she had remembered it. It stood in the centre of a clearing, the branch that so fascinated her running almost horizontally about three feet off the ground, and about nine inches in diameter. And there, in the centre, was the protuberance she had seen earlier, standing almost straight upwards, the length and girth of a man's cock.

She moved towards it slowly, suddenly guilty about her intentions. When she reached it she turned around so that she could place her hands on the wood. It felt rough and warm to the touch, and, as she groped higher, her fingers closed about the broken branch.

She ran her fingers up its length. It was smoother than the main branch, but with a number of knobbly lumps down its length. She thought of what these might feel like inside her, and a new spasm of desire shook her body.

Her mind was made up. No matter how wanton her behaviour, she badly needed filling with something long and hard. She was so wet now that drops were forming on the brass ring and dripping down onto the sand. With one last guilty look about her, she turned and straddled the tree.

She settled down, enjoying the rough feel of the wood against the tender flesh of her sex. She moved her hips back and forth, revelling in the sensation. When she lifted her body again, she left behind a perfect imprint of her open sex on the wood, formed by the fluids that leaked from her. She moved forward, so that the erect branch was pressing against the bare white mound of her pubis. Then she raised herself up and manoeuvred her body so that the end of the branch was pressing against the entrance to her vagina.

She lowered herself slowly, gasping aloud as she felt herself penetrated by the wooden phallus. She forced herself down, revelling in the delicious sensation as the hard, unyielding wood rubbed against the walls of her sex, causing her juices to run even more copiously. She pressed and pressed until she felt her stretched sex lips come into contact with the base of the branch and she knew the wooden object was all the way inside her. For a second she paused, revelling in the sensation of having her cunt filled after so long. She wondered again at what it was that had made her so totally abandoned to the pleasures of her body. After all it was not so long since she had been technically a virgin, and had eschewed any thoughts of carnal behaviour. Now here she was, so desperate for sexual relief that she was masturbating herself whilst naked in the open air for all to see.

She began to move, flexing her knees and working her body up and down.

"Ahhh!"

The cry came out before she was able to suppress it. The sensation was wonderful, the knobbly surface of the wood stimulating her beautifully as she worked her body up and down, her breasts shaking with every stroke. Already she could feel her orgasm building inside her and she closed her eyes and threw back her head, intent only on her own pleasure.

When the hard, metallic object pressed against her nipple she barely noticed it at first, so absorbed was she in her masturbation. When the second one was pushed against her other breast though, she suddenly stopped moving and opened her eyes. Then she gave a cry of dismay.

There, grinning broadly, their spear points pressed against her chest, were two of the Chief's warriors.

Chapter 25

Lisa's face blushed scarlet as she realised she had been caught in the act. She had no idea how long the men had been watching her, but there was no doubt that they had seen everything and she cursed herself for having left a perfectly good hiding place for such a reason. Why had she been so weak as to have given way to her desires so easily? And what must they think of her, disporting herself in so shameless a fashion in front of them? Even now her hips were moving, driving down against the phallus in the most overt manner.

One of the men tossed aside his spear and shield and moved closer to her. He was tall and black as ebony, his lips thick and his eyes dark brown. She could smell him now, a smell of wood smoke and sweat, and she shied away instinctively as he reached for her breast, grabbing it and squeezing it roughly in his palm. He spoke a word to his companion, and the man laughed, tossing aside his own weapons and grabbing hold of Lisa's arm.

Together they lifted her bodily from where she was perched, the wooden phallus sliding out of her, shiny with her juices. The mens' hands were rough, and they showed no tenderness as they dragged her screaming away from the log and hurled her onto the ground. She tried to get up, but one of the men grabbed her shoulders, pinning her to the hard earth whilst the other kicked her ankles apart. Lisa continued to try to wriggle from the warrior's clutches, but even now the whole scene had a sense of inevitability about it, and when the other man dropped his loincloth and she saw his stiff, rampant organ jutting proudly from his groin like a great black flagpole, she knew there was no escaping what was to follow.

He fell on her, showing no finesse or consideration as he reached for her sex, pulling her slit open with his fingers. He positioned his thick glans against the hot, wet entrance to her love-hole, then pushed hard, ramming his cock into her open vagina, eliciting a cry of surprise from his struggling captive. Almost at once he began to fuck her hard, whilst his friend continued to hold her down.

Lisa strained hard to free herself, but in vain. Even without her arms tied, she was no match for these two strong, lusty warriors. All at once, she realised the futility of her resistance and, with a sob, she stopped struggling.

Sensing her surrender the man who was holding her removed his hands from her shoulders and began mauling at her breasts, pinching the nipples between his fingers, a delighted grin spreading across his features as he contemplated what awaited him.

It was the roughest, most dispassionate onslaught Lisa had ever experienced. Her seducer's hips pounded against her own, and the rough, stony ground dug into her back in the most painful manner.

And yet, once she had stopped resisting, she couldn't suppress the lustful feelings that rose up inside her as he took her. To have a cock inside her was precisely what she had desired only minutes before. And now here she was, being shafted mercilessly by this cruel stranger, his thick member ramming in and out of her, shaking her body with every stroke. And all at once she too was gasping with passion, pressing her hips up against his, suddenly revelling in the rough fucking she was getting

He came suddenly, and Lisa felt herself filled with hot, sticky fluid that pumped endlessly from him. The sensation was too much for her and she let herself go, her shouts of pleasure ringing through the air as an intense orgasm overtook her, her body flailing about on the ground as she accepted his seed deep within.

All at once he was gone. He rose to his feet, his cock wet and glistening, a long streak of semen hanging from the end. But he still hadn't done with her. He came round to her face, grabbing a handful of hair and forcing his still stiff member into her mouth. He held her fast as she licked him clean. Even as she was doing so she felt her thighs dragged roughly apart once more and another stiff penis driving into her.

Her second ravisher showed no more consideration than had the first, his urges like those of a wild animal, a rutting stag that takes his female for his own pleasure alone, seeing her as no more than something to relieve his needs. He came quickly, yet still he invoked a loud and passionate orgasm in the wanton young girl as spurt after spurt of his semen emptied into her already brimming cunt.

Like his companion he did not linger, pulling out quickly. He too made her lick her juices from him before rising to his feet, leaving her where she was, moaning and writhing.

For a while she remained prone, her eyes tightly shut, too ashamed to look at her ravishers. Then suddenly, from all around, voices began to be heard.

The rest of the men emerged in ones and twos from the bush, each one gazing hungrily at the girl who lay before them, her thighs spattered with semen. For a moment she thought they would all take her then and there, but their reticence made it clear to her that this reward was restricted to the pair that had first caught her.

There was much chatter, and she knew that her captors were telling the others how they had found her impaled on the log. Indeed the protrusion was still wet with the evidence of her lascivious behaviour. Then one of the men said something, and there was much laughter from his companions as he produced a machete from his belt and began hacking at the tree branch. Lisa had to roll aside as the woodchips flew from the blade, and in no time the branch was severed.

What happened next took the young captive by surprise. The men undid the chain on her manacles, and fastened her hands in front of her, threading the branch through her arms. Then someone produced some rope and bound her ankles together over the top of the wood. Once she was secure the men each placed a hand on the branch and, with a shock, she felt herself lifted clear of the ground as the men hoisted the makeshift pole onto their shoulders and set off through the bush, with Lisa hanging from it like the hunting trophy that she was.

The men made swift progress, their unfortunate quarry swinging back and forth as they followed the path back to the village. Lisa's bonds were tight and they chafed painfully as she hung helpless between them, so it was a relief for her when the village came into view, though she was filled with trepidation about the welcome she would receive. As they strode in, the people came out to greet them, laughing and pointing at the tethered girl, who blushed deeply, aware that her thighs were dripping with semen. They carried her right to the middle of the square, and lowered her to the ground.

They left her there, her wrists and ankles still bound, whilst they slipped the branch out. Lisa watched puzzled as, amid much laughter, they carried it over to the stage and began lashing the top of it against the totem with stout rope.

By the time they had finished the branch was fast, leaning at an angle of about twenty degrees from the vertical, the top attached high up the totem whilst the base rested on the ground in front of the stage. It had been positioned such that the stump on which Lisa had sought to pleasure herself earlier was pointing outwards.

Once they were satisfied with this, the men turned back to their prize, who still lay prostrate in the dust. They undid her ankles and led her to the branch.

All at once Lisa realised their intentions, and tried to pull back.

"No!" she cried, but the men paid no attention. Instead they took hold of her thighs and lifted her up, spreading her legs wide as they did so. Lisa tried to struggle, but there were too many of them, and they held her firmly as they carried her towards the branch.

Fingers reached for her sex, spreading the lips apart and guiding her towards the wooden protrusion. Lisa gave a gasp as she felt the hard, dry object come into contact with her sex. Then the men pushed her forward and for the second time that day she found herself being impaled on the thick, hard protrusion.

She moaned quietly as she felt herself penetrated, the sensation at once deliciously stimulating and mortifyingly embarrassing before the eyes of her audience. The villagers crowded about, watching intently, occasionally shouting out words of encouragement as the men forced the wood deeper and deeper into her until it would go no further. Her clitoris pressed hard against the branch. Then they produced more ropes, fastening her wrists above her head and securing her ankles to rings in the ground, leaving her legs trapped wide apart. Finally a strap was wrapped about her waist, holding her belly tight against the wood.

Lisa's position was one of complete helplessness, her arms and legs immobilised, her breasts forced apart on either side of the branch, her sex at once wonderfully and viciously penetrated, the chafing of the wood against her love bud bringing a new surge of arousal to her naked body.

She gazed back over her shoulder. The warriors had gathered in a semi-circle, with the crowd of villagers behind them. As she watched, two men stepped forward, and she recognised them at once as the two who had captured her. She gave a sharp intake of breath as she saw that both were carrying long, thin horsewhips made of leather.

The crowd began to shout encouragement as they moved toward her, wielding the frightening weapons as they did so. Lisa pressed herself against the wood, as if trying to pull her vulnerable body away from the pair, but it was a futile gesture.

The men took up positions on either side of their captive. Then, without further ceremony, they drew back the whips.

Swish! Whack!

The two whips fell as one, striking Lisa's pale behind at the same instant, planting parallel stripes above and below the swelling mounds.

Swish! Whack!

A second double blow hit her, one on her back, the other on her legs, each one stinging dreadfully.

Swish! Whack!

Swish! Whack!

Lisa could barely distinguish one blow from the other, so perfectly were they timed, the pain from each reaching her simultaneously.

Swish! Whack!

This time both struck her backside once again, shoving her body forward against the branch and triggering the reaction she dreaded, but that she had known was inevitable. The movement of the wooden post buried so intimately inside her was having its desired effect, and she groaned as a bolt of pleasure shot through her.

Swish! Whack!

Swish! Whack!

Swish! Whack!

Still the blows cut into her bare flesh, and still the force rammed her against the branch, causing her hips to move and stimulating her cunt to weep new juices onto the stout wooden object that filled it so completely. Lisa fought to control her emotions, trying desperately to concentrate on the intense pain that seared her with every stroke. But it was the sensation in her vagina that was taking the upper hand and she could feel the hardness of her love bud as it chafed against the wood.

Swish! Whack!

Swish! Whack!

Swish! Whack!

Now, whenever the two whips struck her body, regardless of where they hit her, she was thrusting her hips forward against the tree, the cheeks of her backside alternately clenching and relaxing as she literally fucked the branch, the wood making a squelching sound as the combination of cunt juice and semen leaked out from between her twitching nether lips

Swish! Whack!

Swish! Whack!

Swish! Whack!

"Oh! Oh! Ahhh..."

Lisa's orgasm was noisy and public, her hips jabbing against the wood as she finally lost control and screamed out her passion. Oblivious to the blows that continued to rain down on her unprotected flesh, she was, at that moment, intent only on wringing every last drop of pleasure from the unyielding wooden phallus that filled her so completely.

They went on beating her for another five minutes, blow after blow cutting into her lovely young flesh. But each stroke simply served to prolong her orgasm, and when they finally stopped, their faces dripping with perspiration, Lisa was still banging her hips against the wood, her groans now turned to hoarse grunts.

One of the men moved close to her and she felt his hand run down over her backside, his finger slipping down her crack.

"Ah!"

Once again the tormented girl's cry rang out as he forced his finger into the tight hole of her anus, pressing her body hard against the branch so that the protrusion penetrated still deeper. The action sent a new orgasm through her, despite her exhaustion, and much to the delight of the crowd.

Then they were cutting her down, releasing her wrists and ankles and locking her manacles behind her once more. But any hopes she had that her ordeal was over were dashed as she was lifted up onto the platform.

She stood, hands trapped behind her, her legs akimbo as the men began to remove the branch from the totem. She knew she made quite a sight, the rear of her body striped with innumerable marks from the whips, her nipples standing out long and hard on her prominent breasts. Below her sex lips were puffy and swollen, love juice and sperm streaked down her thighs, the cunt ring constantly in motion as the muscles of her sex twitched intermittently.

Once the branch was removed they forced her down on her knees, her wrists once again released and locked, this time behind the totem. Her ankles too were tied to the other side of the post, then straps were produced. The first was fitted round her belly and round the back of the totem, the thick leather cutting into her flesh as her back was pressed hard against the wood, making the whip marks sting anew. A second was placed just below her breasts, with a third about her neck, pulled just tight enough so that she could breathe, but barely move her head.

The bondage position was the most restricting and uncomfortable she had experienced since her ordeals had first begun, her gorgeous young body held rigid against the pole, her legs spread wide and her breasts thrust forward. The dark, heavy straps made a sharp contrast to the pale, smooth flesh they constrained so completely.

The crowd went quiet, watching expectantly as the first of the warriors, one of the pair who had captured, fucked and whipped her, mounted the stage to stand towering over her small figure. He reached for his loincloth, undoing it in a single movement and letting it drop to the ground. A small cheer went up from the crowd as his cock came into view. It was completely rigid, soaring upward from his groin, long and thick and twitching with arousal. Lisa watched as it bobbed up and down in front of her face. Then he moved forward and she realised what was to come.

He pressed his glans against her lips. At first she kept her mouth shut, unwilling to accept his long, black rod inside. But he pushed forward insistently and, mindful of the consequences if she refused, she reluctantly parted her lips.

At once he was inside, and she closed her mouth about his shaft, tasting the salty, musty aroma of his manhood as he pressed it deeper into her throat.

Once again there was no ceremony. He simply began to fuck her face at once, his hips slamming against her head, shaking her body and reviving once more the stinging from the whipping she had just received. Lisa sucked hard at him, her tongue snaking up and down the length of his organ, suddenly intent on bringing him the pleasure he demanded. His thrusts were insistent, his heavy balls banging against her chin as he pleasured himself.

His orgasm came suddenly, his cock giving an extra violent twitch before Lisa's throat was suddenly filled with his semen, his balls contracting as he pumped his seed into her mouth. She did her best to gulp it down, trying not to choke as spurt after spurt struck the back of her throat.

He spent his load into her, then withdrew, leaving her gasping for breath, twin trails of semen running from the sides of her mouth. But she had little time to recover. Almost at once his place was taken by the second of her captors, and in no time she found her mouth filled by his stiff cock and was sucking hard as he began to thrust into her with all the vigour that his companion had. His member was shorter and thicker than his predecessor, forcing her jaw open wide to accommodate it.

Shortly afterwards her mouth was filled with spunk for the second time, the hot glutinous fluid spurting relentlessly from his throbbing manhood as she swallowed what she could and allowed what she couldn't to dribble down her chin and flow between her breasts.

He withdrew and, picking up his loincloth, jumped down from the stage. Then a third cock was standing before Lisa's face, and she realised with horror that the entire hunting band intended to come off inside her mouth.

The ordeal went on for more than an hour, and soon Lisa found herself unable to distinguish one cock from another as they were rammed down her throat, each one delivering a fresh helping of sperm for her to gulp down. Her jaw ached, her limbs were seized with cramp and the flesh on her back and behind stung dreadfully, but still they kept coming and still she sucked and licked at them, waiting for the gasp of pleasure and the gush of spunk that signified that they had been satisfied.

At last, though, there were no more, and hands began undoing the straps and the ropes at her ankles, though they left her wrists trapped behind the totem. At first her limbs refused to obey her and she remained slumped down on the stage. But gradually she felt her energy return and she hauled herself slowly to her feet, finally standing erect, her back pressed against the totem, her legs placed apart.

Lisa was exhausted, her face, hair, breasts and belly spattered with the semen of fifteen men, her back and behind striped with the marks of their whipping. She stood, gazing down at the crowd still gathered about the foot of the stage, too tired even to feel shame at her degrading behaviour.

They left her there for another two hours, like some hunting trophy on display. Then she was released, the lead attached to her cunt-ring and she was taken back to her cell where, without even pausing to wash herself, she slumped to the ground and fell into a deep sleep.

Chapter 26

Time passed. Days turned into weeks, then into months, until Lisa completely lost track of how long she had been the naked captive of the people of the village. There was a kind of routine to her life now, though she could never quite be certain what each day would bring.

Much of her time was spent in her cage, though the hunting trips became a regular feature of her life, and at least once a week she found herself kneeling on the stage and sucking off a queue of men. They kept the branch too, so that the crowd were regularly treated to the sight of the young white girl pleasuring herself on the wooden knob whilst the whips cut into her behind.

Then, one day, during the hunt, she managed to elude her

captors until nightfall, not realising at the time that in the eyes of her pursuers this meant she was deemed to have won the contest. As soon as it was dark the hunters lit torches to summon her back to the village. At first, though, she didn't realise what was happening and contemplated making a genuine effort at escape, heading off under the cover of the darkness in the hope of finding sanctuary. The bush by night was a very different prospect than by day, however, and the cries of the animals together with the strange shadows that lurked in the bushes soon drove her back to the relative safety of the village. There she discovered that, having won the game, no beating awaited her. Instead she was seated at a table with the warriors and allowed to eat with them. After the meal they made her stand on the table and masturbate to orgasm, but no other demands were made of her and before long she was back in her cage and fast asleep.

Once she realised that there was something to be gained by remaining undiscovered she began to take the hunting games more seriously, finding new and better ways to evade her pursuers and managing to stay at liberty on more than one occasion. She was not always so lucky, however. Once she stumbled into the camp of a group of nomads who chased her through the bush, catching her and dragging her back to their camp, where they laid her out on the ground and fucked her in turn. When the warriors found her, tied to a tree, evidence of her ravishment clear for them to see, they took her themselves before carrying her back for an extra long dose of punishment.

For the rest of the time, Lisa's was a lonely existence, spent pacing her cell. She worked out a series of exercises to perform within the confines of the cage. These became a daily ritual and some days she worked out for hours at a time, much to the amusement of her guards who would gather to watch. This, along with her frequent forays into the bush as the warriors' quarry, and the frugal diet she was fed soon

217

toned her body beautifully. Her skin became tighter and smoother, and her breasts became even more firm as a result of the exercises. The guards ensured that she was kept out of the sun most of the time, so that her skin retained its paleness, a quality that was clearly valued by her captors.

But the one thing she could not grow accustomed to was the continuous forced nudity. The fact that everyone who encountered her was treated to the sight of her bare breasts and sex, and that she was allowed absolutely no concession to modesty. Even when she was standing still she was obliged to keep her legs apart at all times, and once a week a poultice was spread over her pubis and sex lips to ensure that not a scrap of hair grew there. Even after all these weeks she still found her face glowing red every time she was paraded out in front of the village in preparation for the hunt, wishing desperately even for a simple pair of panties to hide her shame.

Then, one morning, she witnessed an unusual ceremony taking place in the square. A group of warriors had gathered in full warpaint, chanting loudly, and at first she thought a hunt was in the offing. Then, as she watched, Lisa saw three youths being led into the centre. They were much younger than the other warriors, no more than seventeen years old, and they appeared nervous as they confronted the more experienced men.

There followed an elaborate ceremony in which the three were made to stand on the stage and recite some kind of chant, after which paint was daubed on their bodies. Then they were led away to a lone hut on the far side of the square and the door was closed behind them.

For the next week the three remained ensconced in the hut whilst older men came and went and the old man who had branded and pierced Lisa performed elaborate rituals outside, making fires and daubing strange shapes on the walls of the hut.

Meanwhile Lisa's life took on a new dimension as well. On the morning after the three men had been shut away, a guard came and led her out to the Chief's house. It was the first time she had been inside the building since her arrival, and she felt a sinking feeling as she was confronted by the Chief's wives, the superior one in the front, her face stern as ever.

They released Lisa's wrists and led her to the middle of the room. There were two more young women there, both dressed in bright clothes, and they giggled at the sight of the naked white girl.

All of a sudden a man appeared carrying a drum made from animal hide. He set it down by the wall, and began to play, beating out a loud and insistent rhythm. At once the two girls began to dance, planting their legs apart and shaking their bodies back and forth, then going through a series of elaborate steps, all the time keeping to the beat. Lisa watched in fascination, enthralled by the sensuousness of the dance as the pair thrust their hips forward in a blatantly sexual movement.

The dance went on for about five minutes before the drummer brought it to an end with a loud crescendo and the two women collapsed laughing to the ground. The wives nodded their approval, clapping their hands. Then the superior wife beckoned to Lisa.

She made a sign to the drummer, who began his beat once more. The woman turned to Lisa and gestured to her and at once she realised what was required of her. They wanted her to do the dance.

Lisa began to move, spreading her legs and trying to imitate what she had just witnessed, her movements awkward, making the other girls collapse into a fit of giggles at her attempt. The woman watched for a short time, then pulled a thin whip from her belt.

Thwack!

She brought it down hard on Lisa's behind, making the girl wince with pain. There followed a tirade of angry words. Then she called to the other pair and made them demonstrate the opening moves once more. After that it was Lisa's turn once again, and this time she made a slightly better job of it.

The training went on for more than three hours, the woman not sparing the whip as Lisa struggled to get to grips with the complicated movements. By the time she returned to her cage she was exhausted, and hungrily devoured her simple meal.

The training went on every morning for the next few days, and each day Lisa's performance improved until the woman found no reason to use the whip on her. Lisa couldn't understand why she was being asked to perform in this way, but she guessed that there was some purpose to it, and the anticipation of what that purpose might be made her somewhat uneasy.

Then, on the sixth day after her first summons to the Chief's house, she was woken early in the morning by her guard, and given some food. A lead was clipped onto her cunt-ring and she was led out of the compound and across the square to a hut on the far side, next to the one daubed with the old man's markings. The guard took her inside, fastened her chain to the wall, then left her there alone, her arms manacled behind her back.

On one side of the hut was a small, glassless window, about four inches square, and Lisa's chain was just long enough to allow her to reach it. She peered out onto the square. At first there was no sign of life, the area being completely deserted, but gradually the villagers began to appear. Then, about an hour later, she heard a drumbeat, a sound that she knew meant only one thing. A hunt was due that day.

Sure enough, a few minutes later, the warriors marched

out and began to parade up and down. Today, however, there seemed even more excitement than usual, and the sound of the spears drumming against shields was almost deafening. Lisa eyed the men as they marched back and forth. It was an elite troop, she knew, each man an experienced warrior. There wasn't one out there who hadn't on some occasion been the first to capture her over the past few months, and she blushed as she realised that every man on the parade had fucked her, many more than once.

Suddenly the drums went silent, and from his compound on the far side, the Chief emerged, striding to the centre and taking his place on the stage. There was a sound from the hut next to Lisa's, and she watched figures emerge from the doorway. It was the three youngsters, dressed in the garb of the warriors, their bodies painted brightly, though without the feathered headdresses their counterparts wore. A cheer went up from the gathered village folk as they marched out to stand before the Chief.

It dawned on Lisa that this was some kind of initiation. Clearly the young men were new recruits to the warriors. They had spent the previous week isolated, presumably being psyched up for this, their first hunt. They appeared extremely excited now, their eyes wide as they positively danced out to greet their chief amid much drumming and banging of shields.

What puzzled Lisa, though, was what her part was to be in this ceremony. Normally they would have come for her by now, yet here she stood alone in this strange place, a mere spectator. Wasn't she to be their quarry that day?

Her question was answered almost at once, as a goat was led out into the arena. Lisa watched as the familiar ceremonies were enacted, then the unfortunate creature was chased out of the village. Not long afterwards the warriors followed, the excited youngsters at the fore, whooping and shouting as they ran.

For the next two hours Lisa was left alone once more, still puzzled as to why she was being treated in this way. In many ways the anticipation of what might happen to her was almost as bad as the realisation, and she fretted as she waited helplessly to discover her fate.

Then an odd sound reached her ears. One that at first she couldn't recognise at all, though she knew it should be familiar to her. It grew louder by the second and she peered out trying to see what it was.

Then it came to her. It was the sound of a diesel engine! It had been so long since she had heard a motor vehicle in this god-forsaken spot that she had forgotten what one sounded like. Her heart leapt as she considered its significance. A vehicle meant civilisation. Europeans possibly. And a possible escape from this dreadful, savage place. No wonder she had been taken from her cage. They must want to keep her out of sight. She craned her neck to try to catch a glimpse of the vehicle, and was finally rewarded by the sight of a blue Land Rover that pulled up to the edge of the square opposite her hut and stopped.

The doors opened, and Lisa gave a gasp as she watched two men get out. They were white men. The first she had seen since leaving England, an event that seemed a lifetime ago. One was tall, about forty years old she guessed, though it was difficult to tell from that distance. The other was shorter, with a broad belly. Both wore bush hats, and both carried a revolver at their belts.

Lisa wanted to call out to them, and she prayed they would come closer. But they walked away from where she was incarcerated and towards the chief's compound.

The day wore on, and Lisa continued her solitary vigil. A number of people came and went from the Chief's house. Then, after more than two hours, the men emerged again, along with the Chief and his wives. The Chief took up his position in the centre of the square whilst the men went to the back of the vehicle and unloaded a long wooden crate.

Lisa watched as they carried the crate across to where the Chief stood. One of the men produced a jemmy and began levering the lid off. When it was open he took something from inside. Something long and metallic that glinted in the sun.

It was a modern, semi-automatic rifle.

Lisa's jaw dropped. They were gun runners! She thought back to the day Okama had sold her to the Chief, and the weapons that had changed hands. Obviously the Chief was a source of guns for the rebels, though how he paid for them she had no idea. She watched as he examined the rifle, then passed it to one of his wives who did the same. Three more crates were removed, all containing guns and ammunition. The Chief studied the contents of each one, before nodding and solemnly shaking the hands of the two white men.

The crates were carried off, and the Chief returned to his compound with his guests. Once again all was quiet, and Lisa was left alone with her thoughts.

It was half an hour before she heard the hunters returning, clearly in a state of high excitement. The young novices led the parade, carrying the dead goat on a pole between them. Their faces and chests were smeared with blood, and they were still in a frenzy of excitement, urged on by the shouts and laughter of their older counterparts. They set their prize on the ground and set about dismembering it. Soon the smell of roasting meat met Lisa's nostrils.

The women of the village began setting out tables and logs to sit on in the square, and Lisa realised that the celebrations that afternoon would be special. Garlands of flowers were hung from the trees, and pots of steaming maize meal were laid out as the villagers began to gather.

The Chief emerged, taking pride of place at the centre of the tables. On either side he was flanked by the gun runners. Then came his wives, followed by the rest of the village.

The warriors sat on the other side of the square at their own table, where they made a good deal of noise.

A group of drummers took up their places by the stage and began a steady beat whilst the villagers and their guests talked and ate. Lisa watched the proceedings through her window, a sense of foreboding beginning to overtake her as she listened to the rhythm of the drums.

Her anxiety increased when, with a sudden increase in tempo from the band, two figures suddenly emerged from the sidelines and made their way to the centre of the arena. It was the two young women who had shown Lisa the dance in the Chief's hut, and now they began their own dance in earnest, whirling their bodies around and prancing across the ground.

So intent was Lisa in watching the dance that she failed to hear the man enter the hut. The first inkling she had of his presence, in fact, was a hand that stole down between her legs from behind, the fingers sliding into her vagina.

She jumped and turned to see one of her guards grinning at her. He pressed her back against the wall, his hand approaching from the front this time, running down over the bare whiteness of her mons and feeling for the soft flesh of her love nest. Lisa whimpered softly as he penetrated her with a finger, twisting it round and grinning at the immediate reaction in the young girl. He slid the finger out again and held it to her lips for her to lick clean. Then he undid the lead from her cunt-ring, removed the chain from her manacles and indicated the door. Lisa held back, a questioning look on her face, her innocent young eyes wide. The man grinned again, then went into a ridiculous charade, wiggling his hips and waving his arms about.

Lisa didn't need any further explanation. It was time for her to dance.

Chapter 27

The noise of the drums seemed to grow louder as Lisa stepped from her hut. It was late afternoon, and the sun was still bright, the air heavy with wood smoke. The guard made her wait by the door of the hut as the other women finished their dance. For Lisa it felt odd to be standing in the open with her hands free. Normally they were kept trapped behind her back at all times in an effort, she suspected, to stop her masturbating. Now, as she waited to begin her dance, she found herself wondering where to put them. She wanted to use them to cover her private parts, but she knew the guard would punish her if she tried, so she simply let them hang at her side.

She thought of what was about to happen. Having to appear in front of the village naked was bad enough. She hated the way they stared at her, and hated even more the effect that their eyes had on her, and the way her body responded to their gaze. But today it was even worse. She was not only going to have to perform the dance they had taught her, but she was to do it in front of the two white men as well. Somehow her shame seemed far greater to be exhibiting herself before those men, though she couldn't fully explain why. It was as if the strange and alien culture of the Africans made it somehow acceptable to behave in the way she did. But to do it in front of these two Europeans was something quite different. Even worse, they might be British, and that would make her mortification complete.

The drums suddenly increased their tempo, ending in a crescendo of sound, and cheers and whoops went up from the crowd as the two girls scuttled off. Then the beat started again and Lisa knew it was her turn. She listened for her cue, her heart hammering in her chest, then jumped out from behind the hut.

Standing there, suddenly exposed to the sea of eyes, she almost froze. Then the drummers found their rhythm and she dropped into the dance.

In the relative privacy of the Chief's hut she had been able to put the eroticism of the movements to the back of her mind, concentrating merely on the choreography. Now, though, with all these eyes upon her, she found herself glowing with embarrassment as she went through the motions, spreading her legs and bending her knees, thrusting her hips forward as if fucking with some invisible partner, her cuntring slapping against her love bud, making it harden and stand out from her sex lips.

She moved about with a wonderful fluidity, her firm breasts bouncing up and down with the rhythm of her movements. She held her hands above her head, her elbows bent, her breasts pressed forward. The whole dance was extremely erotic, as if she was offering her lovely young body to those watching.

She stole a glance at the two gun runners. They had clearly been surprised at the naked white girl's sudden appearance amongst the villagers. Now, as they watched her disport her body in such a wanton manner their faces were creased in grins and they were clapping along with the rhythm.

The second phase of the dance involved Lisa moving forward. During rehearsals this had seemed innocent enough, but now she realised it would take her right up to where the Chief and his guests were sitting. She knew she dare not deviate from the movements decreed by the women, however, so she began slowly making her way toward the tables, still swinging her hips and making her breasts bounce up and down to the music.

She was right at the tables now, her body still undulating in a fashion that emulated the most experienced stripper.

226

And as she moved, the thought of all those eyes upon her began to arouse her latent exhibitionism. Intense thrills ran through her as she openly displayed her charms to the crowd. At the same time the friction of the cunt-ring against her clitoris was almost more than she could bear, and she knew that already the lips of her sex were coated with moisture that must be evident to all those watching.

Suddenly, to her surprise, three figures joined her on the square, their bodies moving in synchronisation with her own. The watchers cheered as the young novice warriors danced about the girl, their muscular black bodies making a striking contrast with her petite, pale form. The three appeared to be in a lather of excitement, their eyes ablaze as they hurled themselves about the square, uttering shrill cries as they did so, cries that were echoed by the onlookers.

They took it in turns to dance close to her, their hands held up like hers, matching the thrusts of her hips with their own, the bulges in their loincloths obvious as they pressed their bodies against hers. Lisa's arousal increased with every movement, her nipples standing out firmly from her soft mounds, the sensation when they brushed against the young mens' chests sending pulses of excitement coursing through her body. She could smell the sweat on their bodies as they closed in about her and, on top of that, the all-pervading scent of male arousal, a scent that made the wetness inside her course anew.

The dance was approaching its climax now, the movements of the four dancers almost frenzied as they lost themselves in the rhythm of the drums. Lisa was making little grunting noises of arousal as the mens' bodies came into contact with hers, each one rubbing his crotch against her open sex, then jumping aside to let the next man do the same.

With the final crescendo from the drummers, Lisa came to a halt, her body bathed in sweat. Her chest heaved with the effort of the dance, making her breasts quiver as they rose and fell. But although the dance was finished, the young men hadn't. They closed in about Lisa, their hands groping for her body, squeezing her breasts and reaching up between her legs to feel the heat and wetness there. Then, before she knew what was happening, Lisa found herself being lifted and carried across to where the Chief was sitting.

They threw her down on the table, sending crockery flying and spilling food and drink over her body. Lisa glanced at the Chief, expecting anger, but he was laughing aloud at the young mens' antics, clapping his hands with delight. The three seemed hardly to notice him as they pinned the struggling girl down amongst the discarded remnants of the meal.

Lisa felt her hair grasped and her head pulled round to stare at the groin of the man standing beside her. At the same moment he ripped off his loincloth to reveal his stiff cock. It was enormous, long and black and throbbing with life. Yanking her head forward the youngster rammed it into Lisa's mouth, pressing it all the way in until it reached the back of her throat, momentarily making her choke. At the same moment she felt her thighs wrenched apart and another thick, solid penis was suddenly violating her sex, ramming into her vagina with a force that took her breath away.

Lisa found herself being fucked hard, stretched out on the table amidst the debris of the meal, another cock pumping in and out of her mouth. She had stopped struggling now, aware that the men were too strong for her and abandoning herself to her fate. The rough shagging suddenly rekindled the arousal of the dance, so that her own hips began to thrust upwards against her ravisher.

Suddenly Lisa felt a pair of strong arms about her waist, pulling her from the table and snatching the cock from her mouth. The man who's penis was buried inside her lifted her up and, placing one hand under her backside and his other about her middle, began to dance about the arena as she clung to his neck, her breasts pressed flat against his chest.

Whoops of laughter went up from the crowd as the man danced before them, his cock still deeply embedded in the girl, who gasped with pleasure as she bounced up and down on his rampant rod. She thought of the sight they must make, their skins making such a total contrast, his body heavy and ebony-coloured, hers shapely and white, the thick, black shaft of his cock disappearing between the pink folds of her vagina and his heavy balls slapping against her backside.

All at once he was carrying her back to the table where his two companions waited, both grasping their long, hard members in anticipation of what was to come. This time the man turned his back to the table and prostrated himself along its length, pulling Lisa down on top of him.

Lisa was almost shouting with arousal now, and immediately began pumping her hips up and down, the delicious sensation of his cock moving back and forth within her lifting her to new heights. She raised her head and found herself staring into the eyes of one of the gun runners, and for a second a wave of shame washed over her as she realised what an exhibition she was making of herself. But then her head was snatched round and she found herself once again with a mouthful of rampant cock.

She sucked hard at it, suddenly hungry for the taste of spunk, her hand reaching for his shaft and beginning to wank him enthusiastically. Then she felt something else. Something completely unexpected. A pair of hands were prising the cheeks of her backside apart and something hot and hard was pressing against her anus.

There was a moment of resistance, of sharp pain as her body tried to reject this unnatural intrusion. Then, with a gasp, she felt him enter her, his thick weapon forcing its way deep into her rectum, burying itself until the coarse tight curls of his pubic hair rubbed against the flesh of her backside. Then she felt a hard, stinging slap on her behind, which she knew was the signal to begin moving.

She began to pump her hips back and forth, feeling first one, then the other cock intrude deeper into her body whilst she continued to suck at the member that was being thrust into her mouth. Lisa could scarcely believe what was happening to her. Three thick, black penises were invading her body. Three men were pleasuring themselves inside her, their sweating flesh pounding against her small, soft body. And they were doing it publicly, giving no concession to her shame as they drove themselves hard into her, each one intent on filling her with his spunk, careless of her own feelings.

Lisa was suddenly more powerfully aroused than ever. The cock in her cunt was long and fat, stimulating her wonderfully, the sensation somehow heightened by the equally large weapon that was sliding in and out of her backside. Meanwhile the smell and taste of her third ravisher completed her total absorption with the process of fucking, nothing else being allowed to possibly intrude, not even the thought of the two gun runners who were watching the spectacle of her debasement.

The man beneath her was grunting loudly now, and she could feel the tension building within him as his orgasm approached. The other two were also becoming more urgent in their movements, their hips jabbing forward as the naked girl bucked and heaved between them, her own cries of lust indecipherable owing to her mouthful of manhood.

Then there was hot spunk pumping into her vagina, the man beneath her giving a shout of triumph as he released his seed into her. An instant later more sperm was filling her wanton young body, this time spurting into her arse, the two penises throbbing in unison as they discharged their load into the girl. Barely had she registered this than a third helping was filling her mouth, jetting against the back of her throat as she struggled to swallow it all down.

Lisa's own orgasm was as intense as it was long, her muffled screams going on and on as the muscles of her vagina and rectum tightened around the mens' shafts, milking still more of their seminal fluid from them and prolonging their own orgasms still further.

By the time they withdrew, Lisa was exhausted, lying amidst the spilt food on the table, her sex and rectum red and swollen with the rough treatment she had received from the three. But she was given no opportunity to recover. Suddenly the young men were turning her over, spreading her face down across the table and securing her wrists and ankles to the corners with strong rope, shouting and laughing as they did so. Then they produced long, thin leather belts and began to beat her, the leather cutting into every inch of her skin as they lashed her with enthusiasm whilst the crowd cheered them on.

The beating went on and on, stroke after stroke falling across her pale skin until the flesh on her back and behind felt as if it was on fire. Then, just when she thought she could take no more, they turned her onto her back and began to lash her belly and breasts with equal enthusiasm, bringing screams of anguish from the hapless girl.

As they beat her, somebody picked up a bottle from the table and pressed it between her open legs, pushing it deep into her vagina, changing her screams of pain to shouts of passion as the unknown hand began to frig her. They worked it back and forth in time to the crack of the leather on her flesh, bringing her two more shattering climaxes in quick succession. Lisa's body was a mass of red stripes now, her breasts red and swollen with the punishment she had received.

At last the men grew tired and tossed the belts aside. By this time their cocks were hard again and, barely pausing to regain their breath, they started to fuck her again, taking turns to penetrate her cunt and bring her yet more orgasms

231

as they came inside her one after the other.

Only then was she allowed to rest, left tied across the table her body covered with the red stripes of the belts, spunk trickling from her sex and rectum, her skin smeared with discarded food.

A face loomed over her as she lay there, her breasts rising and falling as she gasped to regain her breath. It was a white face, that of the first of the gun-runners.

"That was quite a show," he said quietly.

Chapter 28

The next morning Lisa woke to find herself back in her cage, her wrists pinned behind her as usual and attached to the bars by a short chain.

She pulled herself painfully to her feet and glanced down at her body. It was still criss-crossed with the thin red stripes of the belts. Even the creamy whiteness of her young breasts was decorated with the marks of the beating.

She staggered across to her water bucket and began trying to clean herself, but it was almost impossible without the use of her hands, and she was grateful when her guard arrived and freed them, allowing her to wash herself under his amused gaze. Then she squatted in the corner and devoured the bowl of gruel he had brought her before allowing him to pin her wrists behind her once more.

But he didn't re-attach her chain. Instead he produced a lead, which he fitted to her cunt-ring. Then he led her out into the compound and towards the Chief's house.

He took her inside. There, seated by the wall, were the two white men. Lisa's face glowed scarlet as she recalled her behaviour in front of them the night before, and she tried to hang back, but one tug at her lead was enough to bring her staggering forward to stand before them, her legs placed apart as her guards always insisted.

"What's your name?"

The question startled her. Apart from the short sentence the night before, it was the first English she had heard spoken for months.

"L-Lisa Sir." The sound of her own voice was strange to her, since it had only been used for screams of pain or pleasure for so long.

"Lisa Carling?"

She looked up, dumbfounded. "How did you..?"

"Just answer the questions, bitch."

"Yes Sir."

"Good." The tall man, obviously the leader of the two, rose to his feet and stood over her. "A lot of people have been wondering where you were, Miss Carling," he said.

Lisa stared at him. She had honestly thought herself forgotten. Fated to live out her days in this scruffy little village as the warriors' plaything. A body to be abused and fucked purely for the mens' pleasure. And now here was a man who knew of her by name!

"You've taken a bit of finding," he went on. "But we've had our spies out. We knew you weren't with Okama any more. He moved on with his rebels some time ago and we'd have heard if you'd been taken along."

Lisa listened with increasing surprise to these words. It hadn't occurred to her that they would try to find her again, let alone that they would succeed.

"Of course," continued the man, "we heard about your night of whoring in the village about a day from here. From there it was a pretty good possibility that the Chief would have you. Pay for you with rifles did he?"

Lisa nodded dumbly.

"Wily old devil. Of course he'll be making a huge profit from us. These semi-automatic rifles are worth a sight more

233

than the blunderbusses he'll have given Okama. Still we'll make a profit from the deal too. There's some people quite looking forward to seeing you again, young lady."

He must have seen the look of surprise in Lisa's eyes, for his face broadened into a grin.

"Oh, yes. Didn't they tell you? You've just been sold again. You're coming with us, darling."

Lisa was astounded. The guns must have been in exchange for her! So the men had known she was here all along. Clearly they had had some kind of go-between set up the deal beforehand. And now she was to move on once more. Away from this dreadful place where they spoke not a word of her language, and where she was kept like a domestic animal, to be used at the whim of the Chief. But where was she going? And what terrors awaited her there? She had no illusions. It was not to freedom that these men were taking her.

The man walked around her, examining her body. He took her cunt-ring in his fingers, inspecting the way her flesh was pierced. Then he ran his fingers over the brand on her behind, making her shiver at his touch.

"Hmm, they've certainly marked you nicely," he murmured. "And your crotch shaved too. That all adds value to a young slut like you. And after yesterday's little show I've no doubt you'll perform when required. You looked like you were really enjoying having that sweet little arse of yours fucked. Like being buggered by the natives do you?"

Lisa said nothing.

"Right," he said, taking her lead from the guard. "Time we were leaving. I trust you haven't got any luggage, judging from the way you go about. Christ I've never seen a girl flash her parts the way you were doing last night. Give you a thrill to show off your tits and cunt does it?"

He gave a tug on her lead, and the red-faced girl followed him out of the hut.

A small crowd had gathered by the Rover and they hooted

their derision as she was led past them. The man placed his hand on Lisa's backside and lifted her up into the rear of the vehicle, padlocking her lead to a ring in the floor. Then he slammed and locked the doors and he and his companion climbed into the front. Next minute there was a whirr and a rattle and the diesel engine came to life. Then, with a grating of gears, the vehicle lurched forward and they were on their way.

The journey seemed endless. For a long time they drove along tracks that were barely discernible, bushes and trees scraping along the side of the Land Rover as they lurched through deep potholes and across river beds. Then they came to a dirt road, along which they were able to travel somewhat faster. Finally they turned onto a fully metalled surface, and the wheels sang as they accelerated away towards their ultimate destination.

That night they camped by the side of the road, erecting a tent and lighting a fire. They ate in silence, Lisa's wrists being freed for the purpose. Then they staked her to the ground and she fully expected to be ravished. But the men seemed uninterested, returning to the fire to drink whisky and talk in low voices.

The next day they were on the road early, and once again continued non-stop whilst Lisa dozed in the rear. She was finally wakened by the sound of the vehicle slowing down and she raised her head to peer out through the windows.

They were in a town. Not one of the tiny villages she had grown accustomed to over the past months but a large, bustling urban area, the streets filled with cars, buses and bicycles. The moment she realised they were surrounded by people she ducked down once more, afraid that the passers-by would realise she was naked.

The Rover wound its way through the busy streets, where horns blasted out and bicycle bells seemed to ring incessantly. Then suddenly the vehicle swung to the left and came to a halt at the curb side. The two men climbed out and slammed the doors. Then. To Lisa's chagrin, they came round and opened the tailgate.

"Come on, out." Ordered the man.

Lisa hung back. The street they were on was as busy as any she had seen since entering the town. Surely they weren't going to make her climb out in her condition? But a sharp tug at her lead confirmed that that was precisely what they intended and, her face glowing pink, Lisa was forced to step out onto the road.

She felt extraordinarily conspicuous, her firm, jutting breasts still bearing the marks of the belts, her sex perfectly visible, the gleaming ring drawing attention to her lack of pubic hair.

She walked down the road behind the men, her hands still pinned behind her. All about people were stopping and staring at the naked white girl being led through the streets by the ring in her cunt, her breasts bouncing delightfully with every step. Lisa stole a glance at the faces turned in her direction. They were a cosmopolitan crowd; black, brown and white skins all in evidence. Across the road a group of African youths were pointing and laughing at her, whilst from the window of an expensive looking car a beautifully dressed young white woman stared at her aghast.

The walk can have been for no more than five minutes, but for Lisa it seemed to go on for ever. On all sides whistles and shouts rang out, many of them in English, and Lisa hung her head as she listened to the lewd suggestions they were making.

At last they stopped outside a door and the man knocked. A few seconds later it was answered by a servant, who raised his eyebrows at the sight of Lisa.

"Is the B'wana in?"

"Yes Sir. Please come in."

The man stood to one side as the strange trio entered the

house and Lisa heard the door close behind her with a sigh of relief.

The man spoke a few words to the servant and he nodded, showing them to a large reception room then heading off again. Two minutes later he was back, and after a few words had been exchanged he took hold of Lisa's lead.

She followed him up a flight of stairs and down a short corridor to a door at the end, upon which he knocked.

"Come."

The servant placed the end of her lead in Lisa's hand, then, opening the door, he pushed her inside, shutting it behind her.

The room was long, with large windows that admitted great shafts of sunlight. At the end were two men, standing at a table with their backs to her. As the door closed they turned and Lisa's jaw dropped.

It was Conrad Lang.

Conrad Lang! The man who had started all this! The man who had single-handedly changed her from demure young woman to slut, slave and whore. She could scarcely believe her eyes. In fact, so distracted was she by his presence that it was a moment before her eyes turned to the second man, and once again she gasped in recognition. It was the man she knew only as Bulcher, the one to whom she had been passing the secrets on the night she had lost her freedom.

Conrad Lang eyed her, a look of contempt on his face. Then he beckoned her closer.

"So, we've found you at last, Miss Carling," he said quietly. "It's been a long time."

Lisa did not reply, but she knew the surprise showed in her face, and this was confirmed by Lang's next words.

"Not expecting to see me, were you? Well thanks to you I'm now out of a job. After your own little cock-up that bastard Dawson was on my case day and night. It was only a matter of time 'till he found out what I was doing, then I was out on my ear. Since then Mr Bulcher here and I have been working together more closely."

Bulcher inclined his head. "That was when we decided to dig up a bit of dirt on Dawson ourselves," he said. "We knew he'd got rid of you somehow, and we were curious to find out how. So we investigated and discovered what had become of you. Or what should have become of you but for Mr Okama's intervention. At the same time we discovered what a lucrative business this is. So we bought ourselves in."

"So now we're in the human resources business," said Lang. "With a little bit of armament supplies on the side. There's no shortage of customers around here."

"But there was one bit of merchandise we both wanted to get our hands on," said Bulcher. "A little unfinished business if you like. It's cost us a lot of money to get you here, Miss Carling, so I do hope you're going to be worth it."

Lang moved closer to her, and his hand dropped to finger the brass ring that hung so prominently from her sex.

"What a crude little ornament," he said. "But I bet it turns you on when you walk about. Let's see."

He slid a finger into Lisa's vagina, bringing a faint whimper from the youngster as he delved deep into her honeypot.

"As I thought," he said triumphantly, holding up his finger. "Wet as hell. I've never known a girl so constantly hot as this one. Here, lick my fingers clean."

Lisa obeyed, keeping her eyes cast down as she did so. Then he ran a finger over her brand.

"Another little body decoration," he exclaimed. "These will make you a very valuable acquisition, young lady. It's not often we get such authentic native decorations. Give me that lead."

Lisa had been holding her own lead behind her back until now. She turned and offered it as best she could to Lang, who took it and tugged experimentally, grinning as he saw her hips thrust forward.

"Very nice," he said. "Very nice indeed. Come over to the window."

He led her across to the window, which looked out onto a busy square. Everywhere there were people bustling back and forth or hawking their wares from stalls set about the street. In the centre was a large block, about six feet high, with steps leading up to it.

"Do you see that block?" he said. "Once a week the auction is held there. Young Negro men, the occasional Arab expelled by his or her family for some misdemeanour, and just occasionally a little prize like yourself. You'll cause quite a stir up there. We'll sell you naked of course. It would be a shame if the buyers didn't get a good look at those interesting adornments to your beauty. I wonder who'll buy you? An Arab sheikh wanting a plaything for himself and his guests, maybe. Perhaps a whorehouse owner looking for something new and unusual. Or maybe just some sadist who will gain his pleasure from inflicting pain on that exquisite little body of yours."

"But that won't be for a while yet," put in Bulcher. "I intend to have a little fun with you first. Down in the basement I've got some wonderful toys I want to share with you. I know you like chains and whips, and I've got some even more ingenious devices to use on you. Even now the servant is down there preparing the whipping post."

Lisa stared dumbly at the pair of them, then out into the square at the auction block. Their words had sent a chill through her and she contemplated her time ahead with foreboding. Bulcher had the cruelest eyes of any man she had ever encountered, and she knew she could expect no mercy from him.

Suddenly, unexpectedly, Bulcher's words caused a surge of lust to sweep through her and she was unable to suppress a slight moan as her nipples hardened and a gush of wetness ran through her sex. She closed her eyes, hoping that the two had not noticed her arousal, but it was a forlorn hope. Lang tugged at her lead, pulling her close to him, then felt her bullet-hard teats.

You really are a sensuous little thing," he said. "Perhaps we'll give you a little relief. Akran!"

The last word was shouted, and moments later the door opened and the servant entered. Lisa gasped as she saw him. He had discarded the long white garment he had been wearing when he answered the door and was now clad in only a black leather jockstrap and black boots. In his hand he carried a thin whip.

"The Memsa'ab is on heat," announced Lang coolly. Fuck her please."

The man grinned, reaching down and undoing the cord that held his jockstrap up. As it fell away his massive black cock sprang to attention. He took the lead from Lang's outstretched hand and pushed Lisa backwards until she felt the hard wood of the desk against her behind. She fell back over it as the man forced her legs apart. Then, with a single thrust, he was inside her.

He managed no more than three strokes before a powerful orgasm shook Lisa's small frame, and the cries echoed about the room as he continued to ram his cock into her sopping cunt whilst she thrashed about beneath him, her mind filled with thoughts of the torture chamber downstairs.

Beside her a grim-faced Bulcher crouched down and picked up the whip.

When the Master Speaks
by Josephine Scott

ISBN 1897809093

In 1869 Clarisse runs away from her country home, and excessive parental discipline, to the delights of London, where she finds discipline can have a deeper and more pleasurable meaning than she ever realized. In 1969 Lauren leaves the country—and a broken relationship—for those same delights where she also finds that love can have painful yet pleasurable overtones. In a house in Fleet Street past and present blend... a fascinating tapestry of pain and pleasure.

Amelia *(A Tale of Punishment and Retribution)*
by Josephine Oliver

ISBN 1897809131

Amelia falls under the sway of a 'Country Gentleman' whose attitude towards women was learned among the slave owners of an American Plantation of the 1850s. He submits her to deeper and deeper discipline and degradation, until at last the tables are turned... and, as Mistress, Amelia knows exactly how to exercise her new won powers.

The Darker Side
by Larry Stern

ISBN 1897809158

What Wendy did, above all, was open my mind to the idea, and the acceptance of that notion, that love has a darker side, that there can be intense sensual pleasure in acts of humiliation and chastisements, that the stroke of the whip can stimulate as effectively as a kiss or a caress. So the stoies that form this volume are drawn from that darker side...

Biker's Girl
by Lia Anderssen

ISBN 1897809042

Set in the near future, this is the story of a beautiful young runaway who glories in sex and exhibitionism, and is an out-and-out masochist. Due to an unfortunate incident she is naked when she meets a group of Biker's and naked she remains through many painful episodes. Then the Biker of her fancies sweeps her off her feet, doubtless to live happily ever after (or rather until Biker's Girl on the Run) as his handmaiden...

See also: Biker's Girl on the Run, Hunted Aristocrat, Training of Samantha

SILVER MINK TITLES

Sonia
by RD Hall

ISBN 1897809212

The strap she relished: easy to tell. 'It covers me as well as wakes me... it is comforting, warm-you work it well-it is fire on a dark night.'
The cane she was still uncertain about. 'You teach me if it means business I think?' 'Yes my little one, yes.'
The whip was small, it was for youngster, yet it gave me the horrors. 'Will, your are not trying! Listen, I will tell you some things from my school days: after you will not shrink from giving me whippings...'

The Captive
by Amber Jameson

ISBN 1897809220

Zarcora is an amazingly beautiful young lady, where a woman's only duty is to obey and pleasure her man.
Betrayed and shamed, when she is sent to another land to be auctioned. Here it is the women who dominate, and the men into whose hands she falls take their bitter revenge upon her. But even in the midst of the worst beatings and humiliation Zacora is bound by her upbringing to please. The man she pleases most is the Pretender to the throne-can her sweet nature affect the behavior of a Kingdom?

SILVER MINK TITLES

Dear Master
by Terry Smith

ISBN 1897809247

Reading a naughty book reveals the truth about herself to Susan Dixon. She needs a Master! Someone to discipline her, mould her, beat her if she is disobedient, change her from the cute and provocative buty very child—like young woman that she is into the alluring sophisticated person she longs to become.

The author sounds like a true Master, a man she can love, a man she can write to *'Dear Master, Please let me serve you...'*

But what of the recipient of this sweet trusting letter? Is he worthy of her or will he take advantage of her innocence, make of her an erotic toy to be used and abused and shared with his friends?

Sisters in Servitude
by Nicole Dere

ISBN 1897809263

When Fran set out to visit her sister on a remote Island she did not expect to be met by her sister's boyfriend—with a pair of handcuffs!

And then to discover that they were both to be trained to the tastes of the sadistic Prince Salman...

Things were to get worse, far worse before they got better!

Cradle of Pain
by Krys Antarakis

ISBN 189780928X

When Jane arrives at the address she has been given, she opens the door on the servitude she seeks - but there is more, much more, for there are others in the house besides the man at whose bidding she has come, a whole Society is based there.

She finds the true submission she seeks in the relentless grasp of the machine they call - THE CRADLE!

Six Recent Titles

Owning Sarah *by Nicole Dere*

When Sarah Lawton wakes to find herself literally naked in Peter Philpott's hands, in his flat, she is subjected to various 'test' of her loyalty and subservience. Shocked at her willingness to endure such treatment, she soon longs only his complete ownership of her. Sold to the aristocratic debauchee Lord Staith at whose luxurious home, in the company of the beautiful but bizarre Lady Pippa and others, Sarah is taught even harsher lessons in obedience.

The Contract *by Sarah Fisher*

When Emily Lawrence signs away her body to pay off her lover's debt she steps into the dark compelling world of passion and pain. In a luxurious isolated mansion Emily discovers her true nature; Sold to the highest bidder, branded and beaten, she finds herself caught up in a web of shame and abuse.

Virgin for Sale *by Nicole Dere*

The coast of Africa - the days of sail. Margeret Hollins, beautiful eighteen - year -old daughter of a British Vice Admiral, is kidnapped with her maid, Cathy Roper. They enter the nightmare world of the sordid trade in human flesh where their only value is in their physical beauty. Cathy betrays Margeret, who is forced to endure the horrors of a slave caravan and a voyage on a slaving dhow, before entering the harem of Prince Abdul Rahman, in the desert kingdom of Al Kharja.

The Story of Caroline *As told to Barbie*

This is the incredible but true story of Caroline, a beautiful young woman caught up in the erotic world of pleasure and pain, bondage and humiliation.

Jane and her Master *by Stephen Rawlings*

A decade ago that master of the classic S&M novel, PN Dedeaux, gave us AN ENGLISH EDUCATION, a version of Charlotte Bronte's JANE EYRE, in which he peeled away the prudish coverings then required, reveal what scholars had always recognised; the seething cruelty and masochism that heaved beneath. In this powerful sequel 'Stephen Rawlings' develops this theme in a way that could not have been done in Victorian times and is daring even today.

Island of Slavegirls *by Roy Bacchus*

The girl was naked, her wrists tied high above her head to a meat hook. Her feet barely touched the duty floor and she hung, slumped against the cracked wall-plaster, in a dusty Singapore cellar. She was blindfolded, her head turned sideways to the wall, her half-masked features erotic to him. Her sexy mouth was soft, full and quivering, her bronzed flesh shiny with the sweat of fear, the slight glow emphasised by the long bl;ack hair. But most erotic of all, the centre of his attention, were her rounded naked unblemished buttocks, contracting and relaxing as her terror mounted. The brothel manager handed her a short dogwhip. "We got a girl here," she said, "she no want fucky-sucky. You punish her, eh Johnny?"

Silver Moon   **Silver Mink**

All our titles can be ordered from any bookshop in the UK and an increasing number in the USA and Australia by quoting the title and ISBN Or they are available from us direct for £5.60 each (UK) or $9.95 (USA) Credit Cards accepted as EBS (Electronic Book Services) £.s are converted to $.s.

We also offer a free 20-page booklet of extracts and maintain a confidential mailing list in both Countries.